MECHANICS OF THE HEART

BY

AGNES H. HAGADUS

Dedicated to all my readers. Without you, I'm nothing. Special dedication to my sweet better half. I love you spitfire. And thank you to our daughter Miss Alex, gone but never forgotten, you are loved

My author page on facebook: https://www.facebook.com/strange1agneshagadus

Follow me on twitter: https://twitter.com/strange176

#2HeartsOneDestiny

"Morning, Frank." A grunt was the response. Rocho knew it was because her boss remained disappointed that she refused to be on 'the front lines' as he referred to it.

Rocho stood nearly six feet tall in flats. If Frank had his way, she would wear six-inch heels, an extremely revealing dress and have her long black locks sculpted as the models on the runway do.

Instead, Rocho had on her usual attire. Grease stained dark blue coveralls with her black locks tucked under her Detroit Pistons baseball cap. Her azure eyes were already covered with safety goggles as she made her way toward the service department.

Restoring old cars or maintaining newer ones were passions of the young woman. Rocho had learned at an early age how to fix anything with a motor. She wasn't certain where she had inherited, as her father was a lawyer. Sadly, she had no idea what her younger brother had chosen as a vocation.

Luckily for Rocho, she had the knowledge to support herself. And it didn't take long to pick up where she had left off the night before. "Son of a bitch." The mechanic hastily retrieved her grease rag. She glanced at her hand. There was a scratch, but luckily no blood. Still, her hand stung.

As did the memories. The sudden flow of images that Rocho attempted to suppress had broken through their barrier. They were of a time when she was young and had trusted her family and a young woman, she thought she would spend the rest of her life with.

Rocho leaned on her elbows against the classic fifty-five Chevrolet she was being paid to restore. She took in several deep breaths as the images continued to assault her.

A petite sandy blonde young woman was pointing at Rocho. Tears were streaming down cherubic cheeks. Her mother and father shaking their heads in the front row of the courtroom. The mechanic staring into those deceptive brown eyes and wondering how she could have been so wrong about one person.

"Everything all right back here?" Frank's booming voice brought Rocho back to the here and now. She had become entranced in the reason she was a wanderer. Why she rarely remained in any town more than a year. Tops.

Rocho was not exactly a free woman. "I'm fine. Just scraped my hand a bit." The mechanic attempted to focus on the here and now once again.

But the images were causing her to become nauseous. Rocho swallowed hard as the scene shifted. Instead of the young woman, it was her family. At different intervals, each one turned their back on her. She wasn't even allowed back in the house. When she left her hometown, she had nothing but what was on her back and in her pockets.

As usual, Rocho forced herself to repair what could be repaired. The past could not. She couldn't be tried again and be found innocent. She couldn't seek forgiveness from those that weren't willing to listen.

So, the Bel Air would be Rocho's solace. Most likely, she would work through lunch. She would help rebuild her walls by restoring the once beautiful powder blue beauty.

The hairs on the back of Rocho's neck stood on end. She sensed someone watching her. Her azure eyes managed to locate who was staring. She found herself caught in a sea of green. There was a depth in those eyes that caused the mechanic to swallow several times.

Rocho blinked and the petite blonde had disappeared. She shook her head wondering if she had actually seen what she had thought she had seen. Besides the emerald eyes, the woman had appeared so much like Juliette. The young girl who had accused Rocho of rape and had her convicted. And in a way, exiled to this small town.

OOOOOOOOOOOO

The petite blonde impatiently tapped her foot against the floorboard. Sylvia was tired of traveling. She was tired of not seeing her father. She was tired of the woman driving her to the small town where she was raised.

Yet, Sylvia hadn't the strength to break off the relationship. They had lived together for the past year and a half. Yet, there hadn't been the sparkage Sylvia had been looking for. And there was no sparkage in sight.

Sylvia sighed heavily as the sign informing them they were only five miles from Portland, Michigan came into view. The small town had a population of just over six thousand. Yet, the woman loved the town and had missed the uniqueness of living in a small town.

Her father, Frank, wanted her to take over the family business. While Sylvia knew how to run the service department of the dealership, she had not known how to run the business side. That had led to four long boring years at The University of Michigan. While the courses had been boring, the sports offered and the women available had made it tolerable.

The young businesswoman smirked at the thought of the women she had once enjoyed. There weren't hundreds, but Sylvia had enjoyed the female form while studying the dry world of business.

And then Sylvia had met Laurie. She was tall, dark and gorgeous. Something had attracted her to the woman. Was it the fact Laurie wore mostly black and leather jackets?

Sylvia's head snapped when the car suddenly came to a screeching stop. "Sorry bout that." Laurie's dark eyes were apologetic. It was a look Sylvia was becoming accustomed to. "I thought the light wasn't going to change."

A shrug was the response, though internally, Sylvia hated the unnecessary abuse upon her classic nineteen-hundred-seventy-six Pontiac Trans Am. She made a mental note to do a quick inspection of her car once settled.

Emerald eyes scanned the scenery. Not much had changed since Sylvia had last been in Portland. She hadn't been back since she had left for The University of Michigan, even though it was only about a two-hour drive.

Her heart wasn't in coming back even though it had been six long years since she'd been home. She was now twenty-four and free. But what freedom did she really have?

Sylvia's heart wasn't in it because she didn't want to take over the business. She wanted to be in one of the bays. Merely doing an oil change was nearly as enticing as a woman in a bikini.

The thought caused a wry smile to form upon Sylvia's features. "Something amusing about being back in such a hick town?" Her girlfriend's laughter followed the abrasive comment.

A cringe flowed through Sylvia's body. This was one of the reasons she had thought about breaking up with her girlfriend. Laurie hated small towns. Though Sylvia wasn't looking forward to sitting in an office, it wasn't because she had grown up in a so-called hick town.

"Please don't refer to my hometown as a hick town." Sylvia's green eyes had turned hunter as she attempted to calm her anger. "I know there isn't a great deal to do and some of the people are set in their ways, I happen to like my hometown."

"Is that why this is the first time we've been back in the year and a half we've been together." The car once again jerked as Laurie nearly missed the turn into the dealership.

"I don't want to argue our first day here." Sylvia waited until the Trans Am had come to a complete stop. "I'm going to find my father. You can entertain yourself however you see fit."

Though Sylvia was angry, she carefully shut the door to her baby. She should have driven. The way Laurie drove the precious vehicle caused her to want to pull the car into an open bay and do a little tinkering.

Instead, Sylvia stalked through the open bay doors. She came to a screeching halt when a vision caught her eyes. It wasn't the powder blue fifty-five Bel Air. It was the mechanic working on the classic.

Even in the dirty coveralls, there was no doubt in Sylvia's mind the mechanic was all woman. The azure eyes were mesmerizing. Her heart pounded in her chest. It was nearly overpowering the sound of her father's voice.

It felt like an eternity that Sylvia stared at the enticing woman. In reality, it was only a matter of seconds. Finally, she forced her feet to move.

Being home and working in an office might not be so bad. It was the final thoughts Sylvia had before she turned her attention fully to her father.

Chapter 2

Rocho stretched. Her stomach was informing her that she had worked past lunch once again. Glancing at the clock on the wall, she had nearly worked past closing time.

A small grin was on the mechanic's face as Rocho realized she had the luxury of working through lunch without being interrupted. She was the lead mechanic. In other words, she chose which vehicles she worked on and what hours she worked.

Another of the perks was that Rocho had her own locker room. The mechanic couldn't wait for a scathing shower to wash away the well earned sweat and grease from her body.

But then what? As Rocho slowly made certain her tools were secured, as was the classic beauty, her mind wandered back to the emerald eyes that had captured her. And the memories those eyes continued to attempt to force from behind their barrier.

With the practice of months working in the same place, it didn't take long for Rocho to strip out of her overalls and the shorts/t-shirts she wore beneath. Not bothering with a robe, she made her way to the shower.

The water was hot. The soap was abrasive. And the memories were vicious. But not all of them. Those were the ones Rocho attempted to concentrate on.

Like asking Juliette out for the first time. The first sweet kiss they shared under the bleachers. The flowers the mechanic would leave taped to Juliette's locker, always cautious so that no one would know they were from her.

Sitting under the cloudless sky. Attempting to make shapes out of the stars. Juliette wanted to be an astronomer. For her, it was the actual constellations. But for Rocho, she loved to see the shapes. And make up stories to go with them.

Rocho was so involved with her memories she didn't hear the opening and closing of the locker room door. When she finally turned off the water, she heard the sound of someone else's breathing.

Cursing and wishing she hadn't abandoned her robe, Rocho hastily covered herself with the large bath towel, grateful she always purchased the largest one possible. "I know someone is out there. This is the women's locker room. And it's private."

"I know." The voice was female. That meant Rocho would not, hopefully, have to show off the moves she had learned over the years. "I'm looking for Renee Bishop."

A shudder ran through Rocho's body at the use of her given name. "The name is Rocho." She held the towel tightly, especially to her full breasts, as she made her way out of the shower and into the locker room area.

Standing just inside the entrance was the blonde woman that had been torturing Rocho's thoughts nearly the entire day. This up close and personal, the woman was breathtaking.

Sylvia had to swallow several times when the barely covered form of her lead mechanic exited from the shower. Rocho was trouble. With long legs, brilliant azure eyes and black hair that was begging to have her hand run through it.

"I'm sorry. My father didn't tell me you had a preferred name." Sylvia maintained her distance. Partially it was to give her employee the illusion of privacy. Mostly, it was because she didn't know if she could trust herself so close to the naked woman. "My name is Sylvia. I've been attempting to introduce myself to everyone."

"And saved the best for last?" Rocho noticed the blush that graced her boss' face. There had been rumors of the elusive daughter's return. But she hadn't expected it so soon. Or for the prodigal daughter to be so breathtaking.

Sylvia couldn't help chuckling softly. "Something like that." The young woman managed to stare at her burgundy sneakers that matched her jeans. The black t-shirt would be replaced with something more 'professional', as her father would prefer.

Setting speed records, Rocho dressed in form fitting black jeans and a navy-blue sleeveless t-shirt. She hadn't expected to entertain anyone and felt underdressed with her boss standing in the locker room.

After hearing the clearing of a throat, Sylvia brought her gaze so it was locked with intense azure. "Actually, my first love is as a mechanic. I grew up in my father's mechanic bay. But I knew he wanted someone to take over the business so I sacrificed my first love to keep the business going."

Another coloring of cheeks was in order for Sylvia. Especially when a dark eyebrow rose. "Sorry. I babbled. And was unprofessional. What I meant was I saved my lead mechanic for last because it is my love and is more important to a dealership than the salespeople."

Rocho attempted to maintain a stoic façade. There was something about this young woman before her that amused her. "Not many people realize that it isn't the sales that make or break a dealership, but people coming back to maintain their vehicles."

Sylvia nodded in agreement. "I meant to catch you before you were done for the day. I wanted to discuss if there were things you haven't been allowed to do that you think would help with customer satisfaction."

The lead mechanic crossed her arms over her chest. While Frank had given Rocho nearly free rein, there were a few suggestions she'd compiled but had never thought Frank was serious. Was her new boss serious about listening to her?

"I have a few ideas." Rocho continued to study Sylvia. For a moment, it wasn't because the young woman was so appealing. It was because she wanted to see how sincere her new boss truly was.

"Excellent." Sylvia's smile could only be described as radiant. "If you don't mind, I'd like to do this outside of work. I'm busy tonight, but I'd like to take you to dinner. I can write it off as a business expense. Though there aren't many places in Portland to really sit down and have a good meal."

Without thought, Rocho was speaking. "I could, if you want, cook for you. My place is rather small. But it would be ok for just the two of us."

Emerald eyes grew wide. Sylvia had been joking. There were a handful of places she missed dining at since being away so long. But to spend time with the beautiful mechanic alone and secluded was tempting. And dangerous.

"I'm sorry." Rocho witnessed the widening of the emerald eyes. She assumed she had startled the young woman. "I didn't think before I spoke. I don't usually attempt to wine and dine my bosses."

Sylvia hastily recovered. "It was a surprise, I'll grant you. But I think I'd like to take you up on that. If Friday is all right with you? I can still write it off as a business expense if you save me the receipt."

"When I offer to make dinner for a lady, no matter the reason behind it, it's always my treat." Rocho wondered where this bravado was coming from. After all, she normally secluded herself from the female population. She hadn't been with a woman in nearly two years.

Forcing her eyes not to widen once again, Sylvia couldn't help the sensual smile gracing her lips. As much as she would love to continue flirting, there were too numerous reasons to end this little dance now.

One was the business aspect. Dating an employee was fraught with danger. Then there was what should be the most compelling reason. The woman who was waiting at home for Sylvia's return.

"I'll keep that in mind." Sylvia cursed herself. "But I insist on paying for something or bringing the beverages. It's only fair." Mental slap as the flirting continued.

Rocho hadn't meant to discover her boss' interest in women. She definitely hadn't meant to discover Sylvia was interested in her. But she had. And now she had to live with it.

"Good. Now if you'll excuse me, I skipped lunch. I need to eat before working on my own lil project." Rocho graced Sylvia with her most charming smile.

"Don't want you passing out." Sylvia opened the door to the locker room. She held it open and studied how the tight-fitting black jeans moved with the long lean legs. "You'll have to, when we have dinner, show me your project."

"Perhaps." Rocho found herself winking. Internally, she was cursing herself. Women were trouble. There was no way she should continue to flirt so shamelessly with Sylvia. It didn't matter she was her boss. She was female. Enough said.

"I can be very persuasive." Sylvia could feel the mental slaps with each word spoken. Flirting had never been her strong suit. Yet, here she was. Beyond flirting.

Sylvia stopped in her tracks. She had forgotten Laurie would be picking her up with her baby. The expression on her girlfriend's face informed Sylvia how unhappy Laurie was.

Rocho had kept walking a step or two before realizing Sylvia had stopped. Azure eyes danced between Sylvia and the woman with dark complexion and dark eyes. Instantly, the mechanic knew the shameless flirting had been even stupider. These two women were in a relationship.

The businessperson within kicked in. "Laurie, I'd like you to meet Rocho our lead mechanic. Rocho, this is my girlfriend. Maybe one day you'd like to see my baby."

The mechanic didn't even think about 'baby' meaning anything other than a classic car. "Perhaps when we have our business dinner Friday. Until then, you two ladies have a good evening and a good rest of your week."

Sylvia watched as Rocho bowed before taking her leave. Time escaped the business owner as she watched the mechanic walk with strength and purpose.

It took a hand waving in front of her face for Sylvia to come back to the here and now. "Sorry. Was thinking about the things I need to discuss with Miss Bishop. Now, where's my keys. I want to take you out for dinner."

Laurie shook her head as she handed over the keys to the precious Trans Am. "You better make it more than dinner. I saw how you were drooling over your so-called mechanic. And what's this about a business dinner?"

Jealousy. Sylvia hated it in her lover. Normally, there was no reason for it. Sylvia was a one-woman woman. Picking up her pace, the business owner was at the door holding it open. Already she knew it was the last that needed securing.

It took Laurie some time to exit through the door being held open for her. Sylvia took her time punching in the code. "Even you have to admit that Rocho is sexy. So if I was drooling, it was appreciating a good looking woman. That old saying I'm in a committed relationship, not dead. As for dinner, it's this Friday. I'll be meeting Rocho at her place. If you want, I'll ask her to set a place for you. Though it's just going to be boring things discussed about how to improve the mechanic bay."

"I don't believe a word you are saying." Laurie slammed the door to the Trans Am. Sylvia wanted to say something but knew it would aggravate her girlfriend further. "Just take me home. I bought a frozen pizza. You can have that. I'm going out without you."

Sylvia hesitated in starting her baby. She should insist their first night in her home town be spent together. But she didn't really care if they spent any time together. It was a mess she should have cleaned up before moving Laurie with her.

The roar of the engine startled Laurie. Sylvia grinned evilly as she shifted her baby into gear. Without leaving any treads behind, she had the classic roaring down the road. She was driving so fast Laurie was bracing herself.

If Laurie wanted to play games, Sylvia would oblige her. Her mood darkened a little at the thought of Rocho. She didn't want to play games anymore. Yet, she had flirted with the mechanic. Was she using Rocho to upset Laurie?

Chapter 3

"Hey, Barker." Rocho chuckled at the name of her neighbor's pup. Half the time, she felt as if the young Dalmatian was more her pup. She rarely saw the family next door playing with him. If they didn't take him in during winter, she might just have to say something.

Rocho shook her head. Reality was she most likely would not be in Portland past the autumn. After all, she had been in the small town for just under a year now. In the past, a year was the limit before she moved on.

The mechanic made her way out back. Rocho cautiously opened the garage door. She had an internal, self-rigged security system. If the weight was moved too speedily, an alarm would sound.

Her stomach growled at Rocho, but she ignored it. Instead, she just had to check on her baby. It wasn't of the four-wheel variety. It was of the two.

It was a Honda four-fifty-cc police special. It would probably surprise Sylvia that Rocho had chosen a motorcycle to restore over a vehicle.

Each place Rocho had lived in, she had chosen a different motor vehicle. This was the first time she had come across the classic motorcycle and just had to restore it.

The Fuzz, as Rocho termed her discovery, was nearly completed. The real issue was finding genuine parts. Everything appeared as she had left it the night before.

Too tired and hungry to be able to safely concentrate on restoring The Fuzz, it was inside to a frozen dinner, a glass of chocolate milk and her one weakness of double chocolate cookies. She attempted to limit herself to two a night, but it was difficult.

Azure eyes blinked several times as Rocho relaxed in her recliner. She glanced around the room before sleep could claim her. What had she been thinking inviting her boss here?

There was only one other recliner in the room. The television set was an old box set that had come with the place. The stove was probably older than she was. Hopefully it could make the meal she had in mind. Then there was the tiny bathroom and a lone bedroom.

Why the number of bedrooms was a factor was beyond Rocho. They would have to dine sitting in the recliners with tv stands. Unless the weather was all right. Then they could eat out in the nearly nonexistent backyard.

"Stop it!" Rocho yawned as she vehemently chastised herself. "This is a business dinner. That's all it can be. You don't do women anymore. And she has a girlfriend."

Staring at the blank television for several moments, Rocho decided it was time to call it a night. Hastily, she washed what few dishes she had dirtied before making her way to the bathroom. Once all her evening rituals were taken care of, she attempted to settle herself in bed.

Instead of sleep finding her, Rocho found herself staring at the weathered ceiling. Images would not be forced from her mind, no matter how many times she attempted to force them out.

"God damn you Juliette!" Rocho could feel the sting of fresh tears. She hadn't cried since she had moved five years ago. It had been the last time she had attempted a relationship.

The words of hate. The threats to call the police. Rocho squeezed her eyes shut. If she didn't manage some sleep, she wouldn't be able to work on the Bel Air.

Hating to do it, Rocho slunk out of bed. She took only one of the over-the-counter sleeping pills. Hopefully it would take the edge off and she would manage at least for four hours.

OOOOOOOOOOOO

Instead of allowing Laurie to use her baby, Sylvia had dropped her girlfriend off at one of the places she knew her girlfriend would hate. The Wagon Wheel was a restaurant, bar and bowling alley wrapped up into one. So not someplace her high-class girlfriend was accustomed to.

While there was a part of Sylvia that was enjoying the thought of her girlfriend in a bowling alley, there was another part that was angry. But it wasn't only her girlfriend she was angry with. Sylvia was angry she hadn't even spoken to Laurie about how unhappy she was before they had left school.

If she had, Sylvia might be in a position to attempt something, other than a business relationship, with Rocho. There was friendship. But Sylvia had very few female friends.

When Sylvia was this angry, there was only one way to release the tension in her body. Working out would help maintain her shape and it would work off the anger.

Sylvia made her way through the small apartment she had leased. Actually, her father had leased it for her since she refused to purchase a home or move into the large home she had grown up in. The major drawback of any of the places was the lack of privacy.

It wasn't even privacy of being in a relationship. As Sylvia had grown older, her father had been more and more in her business. Especially after she had confided in him that she was a lesbian at twelve.

Luckily, the small apartment complex had the advantage of a small gym in the main building. Changing into shorts and a sleeveless shirt, Sylvia walked the short distance to the main building.

Her workout began as usual. A quick warmup on the stationary bicycle was followed by a twenty-minute workout on the treadmill. The final way to punish and exhaust the young woman was lifting weights.

Sylvia was sweating profusely by the time she had finished with her workout. Her body felt amazing, yet she felt exhausted. After a quick meal, she hoped she would be able to fall asleep before Laurie returned home.

Home. Sylvia sighed as she dodged one of the neighbor kids on a bicycle. This apartment wasn't home. It wasn't because of the location. It was because of the person she shared it with.

Enough wallowing. Sylvia used her key to enter through the security door. Another mini workout was in the wings as she had agreed to the apartment on the third floor.

After entering the apartment, Sylvia headed for the shower. It was a quick one to wash the sweat and stench from her body. Grateful for her short wash and wear hair, she didn't even bother blow drying.

Cringing at the thought of sharing the same bed as Laurie, Sylvia was tempted to check into the only small hotel in town. At the very least, she thought about using the spare bedroom. But that was not the woman her mother had raised her to be. Then again, her mother had been taken from her far too soon.

The stray thought of her mother produced a genuine smile. If only her mother had lived to see her as an adult. But breast cancer had a way of shortening lives. Cancer sucked. Big time.

Attempting to settle, Sylvia found her thoughts straying to a certain tall, dark and dangerous mechanic. Dangerous only because she was the kind of woman who Sylvia normally was attracted to. The kind who shared her interests. Who seemed not minding residing in a small town.

Friendship. Sylvia had to remind herself that was all she could expect out of Rocho, outside of one of the best mechanics in all of the wolverine state.

Blurry emerald eyes attempted to penetrate the darkness that surrounded Sylvia. Something had awakened the young woman. Sleeping so soundly that her mother used to joke she would be mistaken for a corpse one day, it was unusual for anything to wake her.

Reaching for her cellphone, Sylvia knocked it off the nightstand. She was grateful she had allowed her father to furnish her apartment before her arrival. Finally fishing it from the floor, she realized she had missed ten text messages and five phone calls from Laurie.

"What the fuck?" Not normally one to curse, except when really upset, Sylvia couldn't help it. The urge to curse became nearly overwhelming when she listened to the string of messages left.

"Who the fuck is Stacy?" Sylvia was now fully awake. She glanced at her alarm clock. Nearly six in the morning, her alarm would have been chirping in another half an hour anyways.

"So, you found a ride home." Sylvia shook her head. The last message had not been intended for her. Or had it been one of those old-fashioned butt dials.

No matter how it happened, Sylvia now had the proof she had always lacked while living off campus. The city was so large, it was no wonder she had never caught Laurie with another woman.

Portland was a small town. But it wasn't the reason Sylvia had caught her girlfriend cheating. It was technology. Now Sylvia had to think of how she wanted to handle the situation.

Irony of all irony? Sylvia's first thought was to contact Rocho. To see if her employee wanted to lend her an ear. Or better yet, a shoulder. Or something more.

Chapter 4

Rocho glanced at the clock over the entrance to the mechanic bay. It was creeping until closing time upon Friday. The week had come and gone. Each night had ended the way Monday had, sadly, with the mechanic succumbing to the need to taking a sleeping aide.

Closing time meant it wouldn't be long until Rocho would be making her boss something in the privacy of her tiny home that, until now, had been only for the mechanic.

After the incident on Monday, Rocho had also taken to showering at home. Tonight would be no exception. While Sylvia had remained distant, the mechanic didn't want to take any chances.

The clearing of a throat startled Rocho. She luckily caught the wrench she had in her hand. Already, there was the scratch from her previous accident she had to repair. She didn't need a dent, as well.

"I'm sorry to disturb you." Rocho took in her boss' condition. There were dark circles under her eyes. There was little to no sparkle in those amazing emerald eyes. Even her manner of dress was dull somehow in a grey pantsuit.

"It's all right. I was actually about to wrap things up for the evening." Rocho began placing her tools in their spots. "After all, I have a dinner to make for the boss."

The smile Rocho attempted was not convincing. It wasn't because she didn't want to spend time with Sylvia. It was because of the continued memories her boss provoked. The ones that forced her each night to take a sleeping pill.

"Sucking up already?" Sylvia's eyes, momentarily, had the sparkle in them. They quickly faded like the last of the fireworks on The Fourth of July. "I just wanted to confirm our meeting/dinner conference. I have been so caught up with attempting to learn everything from my father. He wants to take a vacation in two weeks, before fully signing the dealership over to me. Not sure if I'll be up to speed by then."

Rocho had secured her tools and was now wiping the grease from her hands. She wanted a shower badly from the sweat that always came from wearing the thick coveralls. "When it comes to the service department, you can lean on me. I know it seems I'm always working on the Bel Air here, but I do take time to make certain things are running smoothly."

"That's appreciated." Sylvia ran her hand through her short locks. Rocho hadn't noticed the shorter locks until that moment. It wasn't a drastic new look. Just a trim and shaping that accentuated her boss' natural beauty. "So far, you are the only one I haven't had a major sit down with, yet you are the only one I feel I can count on."

There was a slight tinting to Rocho's cheeks. "I live to serve." In the back of her mind, she wanted to scream that she would soon be leaving. That her year limit of remaining anywhere was just around the corner. That no one should count on her. That she would soon be running away. And no one should trust her.

"That's a dangerous offer." Sylvia mentally scolded herself when thinking of the personal ways Rocho could serve her. Especially after the way Laurie had begun treating her.

While neither was happy in the relationship, Sylvia would never stoop to the level of cheating. It wasn't her style. It would never be her style.

"Life can be dangerous." Rocho visibly grimaced. She was flirting shamelessly with her boss. Hades, she was flirting shamelessly with someone with tits. Not good. That was more than dangerous.

Sylvia didn't notice the flirting. Her mind went to her mother. "That's true. If it weren't, my mother would be here." She didn't even realize she had spoken the words aloud until she felt the hand upon her forearm.

Concerned azure met sad emerald. "I'm sorry. I didn't mean to worry you. It's a personal story. I'll just say that my mom died when I was twelve of breast cancer."

Rocho couldn't help squeezing the skin beneath her hand before hastily removing it. "I'm sorry. Sometimes, no matter the age, life isn't fair. But the younger one is, the more unfair it is."

"Yeah." Sylvia swallowed hard before forcing herself to transform back into the professional she had been when she walked into the room. "Now, about this evening. I was thinking around seven. If that's convenient for you."

The part of Rocho that yearned for basic human contact wanted to know more of the personal story. But the part that knew this had to remain professional knew there was only one answer. "That's perfect. I can get the groceries I need and get cleaned up. You offered to bring the beverages on Monday. I don't consume alcohol so for me any cola or juice will do."

A blonde eyebrow rose at the thought of someone else not partaking of spirits. Sylvia had only once been drunk out of her mind. It was enough for her to swear off drinking. Unlike Laurie who still enjoyed a night on the town. As evident by the voicemail that remained on her cellphone.

"Again, I think something can be arranged." Sylvia smiled halfheartedly. With the thoughts of Laurie running through her mind, she couldn't manage a genuine one. "I have one thing to take care of before I leave. I'll make certain everything is secured before I leave."

"As you wish. Boss." Rocho winked at the lovely lady before making her way toward the locker room. She might not shower at work, but she would still leave her dirty overalls there. She would take her Pistons cap with her.

After making certain her hands and face were thoroughly scrubbed, Rocho made her way through the bay she called home. She would have to skip working on the Bel Air on Monday. Paperwork was calling her name.

There was no vehicle waiting for Rocho. She had purchased a bicycle. Why? Everywhere she went, she sold her vehicle after moving. It was so her parents could not trace her whereabouts. Living in a small town made it easier to get around by pedal power.

It took just over an hour for the quick trip to the local supermarket and trip home. Deciding a shower was in order before beginning to cook, Rocho was still toweling her long locks off when there was a knock at the door.

"Son of a bitch." Rocho hastily dressed in her clean black workout shorts and grey sleeveless shirt. She didn't even bother with her usual sports bra.

Her dark hair still dripping when Rocho opened the door. Her breath caught in her throat when the beauty was revealed. Sylvia was dressed in black slacks with a V-neck silk ruby-red top. Her hair was feathered carefully.

Sylvia had a similar reaction. Seeing her employee in next to nothing was not something she had prepared herself for. She hadn't thought Rocho would dress in business attire like she had, but something casual.

"I'm sorry." Rocho had to clear her voice as it cracked. "I'm running a little behind. I normally walk or ride my bike everywhere I go and time escaped me."

The businesswoman was charmed at how nervous her employee was. "You didn't exactly fail to notice the time. I'm about forty-five minutes early. For that, I'm the one who needs to apologize. I hope you don't mind."

Rocho vehemently shook her head as she stepped aside to allow Sylvia entrance into her humble home. "If you'll just make yourself comfortable, I'll change into something a little more appropriate for a business dinner."

"Take your time." Sylvia watched her hostess disappear. She first made her way into the kitchen. She placed the grape juice and cola in the fridge. She noticed the salmon and wondered what her employee had planned for her.

After glancing down the narrow hallway Rocho had disappeared down, Sylvia made her way into the living room. She knew her father had just given the lead mechanic a raise. She knew Rocho could afford something with more substance.

Sylvia wasn't judging her employee. It was more wondering if this was part of Rocho's personality. If she was the type of person who less was more. In other words, a woman after her own heart once again.

The chair Sylvia chose was well-worn but still extremely comfortable. In fact, if she allowed herself to fully relax, she could easily fall asleep.

As it was, Sylvia was startled when the clearing of a throat caused her eyes to open. Once again, the young woman had her breath taken. Rocho was dressed in a simple black V-neck t-shirt and form fitting black jeans. Black was definitely the raven-haired woman's color.

"Sorry. I didn't mean to drift off on you. This chair is so comfortable and the place so relaxing." Sylvia watched as Rocho hovered in the doorway. When her employee remained silent, she decided to open the discussion. "Would you like help with dinner? There's not a great deal to discuss as your department is the best run. But there are a few points we need to discuss."

"I can handle dinner. But if you'd like to pour us something to drink while I whip up one of the few things I know to make…" There was a twinkle in azure eyes. Rocho couldn't help it. There was something about Sylvia thought brought out the flirt in her.

"I brought cola and grape juice." Sylvia regretfully rose from the chair. Inwardly, she groaned when she was forced to stand. She had been on her feet more than she was accustomed to. And there was sleeping alone.

"Mmm. I think cola would be best as I'll be using lemons for the salmon." Rocho hesitated with her hand upon the refrigerator door. "I forgot to ask if you had any allergies."

A slightly embarrassed mechanic stood before Sylvia. "And I didn't say I don't. Of course, the last time I had someone make dinner for me, outside a restaurant that is, I can't even recall. I'm a little out of practice."

"Still, I feel like I'm out of touch with just the basics of being a good hostess." Rocho retrieved the cola, along with the ingredients she would need to make the lemon peppered salmon with buttery garlic asparagus. A small side salad had already been purchased at the store.

"And I feel like I'm out of touch with life outside of school and work." Sylvia hadn't meant to say the words out loud. Somehow, she felt comfortable with Rocho. Enough to say things she wouldn't normally.

"I guess we're both learning to be gracious outside of work." Rocho covered both the salmon and the asparagus. She placed them in the oven before setting the timer. "It'll be another twenty minutes. We could have the side salads or wait."

"Wait. I just want to sit and relax for a bit." Sylvia had rummaged in the cupboards and located glasses for the cola. "You lead the way."

It didn't take long to settle next to one another. "Let's get this out of the way so that we can enjoy your wonderful smelling dinner. I just have two things to ask. How do you do scheduling so efficiently and how do you keep man hours down?"

Rocho took a sip of her cola before placing it on the small stand that separated the two recliners. "Easy. I searched out the best possible computer program and made certain everyone, including the mechanics, knew how to use it. As for man hours, I'm salaried. So if there's something too major or complicated, I'm the one that takes over at the end of the day."

Sylvia shook her head. It was that simple. "That wouldn't work in most garages." She tilted her head. "But then, you aren't like most lead mechanics."

"No, I'm not. And the fact is I'm probably not going to be around after the lease runs out in this place." Rocho figured she owed her new boss the news up front. After all, her not being the lead mechanic would affect the business.

Chapter 5

Sylvia watched as Rocho made her way to the kitchen. The timer had interrupted her reaction to the fact her lead mechanic didn't plan on remaining employed by her.

Uncertainty warred within. There was a part of Sylvia that would say it was because of the huge loss financially to her father's, and soon to be hers, business. But the more pressing reason was she already found she had a connection to Rocho. Something she'd never had to anyone. Whether as a friend or lover.

The young woman barely noticed when a television tray was placed before her. Sylvia did glance up when Rocho's shadow crossed over her as she placed the plate of salmon, asparagus and salad upon her tray. "I brought the two liter. Do you need a top off?"

"Thanks." Sylvia remained silent as Rocho retrieved her own meal and topped off her own drink. She waited until the mechanic was seated before asking the question that burned since Rocho had let slip she might not be around soon. "Can I ask you why you might leave? Is it monetary? Work conditions? Living conditions?"

Rocho chewed on the bite of salmon. It was zesty, just the way she liked it. She hoped it wasn't too zesty for her boss. "Well, it's more personal than anything else. I won't go into details, but for certain reasons, I haven't lived anywhere beyond a year since I was eighteen."

Sylvia pushed the lettuce across the plate. "I can understand not wanting to share details. I have some of my own. It's just that I could really use your continued work skills and ethics. There aren't many like you in the world anymore."

It was Rocho's turn to pick at her food. For once, it wasn't something microwaved or boiled or from a fast food restaurant. She should be savoring it.

But Sylvia's defeated tone of voice was breaking Rocho's heart. Placing her fork gently on the plate, she turned to look at her boss. All she could see was smartly styled blonde locks as Sylvia's head was focused solely on her plate.

"Maybe, just maybe, we could discuss something that could keep me here a little longer." Rocho couldn't help smirking when Sylvia's head whipped up. "I don't need money. But there might be something else you can do for me."

"I need a great deal of help in the sales department." Sylvia held up her hands to forestall any argument against Rocho joining the sales' force. "Dad already informed me that was a deal breaker. Though I do have to agree with him. Your looks alone could bring in customers by the wagonload."

Rocho shook her head in disagreement. "I won't be your poster girl. I won't be upfront. In fact, I hate even being your lead mechanic. Except that it affords me the ability to work on the cars I choose. Besides, I disagree. You don't want someone like me in contact with people. Especially women."

A blonde eyebrow rose at the last vehement statement. Someone had hurt Rocho horrifically in the past. And not just someone. Someone of the female persuasion.

Sylvia had already surmised there was an attraction between them so it wasn't a shock that a woman was behind the scorn she heard in Rocho's voice. It was the story behind it.

Was it something like what Sylvia had experienced? On the three occasions she had attempted a relationship? Cheating. At this point, Sylvia was ready for a meaningful relationship or none at all.

"We'll disagree on wanting you with customers." Sylvia took a moment to sip her soda. "But what I do know is that I would be hard pressed to replace you in the mechanic bay. Both as a mechanic and as a supervisor. So, if we can work something out where you choose to stay indefinitely, I'd greatly appreciate it."

Indefinitely. It wasn't a term Rocho was accustomed to thinking in. After being caught after remaining in Lisbon, Ohio for eighteen months, she had decided a year was the longest she could remain. Sometimes, she only remained six months, if she could find a shorter lease agreement.

"I can only agree to remain until I have to decide whether to renew on this place." Rocho drained her cola. She was suddenly thirsty at the thought of remaining beyond a year. "More cola?"

"I'd joke that you were attempting to get the boss drunk." Sylvia winked to take the sting out of her words as they both knew it wasn't possible. "I'd appreciate it. Though I'm going to have to have to leave soon. My girlfriend is expecting me."

Rocho was both saddened and grateful her boss had a girlfriend. While the attraction remained, it was yet another reason she would not act upon it.

But the growing friendship that seemed to be between them was enough to be concerned about. Rocho refilled both of their glasses. "I wouldn't want your girlfriend thinking I was seducing the boss in an attempt to get a raise."

Sylvia knocked over her freshly filled cola. She hastily placed the television stand out of her way and stood. "I'm so sorry. That was so clumsy of me."

Without a thought, Rocho was off to retrieve a towel. When she arrived in the living room, Sylvia was attempting to clean the spill with Kleenexes. "I've got this. Why don't you finish your dinner? After all, you have to get home soon."

"Thanks." There wasn't much left of Sylvia's appetite. While she had a noncommitment from Rocho to remain in her employment, it was the referral to cheating that had Sylvia on edge. She managed to consume the rest of the meal her employee had been so kind to make for her. "I guess I should be going."

Rocho rose from her seated position. She'd managed to consume the remainder of her meal as well. "I'll walk you out." As they made their way to the door, a stray thought entered the mechanic's mind. The filter on her brain appeared to be off as she couldn't help with her request. "If you aren't busy tomorrow or Sunday, I'd like to show you my personal project."

A timid smile was upon Sylvia's face. She had to have a little conversation with Laurie. They hadn't spoken, not really, since she'd received the voicemail. But she wasn't ready to face her girlfriend, just yet.

"I assume it has something to do with the mechanical world." Rocho nodded shyly. Sylvia's smile was heartwarming and genuine. "I'd like that. Very much."

Chapter 6

"Why do you have to go?" Laurie stood in the entrance to the bedroom. It wasn't the one she had been sleeping in. She had finally been relegated to the spare bedroom.

"Why do you have to party every night at The Wagon Wheel?" Sylvia wasn't yet ready for her get together with Rocho. Only because of the time. She was already dressed in a greased stained tanned t-shirt and ripped blue jean shorts. The only thing she would gather to top off her outfit was The Detroit Tigers baseball cap her father had had since they'd won the championship in nineteen-hundred-eighty-four.

Laurie closed her eyes. "If you were home at night, instead of working late hours, I might not have to go out and find entertainment."

There was the opening Sylvia had been waiting for. She didn't want to start something when there wasn't much time before meeting with Rocho. But it seemed it was now or never.

Without missing a beat, Sylvia retrieved her cellphone. She dialed her voicemail and entered her password. While placing the phone on speakerphone, she made certain to watch her girlfriend's expression.

Green was an interesting color. Sylvia hadn't been ready for the expulsion of the breakfast they had shared upon the bedroom floor. She sighed heavily knowing she would have to be the one to clean it up. Like she was having to clean up the mess her father had made of the business.

With the exception of Rocho and the service department. Hopefully, after Sylvia cleaned up this mess, she could escape for the afternoon with her employee. Forget everything else and just enjoy an evening with a friend.

Not even attempting to comfort her ex-girlfriend, Sylvia grabbed some old towels from the bathroom. She soaked one and doused it with soap.

Sylvia's voice remained neutral as she focused on scrubbing the mess Laurie had made. "This isn't exactly your fault. I wasn't happy before we left school. I felt we had been drifting apart for quite some time. But I never thought you'd actually cheat on me."

The voice was weak that managed to speak. "That first night. I just wanted to find a place we could enjoy. When you refused, it felt like you were refusing to spend time with me. Like you have for the past six months."

"I guess we both have been avoiding the truth." Sylvia was on her knees. The mess, at least the mess made by Laurie's stomach, was cleaned up. "I don't know what to do. I can't stay with a cheater. As you know, my last two girlfriends cheated. It's something I can't forgive."

"Even if it was because I was feeling neglected and drunk off my ass?" Laurie asked in a hopeful tone. Sylvia merely shook her head. While she had a fear of people leaving her, she wouldn't be cheated on. "I don't have a job. I don't have a place to live. It's going to take me a while to find both."

"I know. You can stay here for a while. I can't say indefinitely." Sylvia rose to her feet. "There's too much going on at work. I need to focus my time there."

"So why spend time with your employee?" Laurie's jealous streak was showing. "You already had your so-called business dinner. What more is there to discuss?"

"Something you don't know much about." Sylvia made her way to the bathroom. She hastily washed out the towels and then her hands. Standing in the doorway to the bathroom, she studied Laurie.

While Laurie was as beautiful as ever, there was something about her. Something Sylvia had never seen before receiving the voicemail. "There's something we never had. Something none of my past relationships have ever had. And that's friendship."

OOOOOOOOOOOO

Rocho had made a quick trip to the market when she had awakened. She had made it part of her jogging. Normally one to use her workout equipment, she had decided a brisk jog the five miles would work just as well.

Using the reusable bags, they actually had worked as counterweights. It had made the jog back to her small house even more of a workout. Rocho was breathless by the time she had returned and began putting away the groceries.

Not certain how long her boss intended to remain, Rocho had purchased more cola and fruit juice. There was also something for a light lunch that even the mechanic couldn't mess up. After all, she'd already used up her one cuisine already.

Why was Rocho so obsessed with wanting to make certain Sylvia was impressed? That her boss enjoyed her time with the mechanic?

Rocho sighed heavily as she placed the last of the groceries in their place before making her way to the bathroom. The mechanic had just enough time before her boss was to arrive and to get her beauty ready for its showing.

The knock on Rocho's door was unexpected. The dark-haired woman glanced at the clock on the oven. Sylvia would be really early. Plus, she hadn't heard a vehicle.

Azure eyes widened a great deal when she took in the short, chubby man who was her landlord. "Mr. Emerson, I wasn't expecting you to call or come over for at least another two weeks."

"I understand." The man fiddled with the envelope in his hand. Finally, he hesitantly opened the screen door, the only thing separating him from his Amazon of a renter. "I just received this in the mail. Some city ordinance bullshit, pardon my language. Basically, this area will no longer be zoned for renting at the end of the year. I can only sign you up for two more months. Then I have to clean it up and get it ready to sell."

Not bothering with opening the envelope, Rocho handed it back to Mr. Emerson. "I wasn't certain about residing long-term. But I think I'd like, if you can spare it, to sign on for another two months. It'll give me time to think if I'd like to remain in Portland or move on."

Not one to hedge his bets, Mr. Emerson had to make a suggestion. "There's also the possibility that you could buy the place. With all the rent you've paid, I'd count it as a down payment or something like that."

"Now that's something to add to the food for thought." Rocho felt a great uncertainty in the direction her life was heading. "No hard feelings, either way. I want to thank you for giving me a chance when no one else in this town would rent to a virtual nobody."

There was a coloring that reached Mr. Emerson's toes. "You had the cash. That's all I needed to see." The landlord managed to wink. "I'll see you in two months. Just keep in mind, I'll give you a good deal on the house."

"I will." Rocho watched as her landlord made his way to the next-door neighbors. "Looks like Barky might have to find a new home."

"Who will have to find a new home?" Rocho jumped at the sound of Sylvia's voice. The businesswoman couldn't help the amused expression upon her face.

"Well, perhaps my next-door neighbor and their dog." Rocho. "And maybe even me." When the blonde eyebrow rose, the mechanic sighed. "You just missed my landlord. Apparently, there's some kind of zoning change. Renting won't be an option in this area."

"Oh." Sylvia didn't know what to say. Her employee had already said she hadn't been certain if she would renew her lease. Now, there was no lease to renew. It, for whatever reason, caused her heart to ache.

"There's the possibility I could buy…" Rocho witnessed the emerald eyes brighten slightly. "But I don't really want to own anything. Now if I could find another place to rent that had a place where I could work on my baby…"

Sylvia's hopes rose and fell in less than a heartbeat. Where she was living now, with her ex-girlfriend, wouldn't allow for anyone working on their vehicles. Still, she had time to work on it.

"Something might just come up. For now, let's get a look at this mystery machine." Her voice was strong, but inside she was aching. Sylvia moved back a few steps so that the tall mechanic could lead the way.

"Speaking of mystery machines, I didn't hear your classic machine." Rocho's long strides ate up the distance to the garage. She unlocked the door and turned to her boss.

"I actually road my bike. I just felt like exercising today. Besides, my ex-girlfriend needed it." Azure eyes grew wide. It wasn't the orientation part. They'd established that. It was the 'ex' part that had caused Rocho's eyes and libido to increase.

"You let someone else drive your Pontiac Trans Am?" Rocho shook her head. "Especially an ex-girlfriend?" There was no way she would allow that. Well, not unless the person had an understanding like Sylvia did.

"It's a long story. I want her out of my life. And to do that, she needs to find a place to live and a job." Sylvia nodded her head toward the door Rocho had just unlocked. "So, do I get to see this mystery machine of yours?"

"Scooby and the rest of the gang couldn't give up the van so you'll be stuck with this." Rocho couldn't help chuckling as she opened the side door.

Rocho preceded Sylvia so that she could turn and watch her boss' reaction. The motorcycle was a rare find. Especially one that had nearly all original parts.

It was worth being rude and not allowing her boss to precede her. There was awe and wonder being expressed upon the beautiful blonde face. Rocho would compare it to someone receiving a gift they'd always wanted.

"Wow." Sylvia turned to look at her employee. "Do you have pictures of the condition this Honda four-fifty police special was in when you discovered her?"

The mechanic couldn't help laughing. "I figured you'd know this beauty." Rocho retrieved her cellphone from the back pocket of her faded, tightfitting blue jeans shorts. "I took the first at the junkyard."

Rocho watched a shiver run across Sylvia's shoulders. She knew it was at the thought that someone had merely tossed this classic, along with other vehicles, that were thought beyond redemption.

Not unlike the mechanic. Azure eyes closed. She had to stop stray thoughts such as those. A gentle touch upon Rocho's forearm brought her back to the present. "Sorry. Thoughts of the past intrude in the present."

Sylvia tilted her head. Instead of asking what she was dying to ask, she decided to wait and see if Rocho ever trusted her enough to divulge whatever it was. Instead, she gently squeezed the forearm under her hand before removing it. "No worries. Just show me the transformation. So far."

Rocho swallowed hard. There were very few in this world like her boss. Having only known Sylvia for a week, she was learning she was a kind and considerate human being. And that was a dangerous combination.

For friendship, it was the perfect combination. But the problem was, Rocho felt something for Sylvia. She was already beginning to come to the conclusion she couldn't control her attraction for her boss.

Wasn't that the real reason Rocho had been so interested when Mr. Emerson had suggestion purchasing the tiny home? As Sylvia commented on each of the pictures showing each day's progress, the mechanic was realizing more and more that she was right where she needed to be.

Perhaps not in this small house with barely even room for herself to move, but with Sylvia. And if the past were to catch up to her? What then?

As Sylvia ran her finger across the front fender of her baby, Rocho knew. Either her boss would stand beside her or she would run, but would die inside and never be the same.

Chapter 7

Sylvia stretched. It had been a long week. After spending Saturday with Rocho restoring the police special, life had returned to what had become normal.

Normal wasn't something Sylvia was liking very much these days. It wasn't sharing an apartment with a woman she used to love, or thought she had. It wasn't sleeping alone each night. It was the blasted business.

No matter what Sylvia attempted to do, her father had nearly bankrupted the dealership and she wasn't certain it would survive. If it weren't for Rocho and the service department, it would have gone under two months ago.

It wasn't merely her father. Sylvia deliberately made her way to her father's office. He had not yet left for his supposed vacation. In fact, he had blindsided her and they were waiting for the paperwork to be drawn up so that she could take over legal ownership of the business.

Once the paperwork was in place, Sylvia would be free to make even greater changes than she had in the nearly two weeks she had already made. Some of the sale's force were not happy with the changes, not because she wasn't the owner, but because she was the owner's daughter.

Waiting for the familiar 'come', Sylvia closed the door behind her after entering. "You're looking haggard." Frank stood from behind the desk. He took his daughter in his arms. "It's not too late to change your mind. The paperwork just arrived. I just have to sign in front of Elizabeth. Then it's all yours. Unless you want me to remain?"

"What I've always wanted was to be a mechanic in the bay." Sylvia giggled like she was still twelve and working in the garage with one of her father's mechanics. "But I also love owning and operating the entire business. Once things are running smoother, I'll get my chance. Call in your hot, young secretary."

Frank released a huge belly laugh. "She's gonna be your hot, young secretary starting on Monday. Unless you decide to go with one of your own. She's young, but she knows her stuff."

"I know, Dad. I've been doing my research." Sylvia waited until Elizabeth had joined them. It was obvious from the way she had positioned herself she had been waiting to be called in. There were no words exchanged as the two signed and the secretary watched and then used her notary public to seal it.

"Well, that officially makes you my boss." Elizabeth held out her hand. She waited until Sylvia took it. She made certain her new boss knew she was checking her out.

"Not until Monday officially, but yes." Sylvia wanted to wipe her hand on her pants. Smarmy was not the proper word for how she felt around her new secretary. "If you'll set up half hour blocks for each of the sales and accounting representatives starting first thing Monday, I'd appreciate it. Just put them on the company calendar."

"You got it, Boss." The redhead winked at Sylvia as she made certain to swing her hips a little more than necessary. She waved before closing the door behind her.

"That's a lawsuit waiting to happen." Sylvia took a deep breath before turning back to her father. "I might just have to rethink hiring a new secretary. I think she's trying to get a raise already."

Frank patted his daughter on the back. "Funny, she never tried anything like that with me in the year and a half she's worked here. But then again, I'm not a beautiful young blonde who's fresh out of business college."

Sylvia sighed as yet another thing was wrong with her life. "How bout your old father takes you to lunch? I know you want to spend tomorrow going over the books one last time before Monday."

"Yeah. Monday is going to be Hell." Sylvia felt her father's arm wrap around her shoulders as he led her toward the front of the dealership.

Her breath caught in her throat as Sylvia caught her lead mechanic speaking to a customer. It was rare when Rocho spoke to someone. She hoped it didn't mean trouble. There was a part of her that wanted to interject.

But there was a bigger part of Sylvia that trusted Rocho. It wasn't merely in business that she wanted to trust her employee. It was in friendship. If not in something more one day.

OOOOOOOOOOOO

Rocho had to concentrate on what her customer was saying. She noticed Sylvia being escorted by Frank out the front of the building. Most likely, the father/daughter duo were having lunch. Something the mechanic would probably be skipping if the current situation couldn't be rectified.

"I understand, Mrs. Williams." Rocho turned her full attention to the older woman. "You are more than correct. You were promised something that wasn't fulfilled. But I can have it to you in twenty minutes."

"That's not acceptable." Mrs. Williams stood nearly a foot shorter than Rocho but wasn't afraid to invade the mechanic's personal space. It was only a matter of time before a finger was poking her chest.

"I understand that as well." Rocho so wished Sylvia was here to give her the ok for what she was about to do. "Not only am I going to give you a discount, but your next three oil changes are on the house."

The grey-haired head tilted. Mrs. Williams took a deep breath. "And what about lunch? I had a lunch reservation that I'm now going to miss."

Rocho inwardly sighed. This was the kind of customer who would attempt to get whatever they could from a company for one minor mistake. Nothing that would harm the vehicle, just take longer than normal.

"I can have one of the secretaries run out and get you something. And before you say anything, it won't be fast food." Rocho held up her hands. "You name the place and what you want and I'm certain it can be arranged. Or, we can get you a gift card for whatever restaurant you wish."

The mechanic was not accustomed to saying so many words at one time. Rocho hoped Mrs. Williams would accept her offer. She didn't feel like arguing with the woman any more than she already had.

"That would be acceptable. But it would have to be at least a fifty dollar one." Mrs. Williams crossed her arms over her chest. "And not for The Wagon Wheel."

Once again, Rocho wanted to roll her eyes, expel her breath or something to show her irritation. "You rest here in the waiting area. In less than half an hour, you'll be on your way. If we can't get a gift card before you leave, it'll be delivered to your home."

"That's better than nothing." Mrs. Williams turned around effectively dismissing Rocho as she stormed into the waiting area, slamming the door behind her.

Taking a deep breath to calm herself, Rocho turned to the receptionist for the service department. "I take it you overheard that delightful exchange."

Martha Neilsen nodded. "I'll get right on it. And I'll offer her coffee, water, soda and whatever else we have lying around. I'll even get the gift card for her out of petty cash."

"Thanks, Martha. You are a lifesaver. I owe you one." Rocho turned to go, but turned back to the thirty something woman. "I just hope our new boss understands all this."

"I know Miss Sylvia. At least before she went off to school." Martha rose from behind her desk having routed her phone to one of the other secretaries. "If the cost isn't too great and it keeps the customer coming back, she'll more than understand. Just go and do what you do best."

An azure eye winked. "Thanks again." Rocho didn't waste another moment. She returned to the service bay. While there was a part of her that wanted to tear Nathan a new one for his screw up, now was not the time. Now was the time to show just how good her magic hands could be.

There was another way Rocho's hands could be magic. The mechanic groaned and chastised herself at the images that conjured. After having seen Sylvia in passing only, it didn't stop the images of the petite blonde or the body beneath the clothing.

After the fiasco created by the rookie mechanic, Rocho had no choice but to speak with either Sylvia or Frank. Nathan had yet to pass the ninety days probation and had already been late on three occasions, missed a day of work and had had to have his work redone four times.

This latest mishap wouldn't have harmed the automobile, but it did lead to a great deal of cost to the dealership. From what Rocho understood, there were some issues with the dealership financially.

It was only ten minutes later that Rocho had the two-year-old Chrysler purring like it was fresh off the lot. She couldn't help smiling as she changed out of her overalls and into a clean pair. It wouldn't do to drive up to the front of the dealership and step out of the car in a dirty pair.

Rocho made certain to adjust the seat before departing the car, even though both her knees hit the dashboard as she extracted herself. She could see the expression upon Mrs. Williams face when she glanced over the top of the automobile.

The mechanic used her long strides to make it to the waiting room before Mrs. Williams could even stand from her seated position. "Here are your keys. You'll find we topped off the gas, along with everything else you asked for. I know our secretaries are good, but I'm certain they haven't returned with your gift card. We'll have it sent to you. I promise."

Mrs. Williams' mouth opened and closed several times before she was able to take the keys to her vehicle. Clearly not having thought Rocho could be as good as her word, she was left speechless.

Instead of saying anything, Mrs. Williams simply left the waiting area. She hesitated at the door to the outside. Her pride, or whatever, keeping her from thanking the mechanic.

Rocho slowly made her way back into the outer service department where several vehicles were waiting some kind of service. She shook her head. The waiting time was unacceptable. Once again, she was standing in front of Martha's desk.

"Martha, you don't have to say she should have signed." Rocho could see the smirk on the secretary's face. "Just have a messenger run the paperwork, along with the gift card, to her house. I just didn't feel like dealing with her. Now, where is Nathan at?"

Martha merely shook her head. She understood where Rocho was coming from. Mrs. Williams was the kind that gave customers a bad name. "I'll get right on that once Heather gets back with the gift card. As for Nathan…" She pointed to the break room.

"You've got to be fu…" Rocho stopped herself. She didn't swear often, but this Nathan character really had her oil beyond needing changing. "I have to remember to email Sylvia. We have to talk about Nathan."

"I could…" Martha pointed to the computer. She glanced up into stormy, azure eyes. Normally the color of a spring sky, they were now the color of a winter storm.

"No, I'll do it. And as much as we are beginning to fall behind, I think Nathan being on break is for the best." Rocho sighed heavily. "In fact, if you see him before I do, tell him to go home. If any questions, see me."

"Will do, Boss." Martha watched the mechanic storm off just as the owner and his daughter made their way back into the dealership. Not having been gone long enough for a sit-down meal, the secretary wondered what was up.

Martha didn't have long to wait as Sylvia bid her father goodbye. The petite blonde made her way directly to the service area carrying takeout. "Have you seen Rocho?"

A sandy eyebrow rose. Martha knew it would be an interesting conversation between the mechanic and Sylvia. "I think she's in the back bay helping with the backlog. She's had to put out a couple fires."

"Backlog? Fires?" Sylvia shook her head. The one department she thought she could count on. "Do you want to share or should I just ask Rocho?"

"I'll just say this. I think you're going to have to put in an advert for a new mechanic." Martha's hazel eyes showed her frustration.

"Thanks for the hint." Sylvia's head hung momentarily before the woman recovered. As she walked past the break room, it opened. Out walked one of the employees she knew she had to rethink her father hiring.

"If it isn't the lady boss." Nathan made a show of sniffing the air. "Did you bring lunch? Or is it just you that smells good enough to eat."

"Excuse me?" Sylvia couldn't help taking a step away from the man. He was only a couple inches taller than her and slightly broader in the shoulders. It was the way he carried himself.

"It's the first thing I thought of when I heard you were taking over." Nathan closed the distance between them. He was nearly touching her. "That there are benefits of having someone of the female persuasion in charge."

Sylvia could sense a presence. When she glanced over Nathan's shoulder, she saw dark eyes. Her own pleading emerald ones begged Rocho to allow her to handle the situation.

Knowingly, Rocho nodded. But she wasn't about to leave Sylvia alone. She leaned against the door to the break room so that there was no escape for Nathan.

"Is that so?" Sylvia straightened to her full height. "Let me ask you something, Nathan. How long have you been working for my father?"

"Just under three months." Nathan couldn't help licking his lips. It wasn't the pleasing scents emanating from the bags. It was the way Sylvia's breasts had jutted out when she had straightened.

"And in those three months, have you shown up on time? Have you learned the ins and outs of how we do things?" Sylvia began circling the unsuspecting young man. She handed the food to Rocho. "Have you worked more than you've slacked off?"

Rocho inwardly smirked. Sylvia had indeed been doing her homework. While she would still have to speak to her boss about the latest embarrassment created by Nathan, firing him shouldn't be an issue.

"I...I..." Nathan took a deep breath. "When Frank, er, your father, hired me he said that work was loose. Meaning we all did our part, but we didn't break our backs."

A dark head tilted. Sylvia nodded her head. "And Frank also informed you that I was the one to train you. Since I am the head mechanic. But you refused to even look at me. You chose one of the least experienced to buddy with. And now your habits are atrocious. And you cost this dealership a fifty-dollar gift card, along with three-hundred-dollar refund to Mrs. Williams."

Beads of sweat were forming on Nathan's brow. Sylvia took over. "Clean out your locker. We'll electronically deposit your pay. And if you ever show your face here again, you'll be escorted off the property."

"Stupid fucking dykes. They always fucking stick together." Nathan shoved past the two women. It was only Rocho's strength that kept her from dropping the containers she was holding.

Sylvia shook her head. "One less headache gone." She turned toward Rocho. "So, we're behind." Rocho sighed and nodded. "If you can wait on eating and have an extra pair of overalls, I could really use feeling grease on my skin once again. Just like last weekend."

"I think I have something that could work." Rocho hastily placed the food in her own small refrigerator. "It'll be safe in there. And I couldn't think of a better person to work with than you."

The pair dove into the workload. It didn't matter if it was a simple oil change, tire rotation or something that had them guessing, the pair truly did work well as a team. And stolen glances couldn't be hidden.

Chapter 8

Sunday. It was the one day of the week when Rocho truly relaxed. After making a trip via walking to the grocery store, she tinkered with her special project. Then, it was time to merely sit back and relax.

Usually, that meant inside while Rocho watched whatever do it yourself show was on. It didn't have to be a mechanic show. She loved anything to do with her hands. In fact, she would love to be able to settle down and actually build a small house for herself one day.

But that would mean Rocho felt safe. While Sylvia made her feel at ease like no one ever before, knowing that her family and her accuser remained out there left her feeling vulnerable. A state she had been in now for nearly a decade and a half.

"Gotta stop that. Tomorrow is gonna be a big day." Rocho knew that the changes Sylvia wanted to implement would slowly begin to take affect the next day.

The service department would see some changes. Rocho would be happy to implement them. Especially would be happy to begin training some of the veterans and hire some new mechanics.

There was one thing Rocho refused to do to help Sylvia. While she was growing fond of her boss, there was a boundary she refused to cross. And that was to put herself out there selling vehicles.

While it was true that Rocho knew more about any vehicle, new or classic, than anyone at the dealership, she just couldn't bring herself to interact with people. Not when it came to attempting to sell them something.

Dealing with the likes of Mrs. Williams was bad enough. It came with being the lead mechanic. And normally something she didn't have to do under normal circumstances.

Just as Rocho took a sip of her cola, Rocho's cellphone chirped. There was only one reason it would ring. When she picked it up, she saw she was right. Sylvia had texted her.

'Laurie took my baby last night for the last time. She did something to the carburetor. Can't work on it at the apartment. Can I come over and you nurse it back together with me?'

Rocho swallowed hard. She'd only had a day away from Sylvia. They'd met in passing on Friday. For the most part, they had stayed on their own side of the dealerships.

Now, Rocho would be working side by side with Sylvia. First, it was on the mechanic's own special project. Next, it was out of necessity and her boss' need to reconnect with the basics of running a dealership.

It was now because Sylvia's ex had mistreated a classic car. That was something Rocho had trouble forgiving. It was something the mechanic had to rectify.

Grateful she had restocked her kitchen that morning, Rocho finally texted back how she was looking forward to getting her hands on a classic such as the Trans Am.

Luckily, Rocho didn't need to change. She was wearing jeans shorts and a black V-neck t-shirt. It was what she normally wore to work on her own motorcycle or just relax around the house on the weekends after working out.

It wasn't long after Rocho had sent the text that she heard the roar of the Trans Am. Sylvia was right. Just by hearing it, the mechanic knew exactly what was wrong. She knew exactly what to do to fix it.

By the time Sylvia pulled into the driveway, Rocho was waiting with the garage door open. She had a can of cola in each hand. She waited for her boss to make it to her before handing her one. "Your ex should be forced to listen to whatever music she hates the most for a week straight after hearing what she did to this classic."

There was an instant smile upon Sylvia's face. "Trust me. When I heard what she had done, I hid the keys to theTrans. I'm arranging for her to lease one of the cars at the dealership. I think I got her a job. In Lansing. Now, if she can just find a place to live."

"I'd be willing to pay for a couple months of the lease, just so she can't touch this car again." Rocho took a sip of her cola before placing it on the table just inside the garage. "Now, let's get started."

It wasn't long before the pair had the Trans Am nearly torn apart. It wasn't necessarily necessary. It was that they were so caught up in what they were doing. Which was having fun exploring the ins and outs of the classic car.

In Rocho's mind, she wanted to make certain there was nothing else wrong with the classic car. They paused briefly for sandwiches and more colas before making the Trans Am whole once again.

Sylvia was shocked when she glanced at her cellphone. It wasn't the fact there were no missed calls or texts. It was the fact it was nearing seven at night. "I think I owe you supper. I didn't realize it was that late. The sun is still shining so bright."

Rocho had been slowly cleaning her tools and meticulously placing them in their labeled places. She hadn't realized how late it was, either.

The mechanic glanced at the sun. Even the temps were still warm. There was very little breeze. It was the perfect June afternoon in Michigan.

After glancing at herself and Sylvia, she realized neither was dressed for anything out. They could order something and pick it up or have it delivered. There was always pizza. "Well, there's only one issue with that." She motioned between herself and her boss.

Sylvia giggled. "I didn't think I'd be here this long. I didn't bring a change of clothes." She eyed her employee. "And I don't think you have anything that will fit me. I'm a sucker for pizza. Anything but anchovies or black olives."

Rocho shook her head. The ease in which the two had formed a friendship in two weeks of working together was beyond her. In fact, any relationship was an amazing thing for the mechanic.

After the pizza had been consumed, along with the rest of the six-pack of cola Rocho had purchased that morning, the pair sat on her back porch. There wasn't much to see. Just her workout equipment and a fence in need of a coat or three of paint.

The sun was just now setting. For June, that meant it was nearing ten thirty at night. "I should probably get going. We both have early days tomorrow. I have meetings all day. And probably so many people to fire." Sylvia's chest rose and constricted with the deep breath she took in an attempt to relax herself.

The mechanic knew that things were not great at the dealership. Rocho distanced herself from the rest of the departments. Yet, she couldn't help overhearing things. Males and females flirted with her.

Then there was Sylvia. Rocho had come to read the young woman's moods. Or at the very least when she was stressed. When she'd first arrived to fix the Trans Am, she had been a bit stressed, but not like she was now.

"I'm just a simple mechanic, but if you need any help…" Rocho's words trailed off when azure locked with emerald. Normally, Sylvia's eyes were the color of spring leaves just making their way into the world.

But at the moment, in the dimness of the evening and the storminess of Sylvia's emotions, they were the color of an evergreen in the autumn. The transformation took Rocho's breath away.

For a moment, Sylvia's face brightened with a genuine smile. Rocho felt her entire body tingle at the sight. This was dangerous times for the mechanic.

"Thank you. I appreciate that." Sylvia reluctantly rose. She stretched before turning toward her employee. No, Rocho was definitely more than her employee. "I think, for now, what I need is to know that at least the service department is running smoothly. If you can weed out the weak mechanics, let me know if they can be trained or not, that will be enough."

Rocho rose to join her boss. "Let me walk you. To be honest, I think I've let it slide a little. I've been working alone too much on the Bel Air. That'll change. But besides Nathan, there's only one other we need to keep an eye on. I'll do that this week. I promise."

"I appreciate that." Sylvia glanced up at her friend. She had trouble, especially here in Rocho's driveway, referring to her as employee. Added to the difficulty was the fact the mechanic opened the driver door for her.

None of Sylvia's past girlfriends, not that she had many, had been so chivalrous as the mechanic was being. "Perhaps we can escape for lunch. Nothing fancy. I can run by the market in the morning. Get us salads. Place them in my fridge."

Sylvia had to leave. Not even her father was this kind to her. The reason they had nearly went to lunch on Thursday was because it was a celebration of a business deal. It wasn't like anything else her father had ever done.

Frank had made it appear he'd been proud his little girl was taking over the reins, but she now knew better. It's why Sylvia had decided takeout, especially takeout for her and Rocho, had been for the best. She'd used the excuse there was more to review before Monday.

"I'd like that. If it's not too much trouble." Sylvia hastily settled herself in the seat. Even though Rocho was the last one in the driver's seat, it was back to the correct position for the shorter woman. "And on one condition."

A dark eyebrow rose in question. "I bring the beverages. Do you like iced coffee?" A hearty laugh escaped the mechanic. "I'll take that as a yes."

"Definitely a yes." Rocho caught herself from leaning in. If she had continued, she would have kissed her boss. Friends kissed on the cheek, but that's not where her aim would have led to. "No flavoring, cream or sugar necessary for me."

"A girl after my heart. Only time I like flavoring is during the holidays. I get addicted to pumpkin spice." Sylvia was nearly disappointed. She'd seen the lean. It would have led to some kind of contact. Most likely a kiss. "I'll see you tomorrow. Sleep well."

"You too, Boss." Rocho stood back. She closed her eyes a moment and listened to the purr of the Trans Am. That was how a classic was supposed to sound. She opened her eyes in time to see the smirk on Sylvia's face as she drove off.

Rocho made her way inside. She didn't bother changing. She merely threw herself on the bed. Slowly rolling over so that she faced the stained stucco ceiling, the mechanic felt the tears beginning to pool.

Why tears? Because Rocho FELT something for Sylvia. In two weeks, it went beyond business. Hell, it went beyond friendship. It was dangerous.

The fact she still had the charge of rape haunting her back in Mississippi meant she should stay away. Yet, Rocho had offered to further invest in the blossoming friendship. She had offered to think about remaining in Portland. Hell, she was thinking of buying this dump of a house or finding a place to rent that would allow her to work on her motorcycle.

Still, when Rocho closed her eyes, all she could see was those emerald eyes. Not the dark ones full of worry, anger and fear. But the ones that were like spring leaves. Fresh and new. Young and strong. Yet timid and unsure.

It made Rocho want to take Sylvia in her arms and protect her. To take all the burdens away from her. But she couldn't. She had enough burdens of her own.

OOOOOOOOOOOO

The dark colored sedan slowly pulled away from the curb. The dark-haired figure inside couldn't help smiling sadly. "It's taken me nearly a decade to find you."

The sad smile disappeared. It was replaced by one of concertation. "Now that I've found you, what do I do?" The dark head shook as if attempting to clear cobwebs from the recesses of its mind.

"Knowing you, I have to be very careful." The dark colored sedan weaved through the small town easily finding the interstate that would lead to the City of Lansing. It was only a twenty-minute drive via the interstate.

"I also want to find out who this new blonde is in your life." Large hands tightened around the black leather steering wheel. "If she is trouble, she won't like what will happen to her."

The headlights were frequent, even on a Sunday night as it was the interstate that connected all the major cities in the middle of the lower peninsula. "I let you down once before. I won't let it happen again."

Chapter 9

Eleven in the morning and already Sylvia was exhausted. She'd only had three meetings and already she was wishing that her day was over.

Or at the very least wishing she was sharing lunch with Rocho. Sylvia wondered how her lead mechanic was dealing with the service department. With the few moments she'd had between meetings, she'd checked the appointments. They were actually ahead, according to the computer.

Sylvia relaxed, if only slightly. She wasn't certain when she and Rocho would have their intended lunch. There were three more meetings she had to have before she could even think about taking a moment for lunch.

The telephone ringing reminded Sylvia of her next appointment. Unlike her father, Sylvia chose to leave the blinds up so that she could see who was outside her office. Her body instinctively shivered in repulsive reaction when she saw who was waiting to be allowed in.

Waiting until the third ring, Sylvia finally answered. "Show Derek in. But be prepared to rescue me." She heard the muffled attempt to cover the giggle before she hung up.

The door was flung open. The man was taller than Rocho by at least two inches. He reminded Sylvia of a sandy blonde surfer. In fact, she imagined underneath the business suit he wore he probably had the abs. His looks probably did bring in the ladies and certain men.

Derek didn't wait to be asked. He settled himself in the leather visitors chair. He leaned back relaxed. He crossed one leg over the other and stared at the beautiful woman who probably didn't know anything about running a dealership. She had probably asked him to help her. After all, Frank had asked him many times his opinion on running the business.

The smarminess emanating from the man was causing Sylvia to feel dirty. "I've been looking at your sales numbers." Derek's relaxed position never wavered. In fact, his smile grew. "While they seem impressive, they are lacking."

"Now wait just a moment." Derek sprang to his feet. "I've checked my numbers. I've studied them. I have since I heard you were coming to take over the business. They are the best of anyone's."

True colors. It's what was running through Sylvia's mind. "As I was saying. Your numbers appear impressive, but your feedback from the customers are far from."

Sylvia handed the pages of comments gathered over the past two weeks. Derek tore the pages from her hand. She gave him a moment to glance through them before speaking. "You refuse to take calls when there are issues. You always give it to other salespeople, taking away from their time with their customers. You don't work with the service department when there are simple recalls. I could go on."

"This is bullshit." Derek threw the pages on Sylvia's desk. "I'm a salesman. Emphasis on sales. That's what Frank hired me to do. Not to coddle the idiots after they've taken ownership. The money is in the bank. That's where the real money comes from. Not the service department."

A headache was beginning to form. It appeared Sylvia would have to school this arrogant jerk about business. "How long have you been a salesman?"

Derek straightened. He fumbled with his tie before looking Sylvia in the eyes. "I've been with your father for five years now. He hired me right out of high school."

A blonde head nodded. Sylvia had already known this, but wanted Derek to calm a bit before she continued. "So partly your lack of understanding can be my father's fault. Because while a good portion of a dealership's money is from sales and leases, it's also from return visits. Aka service department. Parts department. Keeping our customers happy so that they will buy and lease from us again. With reviews like these, they won't. I'm sorry, but you are fired."

"Why you little bitch." Sylvia hadn't been expecting the next move. She hadn't expected to find herself knocked from her chair and on her back with hands wrapped around her neck. "I knew when your father said he was leaving the business to you that I should just begin looking for another job. No skirt is going to tell me what to do."

"Stop." The corners of Sylvia's vision were already turning dark. "I…can't…breathe." She attempted to strike at the back of Derek's head, but she couldn't muster the strength.

Suddenly, without warning, Sylvia was able to breathe. She was coughing as she gasped for air. Her vision wouldn't clear. She attempted to discern the voices. One she knew better than anyone's, including her father's.

"Derek, you little piece of shit." Finally, Sylvia's vision cleared. She could see Rocho holding Derek by the scruff of his suit. Even though the salesman was two inches taller, his feet were dangling off the ground.

Another voice drew Sylvia's attention. It was her secretary's. "I've already called the police. Just calm down." Elizabeth turned her attention to Sylvia. "Are you all right, Boss?"

Sylvia had to take a moment before she could find her voice. When she did, it was rather raspy. "I'll be fine. As soon as Derek is escorted out of here and charged with assault that is."

Rocho instantly shoved Derek into the visitor's chair. She knew that there enough people having been drawn to their location to keep the man from escaping before the police arrived. Her concern now was for her boss.

Kneeling next to Sylvia, Rocho gently inspected the bruised and battered neck. "I had just arrived to see if you were free to have lunch. I didn't hesitate in tearing this animal from you. Is your neck too tender? It's, sadly, already bruising."

Sylvia had to swallow several times. It wasn't from any soreness or pain. It was from the tenderness in the touch of her mechanic, as well as the deep concern in azure eyes. Her voice lowered so that Elizabeth nor Derek could hear. "I'm more scared than hurt, I hate to admit."

"Understandable." Rocho lowered her voice as well. "Allow me to help you up." Before helping Sylvia to a standing position, she righted the chair her boss had been sitting in. She eased the smaller woman into the leather chair. "Try not to talk much until the police arrive. I'm certain the rest of the staff can handle things the rest of the day."

It was tempting. Sylvia knew there were several left on the staff who could handle things. But it wasn't her way. "I just need something cold to drink, a little to eat and to fill out whatever paperwork the police need from me. Then the day can go on like nothing ever happened."

Emerald eyes bore into Derek's pale ones as she spoke the last sentence. She wanted him to know that to her he was nothing. He would forever be nothing but a mistake her father had made and she was determined to rectify.

"Sounds like a plan, Boss." Rocho continued to kneel next to Sylvia's chair. She wanted to make it clear that she might be the 'muscles', but she deferred to Sylvia in all matters.

It was clear Derek wanted to say something. Azure eyes were pleading with him to do so. Not because Rocho couldn't contain her anger. After what had happened nearly a decade and a half ago, she'd successfully done that. It was so he himself would say or do more to place more nails in his coffin.

Time stood still for all of fifteen minutes. The three women glaring at Derek as he breathed heavily. The assault charges could easily be dismissed. And if not, would just be a blip on his record. He had to remain calm and bide his time.

It was well past three by the time statements were taken and Derek had been taken away. It meant the rest of the meetings Sylvia had wanted to take place would have to wait. At least everyone had pitched in and everything had appeared normal at the dealership.

The only department that didn't suffer in the least was the service department. Sylvia shook her head. Rocho had arrived early and made certain everyone was on the same page and had begun working on vehicles that had been dropped off. She was truly beginning to wonder what she would do without the mechanic. A reoccurring theme was attempting to burst forth when it came to Rocho. Don't leave me.

Rocho was working on the Bel Air. Every fifteen minutes she was checking on the service department. She wanted to make certain everything was running smoothly. After this morning, she didn't want Sylvia to be stressed by her department.

Luckily, the rest of the mechanics under her tutelage would workout. They might take a little fine tuning, but Rocho was certain she could turn them into a well running machine.

The mechanic chuckled at her own pun. Rocho glanced at the clock. She sighed as she realized that not only had fifteen minutes gone by, it was closing time. "Time to take off these overalls and help everyone close up for the night."

After making her way back into the special bay, Rocho was stopped by the sight of the exhausted appearing petite blonde. Sylvia was wearing the same tan pleated pantsuit, along with its matching jacket.

Without hesitation, Rocho approached her boss. "How are you doing, Boss?" The mechanic wasn't ready to refer to her boss as Sylvia. Once that happened, it crossed that line they continued to edge toward.

"Been better. But I'm ok." Sylvia ran her hand through her disheveled blonde locks. "After what happened with Derek, I called my father. He's leaving in the morning for his galivanting around the country. I kind of used language he didn't appreciate to tell him what a mess he left me."

A chuckle escaped Rocho. "The businessman didn't appreciate it. The mechanic I occasionally hung out with probably appreciated it."

"Probably not from his daughter." Sylvia shrugged. "I know you have a little more to do here. I was wondering if you'd join me for dinner. I know we've been spending a lot of time outside of work. It's just I don't have any friends, outside of Laurie. And frankly, I'll be glad when she moves on. And…"

Rocho knew this was the moment she had been dreading. Only two weeks now, but she had definitely been dreading it the entire time. It was now or never. "And you would like to have someone to text or have dinner with. Maybe watch a movie with. Or fix up old cars? Sorta what we've been doing?"

The petite frame visibly relaxed. Sylvia could feel a warmth flow throughout her. "Exactly. That is if you plan on remaining. You said your lease is up soon and that you have to move out."

"Yeah. And to be frank, I don't want to buy." Rocho shrugged. "It's not about me not staying anywhere. Though that is a big part of it. I'll tell you later. After I help the gang clean up and we are enjoying whatever for dinner."

"If you don't mind, I'll help you guys out." Sylvia knew she wasn't dressed for it. Even with the dealership not doing well, she still had some money set aside so she could buy new clothing, if necessary.

"It's your business. Not like I can stop you." Rocho chuckled. With Sylvia showing how expert she was with the closing of the service department, they were done in half the time. "I think the gang enjoyed having the owner help."

It was Sylvia's turn to chuckle. "I think it helps to show them I know what I'm doing when it comes to all departments. I know how to do everything on all makes and models. I know what parts to order. I know which banks give the best financing and I know which sales pitches are the best. And I hate paperwork as much as the next person."

The pair laughed together as they made certain no one else was in the building. They had already locked all the other entrances before setting the alarm on the lone door they used as an exit.

Rocho nearly took a step back when Sylvia offered the keys to the Trans Am. In fact, the speechless mechanic could merely shake her head to indicate the negative.

Sylvia smirked. "I know I said no one would ever drive my baby ever again. But I know you well enough to know you would handle my baby with a great deal of care. Besides, we are just driving across town. I've ordered takeout to be delivered to my apartment. It'll be there at seven thirty."

It took a moment for Rocho to take the keys. While she knew she would drive the car as gently as possible, she didn't want to be the one to be behind the wheel should someone else do something stupid like run a red light or stop sign.

Finally, Rocho made her way to the passenger side. Before Sylvia could verbally complain, the door was held open and an ushering motion was being made. "After you, mi lady."

A blonde head shook. Rocho was definitely full of surprises. Sylvia was truly enjoying getting to know her friend. "Thank you gallant mechanic."

They both chuckled at the description before Rocho settled herself behind the wheel. Cautiously, the mechanic adjusted the seat to fit her long legs. The mirrors were next. "Ready?" Sylvia nodded her head.

The engine purred as it had the night before when Sylvia had taken off. The businesswoman was right. Rocho shifted perfectly, never grinding the gears once. The tires never were squealed and the car was eased into motion or slowed to a halt.

Sylvia had to give a few directions once she informed Rocho of where she was residing. There were very few apartment complexes in Portland. Soon, they were parking in the space assigned to Sylvia.

The businesswoman was surprised when she noticed Rocho carefully readjusted the mirrors and driver's seat so that they would be nearly perfect for her. "You didn't have to do that. It's not like my knees would hit the steering wheel."

Rocho glanced at her boss before emerging from the Trans Am. She made it to Sylvia's side before she could exit the classic car. "It's habit, mostly. I've been working in garages of some kind for nearly all my life. It's just become my courtesy. But with you, well, I wanted to make certain it was perfect for you."

Once again, Sylvia couldn't help but think Rocho would be the perfect girlfriend. For now, she would be the perfect friend. "That's thoughtful of you. For customers and for myself.

Now, why don't you come up and I'll show you where I temporarily live. I signed a six-month lease."

"After you." Rocho waited. She hoped that Laurie wasn't upstairs waiting for them. She knew technically Laurie was the ex and she was only a friend, but it would still be a little awkward. Of course, the fact that Rocho had not had any friends in over a decade would lead to awkwardness.

The walk up the three flights of stairs was made in a matter of moments. Sylvia opened the door. The sight that greeted them caused the young woman to curse. "Holy fuck!"

Rocho could easily see over the shorter woman's shoulder. There was a naked brown-haired woman riding the fingers of an equally naked redheaded woman. The mechanic knew, without a doubt, one of the two women was Sylvia's ex.

The brown-haired woman was the first to glance up. "Oh shit." That confirmed who was Laurie for Rocho. The mechanic decided to place herself between the two women. Even broken up, this was not something she would want to come home and see.

"Laurie, get dressed, get the fuck out." It was only Rocho's restraining arm that was keeping Sylvia from going after Laurie. "And forget the lease on the sedan. Consider it void. All I fucking asked was that you kept any activities such as this to the spare bedroom. Even better, at the place of whoever you were sharing them with. But if you can't respect what we had shared for nearly two years, then you don't deserve time. Out. Before I call the cops. After all, you aren't on the lease."

That was a twist Rocho hadn't been expecting. It brought a unique light to the situation. For now, she would remain as a referee until Sylvia needed more.

Laurie hastily grabbed the shirt she had tossed on the floor. She wasn't even certain where her other clothes were. "If you knew even an ounce of fucking passion, you'd know that sometimes you can't control it when it takes over. Sheila has it in spades. Has since that first night when I met her at The Wagon Wheel."

The restraining arm wasn't enough. If it weren't for Rocho's lightening quick reflexes, Sylvia would have tackled the still naked Laurie to the ground. The sultry voice in her ear did nothing to calm the anger the petite woman felt. "Where's your room. You wait there. I'll keep an eye on these two."

Taking a deep breath, Sylvia managed to point toward the master bedroom. Rocho carried the businesswoman in her arms. "Do I have to lock the door?"

Sylvia shook her head. "No. I'm going to call and see if the delivery is still on its way. Then I'm going to rest on the bed. Let me know when those two are gone. Make certain they only take things from the spare bedroom. Please."

"Will do." This was the moment. "Sylvia." Emerald eyes widened. Rocho had skipped over using her boss' last name and directly to her first name. It was a significant step indeed.

It wasn't lost on Sylvia as her anger and frustration were met with a beaming smile. "Thank you, Rocho. Just knock when we are alone again. Please."

"You've got it, Friend." Rocho didn't wait for the door to shut. She made her way back into the living room. She was grateful to discover that the two women were fully clothed.

The one known as Laurie was carrying trash bags toward what Rocho assumed was the spare room. The brown-haired woman turned toward the mechanic. "I hope you aren't after her money. She won't give you a dime. And she's a lousy lover. Can't get a rise out of her. Was better off with my own digits than anything on her. Why I cheated from day one."

It was Rocho's turn to restrain herself. It wasn't easy. She had learned to retrain her anger for herself. But she had not had to restrain her anger when it came to defending someone else. Hopefully, her restraint would not fail her now.

"I guess I'm a different breed than you." Rocho casually leaned against the doorframe. She was enough in the way so that if Sylvia were to exit, she could stop her. "I find a one night stand is ok. I can fuck someone till they can't walk for two days."

Brown eyes grew wide as they took in the tall, muscular body. Rocho didn't mind. While Laurie was attractive, she didn't hold a candle to Sylvia. If only because Laurie had shown her true colors by the way she had spoken to Sylvia.

"But I find taking things slow, like a dance, is so much more fulfilling." Rocho stood to her full height. The brown eyes followed her every move. "Flowers. Candy. Drives in the country. Those are nice, but the girl of my dreams would love working on a car with me. Would love to discuss old and new model cars. Would love to spend a lazy Saturday or Sunday slowly exploring one another's bodies. Sharing every desire and making it come true."

"Yeah…well…" When there was no way Laurie had a good comeback, she disappeared into the spare bedroom.

Rocho couldn't help chuckling to herself. It turned into a yelp when she felt arms wrap around her from behind. When she turned around, questioning eyes were looking into emerald ones.

"I know we're just friends." Rocho tilted her head. "But what you just said meant the world to me. You defended me. And you gave me an insight into you. You, Miss Renee Bishop, are an amazing woman. You'll make a woman happy one day."

The mechanic swallowed hard. "I don't think so." Rocho didn't want to go into further detail. A hand upon her shoulder caused her to look into emerald eyes. "All I can say, for now, is that I'm friend material, not girlfriend material."

"That means Sylvia is stuck where she should be." Azure eyes closed when she heard Laurie's voice. It was as if something snapped inside of the mechanic. Dark eyes grew wide when Rocho turned around.

"If you aren't out of this apartment in five seconds, I won't be responsible for my actions." Azure eyes were now the color of a stormy night. Her skin was flushed. There were beads of sweat upon brow. Her hands were clenching and unclenching.

"You wouldn't…" Laurie trailed off as Rocho took several dangerous steps toward her. "Sheila! Out! Now! Forget anything else!"

Not even the redhead sprinting out of the spare bedroom stopped the slow stalking Rocho had begun. Nor did the hand on the back of her lower back. It wasn't until the door slammed shut that the mechanic managed to snap out of it.

Rocho remained breathing heavy when she felt the warmth of Sylvia's hand on her forearm. She glanced down into frightened emerald eyes. Her voice was barely above a whisper. "I'm sorry. I guess it's best you know now that I have a temper. I should be going."

Sylvia attempted to stop Rocho by tugging on her arm. It wasn't until she was able to step in front of the mechanic that she was able to halt her progress. That was only barely as the momentum of the larger woman nearly bowled the smaller woman over.

"Stop. Please." Sylvia noticed how Rocho couldn't even focus. She was staring into space. "Would you join me on the couch? Please?"

After the second please, Rocho's eyes finally closed. Her head fell until her chin was against her chest. Without looking up, she shuffled over to the couch.

Before Sylvia could join her, the buzzer startled the businesswoman. "Right on time with supper." She shook her head, grateful she had prepaid and pre-tipped. It was only a matter of retrieving the food and returning to her friend.

Rocho sat bonelessly upon the couch. Her mind was racing. The police special was nearly ready. She could close out her bank account and ride until she couldn't ride anymore. She could find the next small town that needed a mechanic. Find a place that would rent with money. Find another project to rebuild. As long as she put mileage between herself and Michigan, it would be for the best.

The mechanic didn't even smell the spicy food that was placed on the coffee table in front of her. Rocho didn't feel the hand upon her thigh. What she did feel was the head upon her shoulder. "It's not safe to be my friend."

"I'll be the judge of that. Now, why don't you tell me why you lost your temper?" Sylvia squeezed the thigh her hand was resting upon. "I know we both have said we had bad luck in the girlfriend department. But what about a friend?"

If she was leaving anyways, what did it matter if Rocho were to tell Sylvia the truth or not? "It's not a pretty picture. That food probably won't be all that appetizing."

Sylvia playfully squeezed Rocho's thigh. "Just tell me your story. I can always put the food in the fridge later. Please, tell me your tale."

Taking a deep breath, Rocho began her tale. It was in a monotone she related her encounter with what she had thought was true love.

"I had just turned eighteen. I didn't want to go off to college, much to my parents' chagrin." Rocho shrugged. "I thought they'd got that when I'd taken vocational studies while in high school. It's where I began my studying fixing anything under the sun."

Sylvia watched her friend closely. Rocho was staring at the darkened screen of the television as if there was the most interesting television show ever playing. She understood. She used to do it while dealing with her mother's death.

"While I had my first job that summer, I met the small garage's daughter." The thought brought a flicker to the corner of Rocho's right eye since she was sitting, in a way, next to her boss' daughter.

"She was seventeen. Her eyes were such a light brown I referred to them as golden. Her hair was sandy blonde, but shone bright in the sun. My days and nights revolved around her." Again, Rocho's eye twitched slightly.

"We made love several times that summer." Rocho did blush quite nicely with this admission. Sylvia had to keep from giggling like a school girl. "After we had a fight over me not giving her a present or something, she went to her father. I found myself being arrested for rape."

Sylvia had wanted to remain quiet while Rocho related her story. But someone accusing someone else of rape was not something she could remain silent for. "Rape?"

Rocho swallowed. Instead of staring at the television, she stared at her hands. If Sylvia had overhead all that she had said to Laurie, she had heard about how she could fuck someone until they couldn't walk right for two days.

"Over a fucking present?" Rocho jumped at the raise in volume. "Sorry. Didn't mean to make you flinch. It's just that rape is no joking matter. And shouldn't be used to get what you want. Period."

The sentiment finally caused Rocho to relax. But not by much. "I managed to post bond. My parents believed Juliette over me. I think they thought because I was this rough mechanic it must be true. Since I had no friends and my family turned their back, I took off. I've been on the run ever since and why I only stay six months to a year in one place."

Sylvia sat for a moment, grateful when Rocho maintained the eye contact. "And if I said, without a shadow of a doubt, that I believe you?"

"I…" Rocho swallowed hard. Her eyes squeezed shut. A single tear was forced out of each eye. As each tear was wiped away, the mechanic realized it was with the most reverent touch she had ever known. "Thank you."

A blonde head leaned back on a strong shoulder. A petite hand sought out a larger, calloused one. "Thank you for being my protector. At work and here."

A thought struck Sylvia. It wasn't the first time. She had the money. Rocho wouldn't have to know. There had to be a small house out there that would meet her friend's approval, both their approval, that she could buy and have an agency lease for her.

Rocho would never have to know. And if the place was perfect enough, Sylvia could work on her Trans Am, when necessary, there alongside Rocho, yet keep the apartment. Now to put her plan in motion.

Chapter 10

Things changed between the two women after the confession Monday evening. In fact, Monday had been quite an interesting day overall. Luckily, the rest of the week had gone smoothly, both professionally and personally, for both women.

Saturday found Sylvia not where she wanted to be. Well, that wasn't exactly true. She wanted to be with Rocho. Because of their work schedules, they weren't always able to spend lunch with one another. Some evenings they spent together, others were spent alone.

This weekend, Sylvia had wanted to spend entirely with Rocho. The motorcycle was nearing completion. She wanted to be there for her friend when it was completed, but this little project had to be completed first.

The Trans Am came to a stop in front of the two-bedroom house. The square footage wasn't much more than the house Rocho was renting now, but it did have a two-stall garage. It was what had drawn Sylvia to it.

It was also within walking distance of the dealership and the grocery store. Sylvia wasn't certain if Rocho would actually ride her classic motorcycle once it was finished. She herself would look into storing her Trans Am once the winter roads began being salted.

The front door opened and the young man stepped out. He had dark hair and grey eyes. He was about Sylvia's height. "Miss Reed?" Sylvia nodded as she met him halfway up the driveway. "I'm Elliot. I was surprised to receive your call. After finding the apartment your father requested, I didn't think you'd be looking into real estate so soon."

"It's complicated." Sylvia couldn't help smirking. "I'm looking to buy so that I can rent. But to a specific person. That I don't want knowing I'm renting to her."

Elliot stumbled as he made his way toward the front of the house. "Um…" He continued and stopped on the front porch. "I honestly don't know what to say to that."

"Just sell me the house. Say you'll act as my renting agent if I do choose to buy." Sylvia crossed her arms over her chest as she waited for a response.

The dark-haired man shrugged. Who was he to argue with a potential sale. "All right. Let me show you around. And don't be afraid to ask any questions."

The front door opened into a small living room. There would be enough room for Rocho's two recliners and maybe a loveseat. A slight improvement over what she had now.

There wasn't a dining room, just a small kitchen that had a built-in oven and stovetop. The refrigerator was larger than what was in the home Rocho currently occupied.

Next was the hallway that led to the bedrooms. Sylvia blushed at the thought as she had never seen the lone bedroom Rocho had. She had used the lone bathroom and the lone bathroom in this home made it pale in comparison.

So far, what she saw, Sylvia liked. Now, it would depend upon what the garage looked like on the inside. Thankfully, the two-stall garage didn't disappoint. There would be plenty of room for even a large classic vehicle or two, plus Rocho's classic motorcycle.

The real estate agent and businesswoman exited through the garage door. Sylvia's mind was racing. She knew the listing price and knew what was in her bank account. She knew she would receive Rocho's rent money.

For the next few months, Sylvia was forgoing her salary at the dealership. It would help bring it out of the red and back into the black. There was the rent of the apartment she was maintaining. Her head hurt a little as she attempted to factor everything in.

In fact, Sylvia didn't even hear Elliot when he asked for the second time if she was interested. It took a hand upon her forearm to shake her from her thoughts. "Sorry about that. I was using my internal calculator. I'll take it. If the owners will come down two thousand dollars."

Elliot couldn't believe his ears. Normally a client would counteroffer with five to even ten thousand dollars lower. "That shouldn't be a problem. The only thing we'll need to discuss will be this renter and the agreement."

"We can do that once everything is in place." Sylvia held out her hand. Elliot gratefully shook it. "Here's my card. It has my business and cellphone number on it. Use the business one first, please."

The realtor nodded as he watched Sylvia walk back to the Trans Am. He mentally whistled at the way the petite blonde's hips swayed. He whistled even more as the classic came to life. "A beauty like that in a beauty like that."

OOOOOOOOOOOO

Rocho felt a tad lonely. She had wanted to spend the weekend with Sylvia. It was a dangerous situation she found herself in. One she didn't think she would ever find herself in.

The mechanic had a friend. Not just any friend, but a female friend. Beyond that, Sylvia was her boss. Rocho knew she was playing with fire. On so many levels she was playing with fire.

Normally, Rocho would be working on her motorcycle. While it remained appealing, today she felt like taking a walk around the small town she had called home for nearly a year.

In the short time Rocho had lived in Portland, she knew most of the landmarks. There were the usual fast food fares. There was the restaurant one of her customers had told her had been owned by a kind man, once upon a time. There was only the one grocery store, along with the dollar stores. There were a handful of churches.

What Rocho loved was walking the downtown area. There were small businesses still in the classic buildings. Some dated back to around the late eighteen hundreds to early nineteen hundreds. There was the historic bridge that was only wide enough for one car.

Rocho made her way toward the old ballpark and playground. Across the street was the only ice cream place in town. Normally the mechanic didn't indulge in ice cream, unless coffee went along with it. But as the sun was shining down and causing her to sweat, she decided a small, er medium, er large milkshake wouldn't hurt.

Besides, Rocho would continue her walk. There remained so much for the mechanic to see. And she could eat a salad or fish or something for dinner. It would all equal out. It was as good an excuse as any.

Chuckling as she took her first sip of her mocha milkshake, the laughter halted when she heard the familiar voice. Rocho expelled a deep breath when she turned to face Derek. The man was wearing a business suit. In fact, it was the same wrinkled one he had been wearing over a week ago when he had been fired and dragged away by the police.

"If it isn't the dyke mechanic." Rocho glanced around. They weren't that far from the ice cream place. Being summer, kids were everywhere. She didn't want them to see or hear anything this man had to say or do.

"Why don't we take this somewhere else?" Rocho's mind raced. Where? There was another park up the road. One that was used mostly for evening sporting events and were home to The Fourth Of July fireworks. Hopefully that would be empty.

"Why? Don't want any witnesses when I beat the shit out of you?" Rocho cringed when she saw a little girl, probably only about six, begin tugging on her mother's arms.

"No. I just don't want any kids having to see or hear your filthy mouth." Rocho took off running. She hated to appear as if afraid. Yet, she had been running for so many years. Wasn't she really just yellow inside and out?

"Dyke!" Derek stumbled several times. He had yet to stop drinking since being released on his own recognizance. Two things he had been doing. Drinking and looking for the two bitches who had had him arrested.

Finally, Derek's feet were moving steadily. By the time they were, he had lost the bitch. That's when a long leg stretched out. The jerk lost his balance and landed face first on the concrete sidewalk.

Rocho came out from behind the fencing. She was still breathing heavy. After making certain he was out cold, she decided she'd had enough sightseeing. She took the long way home. It meant she would walk past one of the older buildings in Portland. It served as the catholic church, as well as a private school.

Finally, Rocho made it to her home. She smirked as she took the last few swallows of her milkshake. Derek may have shortened her walk; he had added to her workout. And she had still enjoyed her treat.

The sweat was pouring off every square inch of the mechanic. "I hope wherever I do live next it has air conditioning. Damn forgetting to open up what few windows there are."

Rocho set about opening the windows, even though there was no breeze. It had to be better than baking inside. She would take a cold shower and sit in front of the fan for the rest of the evening. Maybe read one of those online fanfics she found herself engrossed in from time to time.

When Rocho slid the glass up on her storm door on the side door, an envelope fell out. A trickle of fear ran up and down her spine. She knew she had locked the door before she had left the house.

Inspecting the outside, Rocho cursed. Someone had sliced opened the screen. "Great. Something I'll have to replace before I move out."

The mechanic knew she was focusing on the repair because of what the envelope could contain. Swallowing hard, Rocho returned inside. She bonelessly slid into her chair.

For an eternity, Rocho held the envelope in her hand. Only her initials of R.L.B. were upon it. Finally, she cautiously opened it. The writing was unfamiliar. As were the words.

Dearest Renee (Rocho),

I'm sorry I didn't stand up for you back in the day. In my defense, I was quite a bit younger. But I'm grown and in a position to help you. If you allow me to. Sorry for the cloak and dagger. I just don't know if you are ready for me to be in your life again or for my help. I'll be in touch in a few weeks.

Love,

H.M.B.

"H.M.B?" Rocho stared at the note. There was only one person she knew by those letters. But he was much older than she. In fact, he was the one of the two who had turned his back on her. "If it's you, Daddy, you can go straight to Hell."

Chapter 11

Sylvia knew that it would take at least a week for everything to be processed with the home. She had thought about obtaining a loan. For now, she wanted to leave it with a cash purchase. If money became too tight, she could still travel that path when the time came.

For now, Sylvia wanted to enjoy her Sunday off. To fully do that, she wanted to spend it with Rocho. She hadn't heard from her friend since they'd left work at the same time on Friday night. Not fully unusual, but not how she liked it.

In the back seat of the Trans Am was a picnic basket. Sylvia had swung by the deli in the grocery store. Screw the usual healthy eats. She had bought fried chicken, potato salad, macaroni and cheese and ultimate chocolate chip cookies for dessert.

It didn't surprise Sylvia to see the small garage door was already open and a dark figure lying on the ground. With the purr her Trans Am was making, it wasn't long before the dark head peeked out from beneath the classic motorcycle.

Haunted. As Sylvia extricated herself from her car, it was how she would describe her friend's expression. Temporarily forgetting about the delightful smelling food, she made a beeline for Rocho.

By the time she made it to the garage, Rocho was already standing. Not caring if her friend's hands were grease covered or not, Sylvia took both in a hand of hers. "What's wrong?"

Rocho attempted a smile, but knew it was of no use. With most people, she could put up these walls. There was the stoic façade she was famous for. But when it came to Sylvia, her boss, no friend, could see right through her.

"I found a note last night." Rocho attempted to look away, but a gentle hand guided her gaze back into the depths of emerald. "If you want, you can read it for yourself."

Sylvia noticed the slumped posture. It was similar to how Rocho had been acting when she had nearly attacked Laurie over the bitch's nasty comments. This must be some letter.

The mechanic hadn't even bothered to destroy or hide it. She took it from the kitchen counter and handed it to Sylvia. After reading it carefully, the business owner wondered what had Rocho so upset. Was it the lack of help so many years ago? Or was it who it could potentially be from?

"Talk to me. I can read the words. I can understand them from my point of view." Sylvia placed a hand upon Rocho's shoulder. "But what are they doing to you? Especially knowing that you could have had support so many years ago but have been on your own. Until now."

The last words were but a whisper. Sylvia was afraid of the rejection. Why? She wasn't certain. She had easily made friends over the years. Maintaining the friendships wasn't a different matter altogether. Same when it came to more intimate relationships. That was probably why. Her fear of one day being left all alone.

When it came to Rocho, she wanted whatever they cultivated to last. Sylvia wanted to have her mechanic in her life as long as Rocho was willing.

It took Rocho a moment to respond. It was a combination of the warmth of Sylvia's touch and words. Both were wreaking havoc with the mechanic's brain. And if she was honest with herself, her libido.

"The thing is, there's only one person I know with those initials." Rocho managed to maintain the steady gaze into emerald eyes. "Henry Mason Bishop. My father. But he definitely wouldn't have been too young. And he always would have been in a position to help me."

"Hmm." Sylvia wasn't certain what to think. "Are you certain there is no one else? A cousin?" Rocho shook her head. "Any family member you might have blocked out because you haven't wanted to think of any all this time?"

Azure continued to stare into emerald. Unknowingly, Sylvia's petite hand began to massage the strong shoulder it was resting upon. Azure disappeared behind heavy eyelids for a long moment as the massaging helped Rocho to think.

"Son of a bitch." Rocho's eyelids flew open. "How the fuck could I forget about my baby brother?" Her hand went to her mouth as she realized how many curse words had escaped.

"Don't worry about the cussing. I grew up around mechanics, remember?" Sylvia enjoyed the nice coloring on tanned cheeks just the same. The joy left her as the seriousness took over. "You think that the note could have been from Henry Mason Bishop, Jr.?"

"It fits. At least being too young." The massaging hadn't stopped. It felt so good. Rocho was struggling with her train of thought. "He would have been around twelve when I left home. Damn, my baby brother is about twenty-six."

"You're quite the old woman." Sylvia squeezed the shoulder she'd been massaging before reluctantly removing her hand. "Hmm. That means your brother and I are about the same age. I hope I get to meet him."

Rocho stiffened at the thought. "I'm not so certain I want to meet him." She took the note back so she could reread the words. While they were the ones she had wanted to hear for over a decade, there was that constant fear of being tricked. Of being forced to face the past in a court of law.

"Why?" Sylvia noticed how her friend had stiffened. "Didn't you and your brother get along?" As far as she knew, she didn't have any siblings. In a way, she was jealous of a potential relationship.

"He was so much younger. He was like a puppy dog in some ways always following me around." Rocho shrugged. "I actually didn't mind it. When I started working on cars, I actually made him my assistant. Until Mom found out. Then she forbade us to hang together. I remember Henry crying and talking back. That had earned him a split lip. Mom blamed me for it."

"I don't think it would ever be a good thing if I ever met your mother." Rocho chuckled. It eased only some of the tension. "It's probably why you've pushed him so far from your memories. He was one of the few bright spots. And when you did have something good, it was hurt because of you. At least in your mind."

"Did you minor in psychology?" Rocho gently teased. Sylvia merely shrugged. "It makes sense though. Famous line from a movie. Sometimes the bad stuff is easier to believe. It's definitely the harder to let go of, sadly."

"Now that I fully understand." Sylvia felt it was time for a little lightening of the situation. "How bout we have a picnic. I just happen to know someone that stopped by and has the fixins for a great picnic. But she doesn't want to eat alone."

Though Rocho's heart remained heavy, she knew she could use a little fun. And fresh air always helped her feel better. "I didn't eat breakfast. After reading the note, I skipped supper last night as well."

"Then my big, strong mechanic needs feeding." Rocho blushed at the words. "Come on, you." Sylvia dangled the keys to the Trans Am. "Would you care to do the honors again? I thought we could find a nice spot along the River Walk."

"A walk and a picnic." Rocho could feel her body relaxing. But then, Sylvia had that effect on her. Well, her libido was ignited by her friend, but the rest of her would relax considerably.

It wasn't long before the pair were situated on one of the picnic tables just off the paved trail. The city had left most of the woods intact and it was simply beautiful.

But not as beautiful as the woman sitting across from her. Rocho knew it was a dangerous slope on which she was treading. Still, she couldn't help admiring the woman.

But it wasn't merely Sylvia's silky blonde locks. It wasn't her curvaceous body or perfect face. It was her intelligence and inner beauty. And the fact that she knew nearly as much, if not more, than Rocho when it came to automobiles.

Rocho didn't want to spoil the afternoon, but she had to inform Sylvia of her encounter with Derek the previous day. "I almost forgot with coming home and finding the note. I ran into a very drunk Derek yesterday."

"Good thing you waited to tell me until after we'd had lunch." Sylvia reached for the cookies. "Though with news like this, I could use something sweet." She took a cookie for herself and offered one to Rocho.

The mechanic gladly took her own. Before taking a bite, she figured she better finish the tale. "I had been on one of my walks around town. Had just treated myself to a mocha milkshake when Derek, still in his suit he was fired in, started calling me a dyke. He was drunk off his ass."

A deep breath escaped Sylvia. Derek had worked at the dealership for an extended time period. If he was acting lewd, it still could reflect on the business.

"After a second round of being called a dyke, I took off running. I momentarily lost him." Rocho took a drink of the milk she had brought. It would help wash the cookies down. "I hid around a corner behind a fence. It took him a moment, but when he caught up, I tripped him knocking him out. I left him lying on the sidewalk."

Once again, Sylvia found herself sighing. "This could get ugly with him." She shoved the rest of her cookie in her mouth. Just then, a slight breeze caressed her skin. It caused emerald eyes to close. With the end of June came the rising of the summer temperatures.

"Sadly. I'm sorry if I added to it." Rocho finished her cookie and chased it down by her milk. It was the last thing she wanted was to have anything reflect badly upon Sylvia.

"Actually, the witnesses, if there are any, will say you ran." Sylvia patted her friend's forearm before snagging her second cookie.

Running. Rocho couldn't respond. Instead, she also snagged her second cookie. Instead of looking at the beautiful woman sitting across from her, she was looking at the beauty surrounding her.

There was a nice mix of pines, oaks and maples surrounding them. If Rocho were to ever have a place of her own, she would love to have a mix of sugar and red maples. The colors would be amazing when autumn was upon them.

Sylvia watched intently as her friend was lost in the foliage that surrounded them. There was more to it than the beauty of their surroundings. Should she pry?

"Rocho?" It took what seemed forever for the mechanic to tear her eyes from the trees and bring them to her sexy boss. "Did I say something that upset you?"

"Trigger." Rocho shrugged. "It goes back to what we discussed before." She reached out blindly and grasped Sylvia's hand. "I've been running since I was eighteen. And I haven't stopped."

"Well, there might be a situation opening up." Sylvia didn't want to place the cart ahead of the horse before knowing for certain. "My friend has been renting to someone, but the renter is moving out of state."

"So, it would still be renting." Sylvia nodded. It would give Rocho an out. But it would also mean she would have lived in a city for more than a year for the first time since she had begun running. "Tell me about the place."

It was all Sylvia could do not to allow her radiant smile to shine through. "Wellllll…" She giggled with the look of anticipation on Rocho's face. The lost look, or was it punishing look, was gone. In its place was one of genuine interest.

Chapter 12

A week and a half had gone by. Fourth of July was only two days away. Sylvia had hoped she would have heard from her realtor so that Rocho could be moved into the house by now.

Even with the frustration with the housing situation, there was one bright spot. The dealership was slowly inching its way back toward the black.

One reason was Rocho. It wasn't merely keeping the service department running smoothly. About a week ago, Sylvia came across the mechanic assisting one of the salesmen. She had been discussing the finer points of each model of a car. Basically, she had sealed the deal.

Now was a hectic time for Sylvia. It was already time to the place the current models on clearance and make certain the new models were ordered. She had yet to replace Derek or Nathan. And she needed a manager who could assist her with inventory, at the very least.

The knock on her office door surprised Sylvia. She didn't have any appointments scheduled until four and it was only two. "Come in." Emerald eyes widened when she took in the bouquet of yellow roses. "What the…?"

"There's a card." Elizabeth placed the dozen roses on the edge of the desk. They were out of the way of the phone and computer that way. "I'm dying to know, but I have to get back to work. Let me know who the lucky lady is." She winked before making her way back to her desk.

"I'd like to know as well." Sylvia couldn't help smirking. There had been no one since Laurie. She hadn't been to any bars. She hadn't been to larger cities that had LGBTQ friendly bars. There was always dating sites or apps, but truth be told she was happy spending her free time with her friend. Even if romance was never to be between them.

Elizabeth had placed the flowers so that the card was within reach without having to stand. The pale-yellow envelope wasn't even sealed. 'Hope everything is going smoothly. I'll be in town for the 4th. Love, Daddy'.

"No phone calls. No emails. No texts." Sylvia slumped in her chair. "Yet you can waste your money on sending me flowers." The business owner shook her head. "You couldn't send me a subscription to a car magazine or something I'd truly enjoy?"

Sylvia chuckled as she realized she was talking to herself. "I need to take a mini break, I think." Without another thought, she rose from her desk. She knew she couldn't pass by Elizabeth without telling her. "They're just from your old boss. I'll be back in a few. Just need a walk to clear my head. Page me if you need me."

"Sure thing, Boss." Elizabeth was tempted to see if her boss was telling the truth. Sylvia had been home nearly a month now. Except for the first week when Laurie was around, her boss was alone.

Sure, Rocho and Sylvia had lunch frequently together. And there was an attraction of some kind. But Elizabeth was certain they were merely friends. In the year the mechanic had worked for the dealership, she'd never had a significant other or a friend, come to think of it.

Elizabeth wondered if she had a shot with either one of them. The phone ringing brought her back from her musings. If she did, cool. If not, there were plenty of people out there for her to hopefully find her soulmate with.

OOOOOOOOOOOO

Rocho needed some fresh air. Even with fans and the air conditioning on low, it was smoldering in the mechanic's bay. She made certain each of the mechanics working were drinking plenty of water or sports drinks and taking frequent short breaks, yet not falling behind.

The head mechanic had to admit she hadn't followed her own orders. Oh, Rocho had been hydrating with water. She'd had her favorite iced coffee before work. But she hadn't taken as many breaks as she should so that the others could take their breaks.

The handkerchief was damp still that Rocho used to wipe her brow. As the breeze hit her sweat drenched overalls, a low moan escaped the mechanic. "I really have to take my own advice and take more frequent breaks."

"Yes, you do." Rocho was startled by the slight voice to her right. A bottle of water was slid into her hand. "I've been keeping an eye on you." Martha shook her head as if disappointed. "I don't think Miss Reed would appreciate how you've been pushing yourself."

"You're right." Rocho practically inhaled the entire bottle of water. "Thank you." Azure eyes closed as the breeze picked up once again. It had changed direction. It had also cooled even more.

Azure eyes opened. The sun was beginning to shift. "Looks like we are in for some rain. Hopefully it'll cool things off and not make it more humid and stickier."

"Always a crapshoot." Martha could hear her phone ringing. But she had to take a chance. It was now or never. "We've worked with one another for a year now. I was wondering if you'd like to have dinner one night. Or maybe go bowling."

Rocho turned abruptly so she could gauge brown eyes for their reaction. "While I am a lesbian and you are a very attractive woman, I'm not looking for a relationship. I'm barely even looking for a friendship."

"I see." Martha's brown eyes were now nearly black. "I guess it depends on who you are. If it was Miss Reed who was to do the asking, you would jump at the chance."

Before Rocho could respond, Martha was practically running back into the dealership. The mechanic shook her head. "You always have a way with the ladies, Rocho. So sad."

As if the heavens heard her, thunder shook the entire dealership. Lightning struck close enough that Rocho could actually feel the heat. "Shit!"

Rocho didn't hesitate in running for the shelter of the dealership. She just made it before the sky ripped apart and the rain fell like it hadn't rained in several months.

Someone else wasn't quite as lucky. Rocho happened to see the shadow following her. She held the door open as Sylvia ran into the nearest entrance to the dealership.

"That's some storm." Rocho could only nod in agreement. Seeing a soaking wet Sylvia had the mechanic temporarily speechless.

Luckily, Rocho was able to force herself to speak. "I'll say. I could feel the heat from a lightning strike. Let's get you some dry clothes. It'll be a pair of my overalls, but it's better than those soaked clothes."

Once again, Rocho was shielding her friend from eyes as Sylvia made her way to the back. The mechanic left her friend alone and attempted to check in with Martha. The secretary was now ignoring her. This was trouble.

Five minutes later, a grateful appearing Sylvia returned from Rocho's private locker room. "Thank you." A petite blonde head turned as she sneezed. "Sorry bout that. These are definitely comfortable. Though I hate to meet my potential office manager in these. A tad bit unprofessional." She managed to turn her head as she sneezed again.

"Bless you. Twice." Rocho didn't like how Sylvia was sneezing already. "I think the perfect candidate will understand. And besides, this is a dealership. Even the owner gets their hands dirty from time to time."

"That is true." Sylvia felt a warmth spread over her, though she wasn't certain if it was from Rocho's words, her nearness or from suddenly not feeling a hundred percent. "I best be getting to the office. I'll pick up my clothes on the way out."

"When we do the usual lockdown." It was the term they had given to securing the premises before they went their separate ways for the night.

"I'll see you at six-thirty." Sylvia waved before slowly making her way toward the sales department. It was an area that Rocho normally avoided. But lately, she found herself visiting every so often.

The rest of the day, at least for Rocho, moved smoothly. When the usual meeting time for closing down the dealership came and there was no sign of Sylvia, the mechanic began to worry.

Double checking each of the bays, Rocho checked each of the exits and hiding places customers or employees had been known to be discovered in. Finally, she found herself where she had desired to be in the first place.

Rocho's heart lurched into her throat at the sight that welcomed her. Sylvia remained in the overalls. The mechanic had forgotten the owner's clothes. That wasn't important as the blonde locks were damp and plastered to the drenched forehead. The head was resting upon the desk. A slight wheezing sound was emanating from the slight figure.

"Remind me to have a long talk with Elizabeth the next time I fucking see her." Rocho nearly knocked the vase of yellow roses over in her haste to get to her obviously sick friend.

There was a stabbing in the mechanic's chest at the thought of a secret admirer.

"Friends. Remember? It's more than you deserve, Rocho old girl." Still, Rocho swallowed as her throat burned as she attempted to keep the tears from escaping.

"Now, Miss Reed. Is your immune system low?" Rocho removed her hand immediately as if it had been burned when she checked her friend for a fever. "You definitely caught something in that little dance in the rain you had earlier."

Rocho sighed. It was only mid-week. Sylvia probably had more business to attend to. She wasn't certain who would be available to take care of her. Frank was off who knew where. Laurie was hopefully far from Portland.

The mechanic realized she would be in the same boat if something were to happen to her. Rocho shook her head as she came to a decision. "Let me leave a note for both Martha and Elizabeth. Oh and message Rick. He can handle a day in charge without me in service."

It took longer than Rocho would have liked to leave the necessary notes and instructions. In a way, she was grateful she'd been spending her lunches with Sylvia, as well as time outside of work. Without even realizing it, the mechanic had picked up a great deal about running the dealership.

With ease, Rocho took Sylvia in her arms. "Guess I get to drive your classic once again." The mechanic knew Sylvia actually loved it when she drove. If only because Rocho knew how to make the Trans Am fully purr without harming the classic.

"Only problem with these sports classics is no room in the back seat." Rocho cautiously fastened her precious cargo into the passenger seat. "Sleep well until I can get you home and into a comfortable bed."

Rocho was grateful she had a decent memory as she drove the short distance to Sylvia's apartment complex. She even remembered which parking spot her friend was assigned to.

Once again, Rocho had the precious bundle in her arms. "Now, which key is to the outside door and inside door." The mechanic was grateful she had many skills as she was able to hold Sylvia tight as she fumbled with the keys until she found the correct one.

All those hours of working out came in handy as Rocho climbed the three flights of stairs. Once again, she fumbled with the keys as she continued to hold Sylvia in her arms.

The apartment was warmer than Rocho had hoped. "Darn those energy savers." The mechanic never halted. As gently as possible, she placed Sylvia on top of the blankets. "Let me get you something more comfortable to wear."

The thought of undressing Sylvia caused Rocho to swallow hard. "She's your friend. She's your boss. Nothing more than you taking care of both. Get you libido under control."

Even with the little pep talk, it was a lengthy amount of time before Rocho was able to move from beside the bed. It felt like an invasion of privacy as she opened and closed drawers. Her heart raced when she came across the lingerie drawer.

"Focus, dammit!" Rocho chastised herself once again. Finally, she found what she hoped would work. Soft feeling t-shirts, along with cotton shorts. "Probably what you work out in, but comfortable to sleep in as well."

Rocho turned back to her patient. A moan escaped Sylvia at that moment. "I'm here." Sylvia had managed to roll onto her side. "Sylvia, I'm going to need some help. I have to get you out of these overalls and into something a bit more comfortable."

"Mmm. Calloused hands upon my skin." Rocho swallowed hard. The raspiness of Sylvia's voice was partially due to being sick. But the mechanic knew it was also due to the fact her friend was stuck in a sultry dream.

And that sultry dream was starring none other than Rocho herself. "Oh, boy. I can do this." She had to take a deep breath before undoing the Velcro. Once that was done, she unzipped the long zipper. Her hand coming across the lacy bra and overheated skin.

"I repeat, I can do this." Rocho hastily removed the arms from their coverings and the legs from the pantlegs. She was hyper aware of the softness of the skin and the warmth emanating from the body she was undressing.

"Almost there, Lover." Azure eyes closed. Sylvia was definitely stuck in a fantasy. One that the mechanic had had a few times herself. But she'd never come this close, other than their first encounter, to actually having the fantasy come true. "Then it's your turn to undress."

At the words, Rocho's knees nearly gave out. "I can do this." The words were squeezed through gritted teeth. Her self-control was hastily failing her. "Damn my supposedly dormant libido."

As Rocho hastily removed the bra and panties, along with fighting roaming hands, she realized her libido hadn't truly been an issue until Sylvia had returned home.

Thankfully, it didn't take long to dress Sylvia as the young woman had passed out once again. Rocho covered her friend with the blanket before making her way into the bathroom that was just off the master bedroom.

The cold water seemed to sizzle upon Rocho's overheated skin. She wanted to take a cold shower. There was a problem with that. Without taking the Trans Am across town, she wouldn't have anything to change into.

Instead, Rocho made certain to wash herself as thoroughly as possible giving the circumstances. She contemplated turning the air conditioning down, but wanted to maintain a steady temperature for Sylvia.

Taking a moment to make certain Sylvia remained sleeping, Rocho decided to explore the kitchen. After all, she had skipped breakfast, as usual, and lunch was now six plus hours ago. She didn't think her friend would mind if she stole something. Plus, she wanted to see if there was something mild, like soup, she could have ready for Sylvia when she awakened.

Not wanting to steal too much of her friend's food, Rocho settled for a hastily made sandwich and a can of cola. Not realizing how hungry she was, the mechanic practically inhaled the sandwich and drank half the can before making her way back into the master bedroom.

Sylvia was writhing on the bed. Rocho immediately placed her can of cola on the nightstand. She sat on the edge of the bed. Without warning, she found her arms full of petite blonde.

"Please don't leave me." Rocho felt the warmth of Sylvia's skin upon her own. She also felt the dampness of the tears. It was definitely not from the sweat drenched clothing or skin of her friend.

"I'm not going anywhere." The words were truer than Rocho cared to admit to herself. Absently, she began rubbing Sylvia's back. "Just relax. You need to sleep."

"I don't want to close my eyes." Sylvia pulled back slightly so that she was looking into azure eyes. "They all leave me." Tears were slowly trickling down rosy cheeks. "First, my mom died of cancer. I watched her waste away to nothing. They removed her breasts and everything. And still, she died and left me all alone."

Rocho had to fight to keep her body from stiffening. This was becoming personal. True, she had shared about her dark past. About the untrue accusations. But she had done that while still fully aware of her faculties.

Sylvia was out of her mind with fever. "Shh. You don't have to tell me. I know your Momma passed away. I know she fought the good fight. She wanted to stay with you. So do I. I promise not to leave you."

The words only somewhat seemed to calm Sylvia. "But there are more. Rachel. She left me when we graduated high school. Said she wasn't ready to be out. Yet, she had been cheating on me. Olivia and I were only a month together, when I caught her with another woman. And then there's Laurie. Why am I so unlovable?"

"Oh, Sylvia. You are far from unlovable." Rocho sighed as she kissed Sylvia's forehead. "I love you. If I didn't, I wouldn't even consider remaining in Portland. I will. No matter if I have to stay here until I can find a place of my own."

"Oh, Rocho." Once again, Rocho found she was not prepared when lips found hers. Not only did lips find hers, but a strong, insistent tongue thrust inside. A moan escaped the mechanic before she could find the strength to break the kiss.

"Please don't stop." Emerald eyes were darkened. Rocho knew it wasn't from the illness. It was from desire. "I love you. Please don't stop. Let me show you how much."

"I love you too, Sweetheart." Rocho had to swallow several times before she gently kissed Sylvia on the lips. "Now you be good and get some sleep. I promise I'll cuddle up next to you and be here in the morning."

"You better. I can't lose you. I'd rather lose the dealership than lose you." With those heartfelt words, Sylvia allowed herself to be tucked back into bed. It took a few moments, but adorable snores were emanating from the sick woman.

Once again, Rocho had to take a moment in the bathroom. She stared at her reflection in the mirror. "You are in so much trouble." She couldn't help the bright smile that overtook her.

"But it's the best kind of trouble you've been in for over a decade." That much was true. At least Rocho hoped that it was true. Sylvia wasn't like Juliette. Yet, something always seemed to chase her out of town.

"It has to be different this time." Rocho slowly made her way toward the bed. Steadying herself, she slipped into bed. The moment she was beneath the covers, she felt the warm body mold itself next to her.

It felt…right. Rocho closed her eyes. She was exhausted, even though it wasn't even nine yet. In a way, she hoped she would be able to work the next day so that one of them was there. But in another, she hoped she'd have another day of just the two of them. And if it was spent in bed together, just snuggled together…

Chapter 13

Attempting to be as quiet as possible, Frank closed the door behind him. He wasn't certain if his daughter knew he had a spare set of keys to her apartment. He'd made certain Elliot hadn't told her. After all, what mid-twenty-year-old wanted their father having the key.

Frank glanced at his watch. It was nearing eight. His daughter should already be up. It was Thursday. And if he remembered correctly, today was the day Sylvia would have to have the orders in for the new fleet.

"Sylvia?" Frank placed the keys back in his khaki cargo shorts. His Bermuda shirt clung to him as the storm that had passed through the previous day had increased the temperatures and the humidity ten-fold.

Besides the humming of the air conditioner, there was not a sound in the apartment. "Strange. The Trans Am is in its spot." Frank hated to do it, but he had a bad feeling.

Slowly, Frank opened the door to the master bedroom. "What the fuck!" Two heads popped up at once. One groaned and the other had eyes as big as saucers. "Rocho, get the fuck out of my daughter's bed."

While she wanted to move immediately, Rocho made certain Sylvia's head was resting upon the pillow before sitting on the edge of the bed. "Nothing happened, Sir."

"The fuck it didn't. I believe my eyes." Before Rocho could ready herself, she felt hands on both her biceps. Once she could fight back, she didn't. She allowed herself to be thrown out into the hallway.

"Dad!" Sylvia stumbled when she attempted to stand. While sleeping all night had done her wonders, she remained weak. "Don't you dare touch her!" She had to use the bed to make her way to a standing position. She used it to maintain her balance until she was able to stand on her own.

"Don't you dare defend her." Frank didn't like one of his employees taking advantage of his daughter. "What did she promise you? A good fuck and you'd stay for longer? I knew you were no good when I hired you."

Rocho refused to say a word. She remained where she had landed. She kept her gaze focused on Frank's shoes. She could see by the way he was walking what would happen next. She could have protected herself if she had wanted to.

Sylvia managed to make it to her father, but it was too late. The scream wasn't as loud as it would have been if she were at one hundred percent as Frank's foot made contact with Rocho's ribs.

Somehow, Sylvia managed to throw herself between her father and Rocho. Anymore blows would be felt by Sylvia instead of her friend. Her head was dizzy from the sudden exertion and from her illness.

"Get out of my way." Frank's hands were both clenched fists. "This drifter dishonored us both. She managed to get you into bed nearly the minute I was out of the picture. She's probably trying to get you to marry her so she'll never have to work again."

"Enough!!" Sylvia managed to turnaround so she was leaning back against Rocho. Her head was against a strong shoulder. Without thought, she took a strong hand and placed it on her stomach.

"For your information, I was caught in the rainstorm yesterday while I was taking a break." There was barely even breathing coming from the body she was resting against. "I must have become extremely sick. I don't remember anything after interviewing Marvin for office manager. I believe he starts Monday. But I'm not even sure."

"But…" Frank looked over his daughter and into the azure eyes. There was a blank expression in the them. As if Rocho had given up. "But the two of you were in bed together."

"Fully clothed, Dad." Sylvia wanted to shake her head, but knew it was not a good idea. "Here's what's going to happen. You are going to leave your keys on the counter. You are never to come here unless you call first. And if you ever speak to Rocho like you just did, I'll never speak to you again."

"But…" Frank straightened. He slowly back pedaled toward the door. "But what about The Fourth?" There was a clanging noise as he placed the set of keys on the countertop.

"Either I go alone or with Rocho." Sylvia swallowed hard. Her throat was becoming raw. "Now, leave before I really get upset."

Frank saw the spark in his daughter's eyes. It was the same spark he remembered seeing when he looked into his wife's eyes. The only problem? He didn't like Rocho. She was an amazing mechanic, not bad at business. But she was a drifter. She was not good enough for his little girl.

Sylvia made certain the door was shut and secured before resting her head against the strong shoulder again. There was still little movement, other than breathing, from the strong chest she was using for support.

"Rocho. I hate to do this after what my father just did and said to you, but I need you." Sylvia's words were just above a whisper. Her voice was scratchy. "I need to get to work. There's so much to do. And I need to know if you are hurt. That's first and foremost."

At the words 'I need', Rocho began to come to life. It still took several moments for her to find her voice. "Work, unless you need to be there, is taken care of. I left notes with Elizabeth, Martha and Rick that neither of us would be in today."

Though she was speaking, Rocho's voice was hollow. Sylvia sighed heavily. "Well, that's work taken care of. There was nothing I had to take care of in person. Now, what about you." Sylvia managed to move so that she was looking at her friend.

A gasp escaped Sylvia. The sudden intake of breath caused a small coughing fit that, thankfully, didn't last long. "Sorry about that. It's just that my asshole father left his mark behind."

Not even thinking about it, Sylvia reached out and began tracing the bruises that were in the shape of her father's hand. A slight shiver that could not be contained caught Sylvia's eyes.

When azure locked with emerald, Sylvia immediately understood. They were friends, but there was a strong underlying current of sexual attraction between them. More than just sexual attraction.

"I've had worse." Rocho groaned slightly when she took a deep breath. She hoped her ribs were merely bruised. "Your father jumped to a conclusion. He used my trigger, once again. The one that freezes me. Or makes me…"

Gently fingers stopped Rocho from speaking. "Run." Rocho nodded. "I understand." Sylvia swallowed again. "I want to continue with the sensitive chat thing, but I need a shower. And my throat is sore. Would you mind getting me juice? Can you make oatmeal?"

"Juice is easy." Rocho waited until Sylvia was in a sitting position. After making certain her friend would remain in an upright position, she herself rose. Her groan couldn't be muffled, nor could she stop herself from grabbing her ribs.

"I'll ice them down after we get you taken care of." Rocho leaned against the wall as she caught her breath. She rubbed her ribs. "They aren't broken. It's happened a couple times when I had mishaps a couple times. Bruised can be just as painful, but don't take as long to heal."

After fully catching her breath, Rocho held out her hand. Reluctantly, Sylvia allowed for her friend to pull her to her feet. Once the mechanic was certain Sylvia could stand on her own, she slowly made her way toward the kitchen. "Holler if you need me."

It took Sylvia longer than she would have liked to make her way into the bathroom. Every so often, she found herself becoming dizzy. Normally, she wasn't susceptible to becoming sick. But when she was sick, it knocked her for quite a loop.

After taking a lukewarm shower, Sylvia felt so much better. She still had to be cautious. She wondered if her dizziness was partly from lack of eating. That should be taken care of soon enough. Even if Rocho couldn't handle oatmeal, she could always make toast.

The thought that Rocho was still in her sweaty clothing from the day before caused Sylvia to rummage through her drawers. There was one outfit her girlfriend before Laurie had bought for her as a joke. It was at least a size, if not two, too big. It would be perfect for the mechanic and be comfortable as well. Thank goodness for procrastination on the businesswoman's part in donating it. Plus, it was from her alma mater.

The scent of oatmeal and something else had Sylvia's stomach grumbling. She realized she hadn't had anything to eat since the shared lunch with Rocho the previous day.

When Sylvia finally made her way into the kitchen, she was surprised. She knew it had taken her a bit to shower, but not long enough for Rocho to make oatmeal, toast, slice strawberries, make coffee and pour juice. "Wow. This looks amazing. And smells amazing." Her attempt at speaking caused another round of coughing.

Rocho was instantly by her side. She held the juice to Sylvia's lips. Gratefully, Sylvia took the glass and slowly swallowed two thirds of the contents. "Thank you."

The mechanic nodded and hastily refilled it before placing it in front of the food she'd prepared for Sylvia. "Sit. Eat. If there's anything else or this is too much, just let me know."

Waiting until after Sylvia was seated, Rocho sat next to her at the little breakfast bar. Both ate in silence for several moments. It was a little painful for the mechanic as breathing and moving was difficult.

The juice alone was helping Sylvia's throat. Luckily, her stomach was able to eat all the wonderful food. It was taking the edge off the dizziness she was feeling. It was more about a slight cough and sore throat now.

"That was delicious. I'm nearly ready to head back to work." Just as the words escaped Sylvia's mouth, a huge yawn overtook her.

"I think rest is what you need." Rocho began clearing the dirty dishes. "If you want, you check in with Elizabeth. Then take a nap. I'll clean up. If you feel good enough, maybe see if I can help at the dealership."

"First off, if I stay home, you stay home." Sylvia took on her boss stance. "Secondly, I have some clothing that might just fit you. After you do clean up out here, you get clean up."

Rocho knew that expression. She knew the stance. "You've got it, Boss. Just leave the clothes outside the door. I'll use the spare shower."

Sylvia wanted to say more but was suddenly so tired. Knowing there would be time later to talk and tease, she decided to do as she was told. She made her way into the bedroom. Before she forgot, she left the clothing outside, along with shampoo and soap.

Settling on the bed, she picked up her landline. She had to be one of the few people left who still had one. "Hello, Elizabeth. Still quite under the weather. I'm being well taken care of. Yes, by Rocho. How are things going?"

After listening to a brief report, Sylvia was feeling more relaxed. And therefore, she was feeling more exhausted. "Just one more thing. How is the service department doing? Good. Sorry to do this, but I'm exhausted. If there's anything that does come up either call the landline or Rocho's cellphone if there's no answer. Don't start. Behave. Have a good day."

When Rocho finally finished the dishes, she checked on her friend. She cautiously opened the bedroom door. Sylvia was sound asleep. "Sleep tight. I promise I won't leave you. I might not live with you, but I won't leave you."

"Better not." The mumbled response could just barely be heard. Rocho realized she would have to be careful what she said, even while Sylvia was sleeping.

For the first time since waking up, Rocho couldn't help chuckling. "University of Michigan workout clothing." The mechanic shook her head. "They should fit. So that's a plus, though I'll have to go commando."

It wasn't like Rocho didn't go commando on occasion. It was the thought of being commando around Sylvia. Their relationship seemed to be elevating. She wasn't certain if it were leaps and bounds or baby steps.

There were also the steps backwards. Rocho wasn't certain if Frank breaking in on them this morning counting as backward or forward.

True, Sylvia had defended her quite vehemently. But Rocho had done what she had normally done. She had allowed herself to be beaten instead of fight back. Now if Frank had verbally or physically attacked his daughter…

Rocho shivered to think what her reaction would have been had that happened. "Thankfully Frank was a good father and went after me."

Good father. Rocho sighed at the thought. She made her way to the kitchen after dressing in the shorts and t-shirts both emblazoned with the University's logo. She wasn't hungry yet, but wanted to be prepared when Sylvia woke from her nap.

After having watched Sylvia's appetite, she figured something light but filling would be perfect. There were cans of soup, but that wouldn't be enough. After scrounging in the refrigerator, she found some cheese. Grilled cheese and soup. That should settle well.

Deciding it was time for herself to call work, Rocho made her way into the spare bedroom so that she wouldn't disturb Sylvia. The moment Martha heard her voice, she hung up. "Shit. We have a real problem. One I'm going to have to discuss with Sylvia."

Rocho called the direct line and had Rick paged instead. After receiving a quick update, grateful that things were running smoothly for a Thursday, she decided to once again to check on Sylvia. "Don't leave me!"

Rocho didn't hesitate. She was in the bedroom and had Sylvia in her arms. The mechanic was whispering in a convenient ear. "I love you, Rocho. Daddy is wrong. So very wrong."

This time when the kissing began, Rocho nearly didn't have the strength to put a stop to it. But she had to. There was one thing she had learned from the past. No matter how much she wanted something, she couldn't just take it.

And even if she thought someone else wanted it just as bad. Rocho had to be one hundred fifty percent certain before she gave into her carnal cravings. Plus, she had to have true love behind it. Not what she had as a teenager.

"Sylvia. Please." Emerald eyes opened wide. It was as if she realized what she had been doing. In fact, the young woman began to pull away. "It's ok."

"No, it's not." Sylvia sighed heavily. "I was all over you." Her eyes would not meet azure ones. "It's almost like what Daddy described, only in reverse."

"First of all, you are sick." Rocho took Sylvia's hand in her own. "You were delirious while sleeping." She squeezed her friend's hand to keep her from speaking. "Secondly, it wasn't exactly unwanted."

Emerald eyes grew wide at the admission. She had thought she had felt sparks. In fact, she knew they had come close to kissing at least once. But since then, they had backed off a great deal. She had thought it was because all Rocho had wanted was friendship.

"I thought you wanted to remain friends." Sylvia was leaning slightly closer. She knew what she wanted. She wanted to fall into Rocho's arms and never let her go.

It was odd. With all her relationships, they had been a struggle to begin. Once they'd jumped the friendship hurdle, making love hadn't been what it had been cracked up to be.

But with Rocho, everything was so easy. Just talking or hanging out was simple. Stirrings in her groin just looking at the sexy mechanic had her wanting to rush things along. But she knew of her friend's past and knew things would have to be taken slow.

"It's complicated for me." Azure eyes closed. When they opened, there was such a sadness within them. "I made the first hurdle by even agreeing to remain here with my golden rule of one year." She chuckled to ease the mounting tension.

"The other issue for me is…" Rocho couldn't say the words. She wanted to kiss Sylvia, cold or no, now that her friend was lucid. But she couldn't. Not with the charges hovering over her. Not with her control still so hare-trigger.

"The rape accusation?" Rocho nodded. "I can't say I fully understand. I can only say how it would feel if it were me. So, let me do this." Sylvia placed a hand on both sides of Rocho's face.

Sylvia watched as the different emotions raced across Rocho's face. She waited for the storm to settle before she closed the distance between them.

So that she could still see the expression upon Rocho's face, Sylvia hovered. In fact, she waited. And waited. It was the mechanic that finally closed the distance.

There was passion behind the kiss, but it was mostly tender. It was the kind of a first kiss any couple would love to share. It lasted until Sylvia had to break it as her weak lungs cried out for oxygen.

"I'm sorry. I wish that could have lasted longer." Sylvia rested her forehead upon Rocho's. "I want you to know something. I've never been kissed like that. It was so sweet and tender." She reached up and stroked a cheek.

Rocho was beyond words. Ever since Juliette, she had avoided a relationship. She knew there were things they had to discuss. Where she was to live. Martha not taking no very well. How Frank would take an elevated relationship. The fact Sylvia attempted, on more than one occasion, to have her way with her.

For now, Rocho wanted to snuggle back in bed with her friend. She wanted to make certain Sylvia rested the entire day. That she ate properly. Unfortunately, Rocho would have to leave or they would have to get up early so she could have clothes to wear the next day.

Finally, Rocho was able to form words. "One promise I'll make to you. I'll always attempt to be tender. I'll always be there for you, even if it's only in spirit. But I have to ask that we please take it slow."

"Too slow for kissing?" One of Sylvia's eyebrows rose. It gave her normally innocent appearance anything but. She could be quite devilish when she wanted to be.

"Not that slow." Rocho felt a hearty laugh escape her. "But for now, you need to rest. I'll rest with you. Maybe after lunch we can try some of that tender kissing again."

Chapter 14

Luckily, it hadn't taken Sylvia long to recover. She was back at work first thing Friday morning, as was Rocho. Missing a day kept Sylvia from even taking a break or having lunch with her girlfriend.

Girlfriend. Sylvia took a moment to allow that to sink in before her phone interrupted her thoughts. "Yes, Elizabeth?" It was nearing closing time on Friday night. She hoped she and Rocho could have dinner in her apartment. Or work on the police special. At this point, as long as they spent time together.

"Martha Neilsen from the service department is here to see you." Sylvia glanced out at the thirty something woman. There was anger flashing in her brown eyes. This was trouble. She could sense it.

"Send her in." Sylvia saved the note she was working on. The one she had to have finished before she left. It needed to be finished so that she could finish the orders first thing Monday morning and then begin showing Marvin the ropes.

Martha didn't even wait to be greeted. "I want Rocho Bishop fired for sexual harassment." A foot was tapping and arms were crossed against her chest.

Sexual harassment? Emerald eyes closed. Sylvia knew it wasn't true in her heart. Just the same, she had to take it seriously for the business' sake. "Exactly what happened."

"That pervert keeps rubbing up next to me when seeing what the next appointment is. She repeatedly asks me out, even after I tell her no." Martha glared at her boss.

Sylvia sighed heavily. "All right. Let me contact the dealership lawyer. You can take the rest of the day off, with pay, and head over to Mr. Carnigie's office right away."

"That's not good enough." Martha continued to stand with her angry pose. "I want Rocho fired. Immediately. I don't care if she is your girlfriend."

Anger flared in emerald eyes. Sylvia took a deep breath before rashly answering. "First off, don't be insinuating anything that could reflect negatively against your complaint. Secondly, don't be making demands. Rocho will be dealt with, according to whatever Mr. Carnigie suggests. Do I make myself clear?"

"Perfectly." Martha took several steps closer to the desk. "I quit. I'm getting my own lawyer. And suing you personally, Rocho and the dealership." She stormed toward the door. The secretary turned back toward Sylvia. "And I'll be contacting the media, as well."

Now Sylvia couldn't help the wicked smirk that emerged on the businesswoman's face. "Until this is brought to court, you should know that I can, and will, sue you for defamation of character if you go to the media. So I'd keep your mouth shut."

If steam could come out of someone's ears, Sylvia thought it would be coming out of Martha's. "This isn't fucking over. I'll see you and that bitch mechanic of yours in court."

The slamming of the door didn't startle Sylvia. Neither did the door opening nearly right away. Elizabeth's soothing voice was welcoming. "What can I do for you."

"Start the day over with?" Elizabeth knew it was serious, even with the attempt at humor. Sylvia took a deep breath. "Seriously. I need to get a hold of Mr. Carnigie. I need Rocho in here asap."

"Will do, Boss." Elizabeth knew better, once again, than to ask what was happening. The way Martha had demanded to see Sylvia, along with the request to contact the dealership's lawyer, completely added up.

Sylvia stared at the now wilting yellow roses. Even after the way her father had treated Rocho, she hadn't had the heart to throw them out. Sadly, she hadn't been well enough to watch the Fourth of July parade or fireworks with Rocho as a couple.

The light rapping on the door startled Sylvia. She wasn't certain how long she had been staring at the yellow roses. Not bothering with answering, she hastily made her way to the door and opened it. She was grateful when Rocho was standing there.

For the first time since taking over her father's business, Sylvia closed the blinds. Rocho was surprised when she found her arms full of petite blonde. Wanting to know what happened, she instinctively knew her girlfriend needed to be held.

After breathing in the scent of gasoline, motor oil and what was just plain Rocho for several moments, Sylvia reluctantly placed some distance between them. She wanted to sit on the sofa so Rocho could hold her some more, but knew there would be a call from Mr. Carnigie any moment.

Waiting until Rocho was settled across from her, Sylvia began. "I had a disturbing visit from the ex-secretary of the service department."

Azure eyes closed. Rocho could guess, at least on some level, what the visit was in regards to. She waited for her boss, for in this moment, Sylvia was her boss and not friend nor girlfriend.

"There have been allegations of sexual harassment made against you." Sylvia watched. There was the fight she watched come across her employee's face. It was the remain or flight fight. "First off, I don't believe her. But we do have to mount a defense. For you, myself and the dealership."

Sylvia waited. She knew, though it wasn't an accusation of physical assault, it was still a false accusation. Something

Rocho was already running from. She had to make certain her girlfriend didn't run again.

When after five minutes and no phone call, Sylvia decided she would see if she could get Rocho to speak to her. It wasn't long before she was kneeling beside the mechanic. "Are you going to speak to me?"

In the past, it would be easy. Rocho would have run out of town. There were only a couple months left on her lease and she definitely had enough money to pay it off. She could start over wherever she felt the vibe.

Looking into emerald eyes, pleading with her to stay, Rocho knew she would have to remain. If not for herself, she would have to stay and fight the good fight. "I rarely had anything to do with Martha. I could look up appointments on my own computer, but did check in with her from time to time. She asked me out the day you were sick. I refused. She became angry. I sensed something. But I didn't think this would happen."

The ringing of Sylvia's phone kept her from responding. Hastily picking up the phone, she merely made an appointment to have whoever was best in the office come immediately to the dealership.

"Now that that's settled, let's get a tiny bit more comfortable." Sylvia made her way to Rocho. She pulled her girlfriend to the sofa. She settled the mechanic down, before snuggling against her. "We have about twenty minutes. I don't want to hear another word. I just want to snuggle next to you. I just want you to know that I believe you."

"I know you do." Rocho hugged her girlfriend. For in this moment, she knew that that's what they were to one another. There would be times when they would have to focus more on their business relationship. But there would be times when they needed to comfort one another.

"This might be a conflict of interest, but do you think I could stay with you? The police special is just bout finished." Rocho felt the arms tighten around her. "I can put a tarp over the classic. That way I can take an unpaid leave of absence. Until this is sorted."

Sylvia pulled away. She looked into pained azure eyes. "You're doing this for me." Rocho nodded. "I wish you could remain working. And let me guess. You want to sleep in the spare room."

"Like I said before, I want to take this slow." Rocho kissed Sylvia's temple. "Moving in isn't exactly slow. And Frank won't like it very much. Hell, he'll probably testify for Martha."

"If he does, I'll never speak to him again." Sylvia was about to say more when there was the buzzing of the intercom. "Guess the lawyer is here. Time to see what we have to do to battle the fucking witch."

If she could muster it, Rocho would have chuckled. But she couldn't. Flashes of what had happened so long ago were haunting her. While there was one huge difference, it remained the same. She was being accused of something she hadn't done.

There was a small table in Sylvia's office. She insisted Rocho sit next to her. In fact, Sylvia insisted holding her girlfriend's hand. While business and personal were mixing, she didn't care. And she would tell the attorney just as much.

"This is one of the more difficult issues an employer can face." Mr. Carnigie had arrived himself. His glance went down to where their hands were clasped. "Especially if there is a relationship between the owner and the accused."

Rocho attempted to retrieve her hand. Sylvia only held on tighter. "There's no way of proving it, but the relationship only began three days ago. Wait. Two days ago. Sorry, I was sick and my days are off. Just tell me what we need to do."

"This won't be easy." Mr. Carnigie scribbled on a notepad. "Has Miss Bishop taken a leave of absence from the dealership?"

Before Sylvia could answer, Rocho's sultry voice answered the question. "I've volunteered to take unpaid time off beginning as soon as we were informed of the complaint. The only thing that may seem inappropriate is two factors. As you know, Sylvia and I are in a relationship. Starting tomorrow, I won't have a place to stay, so I'll be using her spare room."

Mr. Carnigie sighed at the information. "That does complicate things. We definitely have to disclose that immediately to whoever Miss Neilsen hires as representation. But it's not the end of the world."

Sylvia squeezed Rocho's hand for encouragement. It was Mr. Carnigie's steady voice as he continued. "My associates and I will be interviewing current and past employees. We'll be interviewing your father as well. And we'll need to do a background check on Miss Bishop."

That's when the room started to spin. Rocho's grasp upon Sylvia's hand was nonexistent. Azure eyes attempted to find emerald ones. But all they could focus on was a face from the past. One that had wronged her. One that she would have to face. Over and over again.

"Rocho!" Sylvia couldn't move fast enough to save her girlfriend from hitting the floor. She hastily checked the mechanic's head for any sign of cuts or bumps. There were none. "Help me get her to the sofa."

It was a moment before Mr. Carnigie did as he was asked. It was even longer before they had Rocho settled on the couch. Sylvia managed to settle her girlfriend's head in her lap.

"I take it that Miss Bishop has something in her past that could affect the complaint?" Mr. Carnigie maintained a distance. As if he wasn't certain he wanted to even be in the same room as the two women.

Sylvia took a deep breath. "It's technically her story to tell. But I'll give the brief story. She was accused, when she was eighteen, of rape. Her family wouldn't stand by her side. She was so young, she ran. She's been on the run ever since."

Mr. Carnigie hastily backed up. He retrieved his briefcase. "I'm sorry, Miss Reed. Your father would never have allowed himself to be in this position. I can no longer represent you or the dealership."

With that, Mr. Carnigie left the office. Though Sylvia knew they needed a lawyer, she didn't much care. She was finding more and more she didn't like how her father had run the business. That included Mr. Carnigie.

"If your brother really is a lawyer, I wish he'd contact us." Sylvia didn't realize she was stroking dark locks. "We could use someone on our side right about now."

The buzzing of the phone was the only reason Sylvia was forced to move from her comfortable spot. She was beginning to worry about Rocho not having regained consciousness.

"What is it, Elizabeth?" Sylvia was short with her secretary. Something she attempted not to do. No matter how difficult her day had been.

There was a hesitation before the secretary spoke. "There's a news crew outside the dealership. Something about a claim of sexual harassment."

"Fuck!" Sylvia glanced at her girlfriend. "I'll be right out. But I need you to do something for me. Can you keep an eye on Rocho? She passed out and hasn't come around. Just let the phone ring for now."

"Anything you say." Elizabeth hung up the phone and immediately made her way into the office. At first glance, she could swear the mechanic wasn't even breathing. "She's not looking so good."

"I'm not feeling so great myself." Sylvia sighed heavily. "Short of the story. As you know, Martha was pissed off. She's accused Rocho of sexual harassment. Mr. Carnigie learned of a blemish in Rocho's past and has quit working for the dealership. So, I need a new personal lawyer for myself and Rocho, along with a business one. That's why the media is here. The employees are free to speak to the media. Even if they give fodder to Martha and her sharks."

It took several breaths for Elizabeth to fully comprehend what her boss had blurted out. "Sexual harassment? That's a lark. Rocho distances herself from everyone, male or female. In fact, in the year she's worked here, you are the only one she's truly spent time with. At the dealership or outside. I had honestly thought the flowers were from her."

"The past is what bite her/us in the ass." Sylvia took a deep breath. "But I don't want to rehash it. And as I told Mr. Carnigie, it's Rocho's to tell. I just hope he keeps client/attorney privilege or I'll sue his ass."

Elizabeth knew this wasn't about the dealership. This was about Rocho. Sylvia had fallen hard. True, she hadn't seen her boss a great deal in the years she had been at school, but love was something easily written across the young woman's face.

"You go deal with the vultures." Elizabeth pulled one of the chairs from the table by the couch. She placed it so she could catch Rocho before she rolled off the couch.

"Thank you." Sylvia straightened her outfit. She braced herself. This was one of the things she had excelled in business school. Giving speeches. Or as her father would have called it 'bullshitting the bullshitters'.

Sylvia could feel the stares as she made her way to the front of the dealership. It wasn't only her own employees. There were her customers as well. There would be business lost over all of this. Just as things were beginning to turn around.

Worst case scenario? Sylvia thought about selling the house she'd just purchased. It placed a smile upon her face. Perfect timing as she confidently made her way through the front doors. She'd also sell the dealership. She and Rocho could find another small town. One that needed a mechanic shop. One that specialized in all makes and models.

There were about three news vans parked out front. Sylvia recognized them from the local stations in Grand Rapids and Lansing, the two closest large towns. There were the local newspapers and what she thought a couple of the local bloggers. This was definitely going to be interesting.

As different reporters shouted out questions, Sylvia held up her hands. It took a moment, but the crowd of vultures finally silenced long enough for her to be able to give her statement.

Remembering what she had learned in business school, Sylvia made direct eye contact with each one of the reporters before speaking. "I'm assuming each of you are here because you were notified that a lawsuit has been filed against the dealership, myself and my chief mechanic."

Once again, the questions began flying. Sylvia continued to smile as the reporters barked one question after another. It wasn't until after they had quieted down that the businesswoman spoke once again.

"I'm issuing this statement. Of course, the accusations are false. We intend to defend the integrity of the dealership, myself and my lead mechanic." Once again, Sylvia made eye contact with each of the vultures. "We'll be asking that you give our associates their space to do their jobs and live their lives, but to question them at their convenience. If they refuse, please respect them. I'll be giving an interview, beyond this statement, at a later time. Yet to be determined. That's all for now."

One of Sylvia's million-dollar smiles was flashed before she hastily made her way back to her office. She wanted to make certain Rocho was all right before she called a meeting of her employees. She was thinking of canceling the rest of the service department appointments and closing early. Giving everyone an early weekend.

There were many shouts to gain Sylvia's attention, but she ignored them. Not good as boss or owner, but she needed to know if Rocho had regained consciousness.

Sylvia's heart began racing when she saw Rocho sitting upright. Her mechanic was pale, but she was awake. That was the best thing she had witnessed all day. "Elizabeth. Would you see if the service department can close early? In fact, can you see if the entire dealership can? But make certain all employees remain for a meeting."

"On it, Boss." Elizabeth witnessed the expression upon Sylvia's face when she had seen Rocho awake. Jokingly, she had flirted with her new boss. Oh, she had been attracted to the petite blonde. But, for some reason, knew they weren't meant to be.

"And sorry about snapping earlier." Elizabeth didn't respond verbally. She winked just before closing the door behind her. Sylvia turned her attention toward her girlfriend. "How are you feeling."

Rocho shrugged. "Did Elizabeth fill you in on things?" The mechanic shook her head in the negative. "After you passed out, I gave a quick description of your past. Mr. Carnigie quit."

The mechanic sighed. "The police special is road worthy. I can get it registered. I can be out of town by Tuesday. That way you won't have to deal with this mess."

"First off, we're in this together." Sylvia sat on the sofa beside her girlfriend. "Secondly, you aren't thinking straight. This mess will be here, no matter if you are here or not, for me to deal with."

Azure eyes closed as Rocho swallowed hard. She'd been so consumed in her own troubles that she had forgotten the troubles involved her girlfriend and the dealership. This time, her troubles went hand in hand with someone else.

"I'm sorry." Rocho couldn't look Sylvia in the eyes. "I'm being selfish. And I'm falling back on what I do best. Running. I just…"

Sylvia firmly grasped Rocho's hand in her own. "It's all right. You've been running for over a decade. You've not had anyone else." She gave a gentle squeeze. "We've said it before. It's time to start believing. You have me."

There was a part of Sylvia that wanted to reveal her backup plan. But there would hopefully be no need for it. She was grateful when Rocho turned her head so that she could stare into sad azure eyes.

Not even thinking, Sylvia kissed Rocho gently. "Hopefully Elizabeth has the dealership closed and everyone gathered in the sales area. We also have to find a new lawyer."

"If my baby brother wasn't being so cryptic, we might be able to get a hold of him." Rocho stood bringing Sylvia with her. "Not that I've had much family, but could use some now."

"I used to." Sylvia placed her arm around her girlfriend's waist as they made their way out to the sales floor. While still out of earshot, she continued. "After the way Daddy treated you, I don't have a father."

Rocho's heart both broke and elated at the words. For the first time in her life, she had someone choosing her. For the first time in her life, she was allowing for someone to get to know her and giving them the option to choose her.

The pair made their entrance into the sales room. When Rocho attempted to break the embrace, Sylvia tightened her grip. "All right. Here's the story. The news crews are here because Martha has accused Rocho of sexual harassment. She is suing Rocho, myself and the dealership. Whether you believe it or not is your choice. Yes, we are now dating, as you can see by our stance. We are closing up early. You are all allowed to speak to the media if you choose, as long as it doesn't interfere when you are on the clock. Any questions?"

There were murmurs that went through the crowd of mechanics, salespeople, clerks, secretaries and financial officers. The only one gutsy enough to say anything was Elizabeth. "So, can we expect wedding bells anytime soon?"

The crowd erupted in laughter as Rocho turned nearly the color of a ripe apple. Sylvia's coloring wasn't quite so bright. "We are taking things slowly. But you can all be invited. If you behave." Sylvia's glare was directed at her secretary.

Once again, there was laughter. It was necessary after the day they had experienced. "All right, everyone. Go home. Relax. Hug your significant others. Hug your babies, two or four legged if you have them. Be grateful for what you have. And see you at your scheduled time Monday morning."

It took a little while for the crowd to disperse. Elizabeth was the last to leave. "Just wanted to let you two know that you make the most adorable couple in the world. Go home yourselves. Relax. I'll have a list of lawyers that specialize in sexual harassment on your desk first thing Monday."

"Thanks, Elizabeth." Sylvia waited until they were alone. "At least we have one ally in this." She turned toward Rocho. "What say we do our usual. Make certain this place is locked up tight, with one twist. We download the security videos and send them to a secure location. Stop for pizza on our way to your place. Work on the police special. And then spend the night snuggled on my couch."

As much as Rocho wanted to remain terrified or numb, she just couldn't. She had Sylvia who was so full of warmth and love. "I love you, Sylvia. And if nothing else, I'm glad we've had these few days together."

It was ominous. But Sylvia fully understood. She took Rocho's hand and led the way as they did their nightly ritual. Neither knew they were being watched. Not just by one pair of eyes, but two.

Chapter 15

Sunday found the couple sitting on the small balcony of Sylvia's apartment. Either the vultures, as Sylvia liked to term the reporters, hadn't discovered her address or were maintaining their distance. If she had to bet, it wasn't the latter.

Rocho had been quiet most of their time together. Sylvia somewhat understood. The past was a funky thing. In this case, false accusations were being leveled. Even with support, it had to be confusing, if not painful.

At least they'd spent some snuggle time together. That was always appreciated as both of them were known to put in at least a ten-hour shift at work. Sometimes even twelve, depending on the day and how busy it was.

The large hand in Sylvia's felt so natural to hold. As did watching as Rocho seemed to naturally scout. It's the term that Sylvia had come up with since spending most of Saturday on the balcony.

It was as if Rocho could sense things that others couldn't. Was it a bird the mechanic heard? Was it a vehicle in the distance? Was it a person walking their dog? And if the breeze changed direction, Sylvia swore she saw Rocho's nose twitch as if her girlfriend smelled something.

When Rocho stiffened, Sylvia knew something was up. "What's wrong?" She glanced around the view allotted her. That was mostly the parking area. There was also the woods just before the interstate.

"I don't know." Rocho slowly rose from her chair. Had she had this sensation when Martha had approached her. She hadn't had it with Juliette or Frank. Of course, she had been sound asleep when Frank had unexpectedly entered the apartment. "Just…something seems off."

At that moment, Sylvia's cellphone chose to ring. "Ominous." There was no caller id. "Even more ominous. "Hello?" She listened momentarily. "Shit. Sorry. Yes, this is Sylvia Reed. Blue. Wolverines. Chocolate cheesecake."

Rocho couldn't help snickering at the obvious codewords her girlfriend had used for the security company. Even though it meant someone had broken into the dealership, it still was entertaining to know exactly what Sylvia chose.

"We'll be right there." Sylvia gently elbowed her girlfriend. "So I love my alma mater and have a sweet tooth. Plus, it's easier to remember. Now, do we take my classic or yours to the dealership? Not sure what happened to set off the alarms, just that the police are on their way."

"Let's take The Fuzz for a ride. See if she's really as road worthy as we think she is." Rocho followed her girlfriend into the apartment. She made certain to lock the sliding glass door before continuing to the only other door to the apartment.

Sylvia shook her head. "I still can't believe you decided to name a classic motorcycle like that The Fuzz." She waited until Rocho was out before turning to lock the door. Her girlfriend had the keys her father had left behind, but still she was the one that normally locked the door.

"What? It makes sense. It's a police special. Therefore, The Fuzz is perfect for it." Rocho was still nearly dying inside. But for Sylvia, she was attempting to enjoy life. Truth be told, she did love their time together. She loved Sylvia.

A blonde head shook. "It does technically make sense. I just think there is something better." Sylvia was giggling and not paying attention when she opened the secured door.

"Sylvia!" At the sound of the unwanted voice, Rocho couldn't move fast enough from keeping the door from closing.

She dug for her key grateful the security key had a marking on it. "We need to have a talk. Without that pervert."

Sylvia could feel the body behind her stiffen. When she'd heard her father's voice, she'd immediately placed herself between her father and girlfriend. She could still hear the sounds as her daddy's foot made contact with Rocho's ribs.

"First off, my girlfriend is not a pervert." Hands on either shoulder were a comfort. Not because Sylvia needed Rocho's strength. It was because the mechanic might just be beginning to believe she deserved the love she was receiving.

"Secondly, I told you there was nothing for us to speak of." Sylvia placed her right hand on Rocho's left one. The comfort was suddenly needed as she felt and witnessed the coldness in Frank's eyes.

"That's before this per…" The low growl escaping his daughter caused Frank to halt his words. "Before the news world picked up on the story of someone at the dealership sexually harassing a longtime employee. Someone I hired and will personally testify on their behalf."

It didn't surprise Sylvia that her father would take Martha's side. "I already knew you'd be testifying against your own daughter. That's fine. Just know that we are through. Forever. And you won't be invited to our wedding, should we decide to have one."

Sylvia squeezed Rocho's hand. It was too soon to say forever, at least to others. But to her, she knew in her heart. This was the first month of the rest of her life.

"And if you read the contract, the fine print, if there is anything amoral that can be proven, I get the dealership back." Frank crossed his arms over his chest in triumph.

"And?" Sylvia could feel the tension in Rocho's body. She also heard the gasp when she asked the simple question.

They really had to get to know one another more. About their dreams and aspirations.

Brown eyes blinked several times. "You would be all right with not owning Portland Auto Center? The business your mother and I built together?"

"You aren't going to guilt me by that." Sylvia took a step toward her father, grateful when Rocho followed her lead. "Momma loved the business. But it wasn't her life. She had wanted to be a nurse. But you guilted her into being your secretary."

"How…?" Frank felt his plan falling apart. He'd hoped that with the publicity that he'd read about he could use it to guilt his little girl into seeing things his way. To use his wife's death to make her see that Rocho wasn't good enough for her.

"How?" Sylvia was now slowly walking toward The Fuzz. "Momma and I spent a lot of time together. You were rarely in the hospital when she was having treatments. Uncle Ethan, her personal attorney, was the one who drove me and Momma. Where were you?"

Frank swallowed. He wondered what his wife was privy to all those years ago. What had she confided in her best friend and mentor? Did his wife know of his extramarital affairs? Did she know about the young woman out there that was Sylvia's half-sister?

"You never really knew Momma, did you?" It was a rhetorical question. And Sylvia really didn't have time to deal with this. The police had probably been waiting quite some time for them at the dealership.

Once again, Frank couldn't stop himself. His wrist was caught before it even made it five inches. "Oww! You're breaking my wrist!"

Immediately, Rocho released the man's wrist. Instead of standing behind Sylvia, she remained standing next to her. She knew it would have been so easy to have continued. Because once again, someone was hurting Sylvia, not herself.

"Daddy, leave. And don't ever come back." Sylvia took Rocho's hand. "I want another ride on your magnificent motorcycle. And I want to wrap my arms tightly around you."

Rocho could hear Frank sputtering like a poorly tuned engine. For a moment, she forgot her troubles. She forgot how negative the world had looked for her a majority of the time. After all, she had Sylvia now.

The ride, as always, seemed to take only seconds, instead of the nearly ten minutes. There were flashing lights and three police cars. Quite the show for the city of around four thousand residents.

"Something major must have happened. Looks like the entire force is here." Sylvia reluctantly released her grasp on Rocho and dismounted. She left her helmet upon the classic motorcycle. She waited until Rocho was beside her.

Someone in a suit approached the couple. Sylvia took the lead, if only because she was the owner. "I'm Sylvia Reed. I own the Portland Auto Center. Can you tell me what happened?"

"I'm Detective Orson Daniels." Instead of offering a hand, the middle-aged man offered a business card. "Nearly every single one of your vehicles, new and used, were vandalized. Even the ones that are inside. Plus, there's damage to the service bay. I don't think there's a computer left that's usable. It's…"

"A total loss." The detective nodded. "I see." Sylvia was now regretting buying the house for Rocho. Sure, there would be the insurance that would cover at least some of the damage. And if they caught the thief, they might be able to sue them. But it seemed like they were out of business.

"You can take a look around. Don't touch anything, please. We're still taking pictures and fingerprints. If you could give your contact information to the officer by the door, I'd appreciate it." The detective nodded before heading back toward the dealership.

Rocho instinctively took Sylvia into her arms. "I don't know what to say." She kissed the top of her girlfriend's head. There were two main suspects as far as she was concerned.

There was the obvious Martha. She would be stupid to with the lawsuit. But sometimes, those that wanted revenge and couldn't see past the fast path to that revenge.

The other was Derek. From what Rocho could see as they slowly made their way to the building, it would take a great deal of strength or rage to do the damage. There was no way any of the cars in the lot could be saved. And she was one of the best mechanics around.

"Maybe the security cameras caught something." Sylvia offered weakly. Most likely, whoever did this had worn masks and gloves. One never knew.

It didn't take long for Sylvia and Rocho to inspect the damage. There were parts of the interior that could possibly be salvaged. But it was a longshot. And the money, even with insurance, was astronomical.

"Looks like we now need to hire a lawyer and to call the insurance guys." Sylvia sighed heavily. "Can we go for a ride?" She needed to feel her arms around her girlfriend.

"Sure." Rocho felt odd. This was a reversal of roles for the pair. Up until now, it was always Sylvia being strong. It was always Sylvia who knew just what to say and do. It was time for the mechanic.

As they made it to the motorcycle, Rocho dangled the keys to The Fuzz in front of Sylvia. "Would you like to drive for once? It seems only fair since I've driven your classic on more than one occasion."

For a few moments, the stress of the confrontation with her father flew away. The scene that remained behind them could wait until the morning. Sylvia had a glowing smile upon her face as she took the keys from Rocho.

"You just want your arms around me." Sylvia winked as she turned to place her helmet on her head. She waited until Rocho had hers on to straddle the motorcycle.

The feel of the classic beneath her and Rocho's arms around her had Sylvia's libido on overdrive. Not that snuggling on the couch wouldn't do that. And when they spent their time exploring one another's mouths…

"Where would you like to go?" Sylvia called over her shoulder. She felt the arms tighten around her. She could remain like this forever.

"Backroads. You know the area so much better than I do." Rocho wanted to tell Sylvia to ride until they couldn't ride anymore. But then, that would mean leaving the Trans Am behind. Not to mention the people that counted on the dealership for a living. They couldn't do that.

Still, it was becoming more and more appealing. Not running away from her problems for once. Rocho held on tighter as Sylvia took a corner a little faster than she might have.

It was so they could start a life together. After they had faced everything. Hopefully Rocho could find the courage to confess her dreams of just being with Sylvia. It's something she never saw coming.

Chapter 16

Instead of working on vehicles, the mechanics were helping the cleanup crew with glass, metal and the worst part gas and oil. It was an ecological disaster that would make the cost of cleanup skyrocket.

The ladies of the office, something Sylvia shook her head at, had volunteered to work on cleaning up the offices. One was never far from the lone working telephone where they had a speech prepared, whether it was for a customer or the news media.

The financial team was attempting to download the records onto new laptops that Sylvia had given the ok to purchase. She only hoped the insurance company would reimburse once the claims were processed.

Sylvia was helping out wherever she could. She was wearing one of Rocho's overalls. They weren't exactly her girlfriend's, but a smaller pair that the mechanic kept around for Sylvia to wear whenever they worked on a vehicle together.

The chirping of her cellphone didn't surprise her. The caller ID did. "Hey, you. Bored already without me?" Sylvia could feel the looks she was receiving but didn't care.

"Missed you the moment the door shut. But I'm calling because I'm assuming you don't know what time it is." Rocho waited for the curse that was coming. She wasn't disappointed. "I just wanted you or someone to be on the lookout for a delivery from The Portland Party Store. Normally they don't deliver, but with an order this large, they said they'd make an exception."

"This large?" Sylvia shook her head. "And how did you pay for it?" A blonde eyebrow rose in defiance, even though Rocho couldn't see it.

Rocho chuckled. "I might live on cash, I still do maintain a bank account. The gentleman who took my order was more than happy to take my account number over the phone." Her voice turned somber. "If I didn't have to stay away…"

"I know, Sweetheart." Sylvia wanted to hug her big softy. Everyone at work thought Rocho was this tough mechanic. And while she'd shown on more than one occasion in the month she'd known her she could kick ass, there was the gentle, caring side Sylvia knew best. "I'll tell the gang who to thank for the lunch. You behave and try to stay out of trouble. I love you."

"I love you." Rocho wanted to say more. She wanted to do more. But for now, she knew she had to distance herself from the dealership. It meant, a majority of times, distancing herself from Sylvia. And that hurt.

The buzzer nearly scared Rocho to death. There were only two people she could think of that would come to the apartment. Hopefully both had learned their lessons and this was a delivery of some kind.

Rocho made her way to the intercom. It was something she wasn't accustomed to. After fumbling with it, she decided to walk the three flights and see what whoever it was wanted.

A young man, slightly taller than Rocho with sandy blond hair, stood with his back to the door. The mechanic took a moment to study the young man. She felt this connection to him and wasn't certain why.

Knowing he could be trouble, even though he was dressed in an expensive appearing charcoal grey business suit, she opened the door. "Can I help you?"

When the young man turned around, it was all Rocho could do to hide the surprise. It was the identical azure eyes that gave it away. After all, the last time she'd seen her brother, he was barely up to her waist.

The first words out of Rocho's mouth were unguarded. "You've grown since the last time I saw you." She stared into identical azure eyes. Fear. It was as clear as day. He was terrified. But of what?

"And you've become more beautiful." Harry shoved his hands in his pockets. He had to refrain from pulling his sister into a hug. "I'm sorry for just showing up. I noticed you weren't in your old place so leaving notes wasn't an option."

"And neither was attempting to contact me at the dealership." Rocho couldn't believe one of her family members had finally, after all this time, tracked her down. But what did he want?

Sure, the note said he was sorry for not standing up for her in the past. Rocho decided there was only one way to find out. "I think it's time we, at the very least, talked about the here and now. I'm curious as to why and now. Why don't you come up? We can have sandwiches and cola or juice or coffee or…"

Rocho trailed off when her brother chuckled. It was a nervous chuckle. "I see you are as nervous as I am about this meeting. Probably more so because I just suddenly showed up. After leaving a cryptic note."

The mechanic expelled a breath. "I'm more than nervous. But let's get out of earshot of anyone listening. Afterall, the media has been camping outside the apartment complex. Been getting complaints from the neighbors. Or questions."

The siblings climbed the stairs in silence. Rocho opened the door and allowed her brother to enter before her. "Welcome to my girlfriend's apartment. It's mine, at least until I can find a place of my own again."

Harry turned toward his sister. "You don't want to live with Sylvia?" With the fire in Rocho's cobalt eyes, he held up his hands. "I have been tracking you, or attempting to. You leave only a small paper trail. But I've been watching the news. That's how I knew who you were dating and living with. How I knew where to find you."

"Oh." It took several deep breaths for Rocho's temper to calm. "Sorry. My temper still flares quite often. Sylvia is helping me to work on it. And in case you're wondering, it wasn't because of me. It's because of her."

The younger sibling tilted his head in question. "What I'm finding is that my temper flares when someone I care about is in danger or being ridiculed. When it comes to me, I run or I just freeze. I still have tender ribs when Sylvia's father caught me in bed with Sylvia."

"In bed?" Harry couldn't help the robust laughter. It was at just how red his older sister had turned. He would joke she was as red as a ripe strawberry, but knew it best not to tease her. At least the sister he remembered from so long ago.

"Sylvia had been sick. I'd been taking care of her." Rocho shrugged. "She said some things while delirious. One of them was about being terrified of me leaving so I held her while she slept. I didn't hear Frank come in."

Rocho revealed her biceps. There remained traces of the bruises Frank's grasp had left. "He grabbed me and threw me in the hallway. I never fought back. Not even when he kicked me in the ribs. If Sylvia hadn't managed to drag herself out of bed and place herself between us…"

Harry shivered at the thought. He was surprised with the ease in which they were speaking. "Is it just me or is it odd how easy you just spilled all of that?" He needed to break the tension and a bit of levity, yet truth, was just the ticket.

"Especially since I haven't offered you a place to sit, something to eat or something to drink now that we are inside." Rocho's cheeks turn a rosy color. "So, something to eat? Something to drink? Sit inside? Outside?"

Once again, Harry couldn't help inwardly chuckling. "How bout we sit in a relaxed area. The kitchen. I could use some caffeine, if coffee isn't too much trouble. And I already had lunch, so maybe just a light snack, if you are hungry."

Rocho took a deep breath. "Sounds like a plan." The mechanic showed her brother into the kitchen. "Have a seat at one of the barstools. Won't take but a moment to get some coffee on."

Harry delighted in simply watching his sister. After she had been forced to leave when he was only twelve, he had missed her something awful. For a sister so much older, she had always taken the time to be there for him.

While the coffee was brewing, Rocho deciding to cut up the strawberries. "You aren't allergic, are you?" She turned toward her brother who shook his head. "So, what have you been up to, Lil Bro."

It was a moment before Harry could find his words. "Missing you." The curse had the lawyer instantly on his feet. "I guess that surprised you. Let's get that under water."

Rocho allowed herself to be guided to the sink. The water stung. It was, gratefully, not a deep cut. After cleaning it thoroughly and drying it with paper towel, she looked him directly in the eyes. "How long have you been looking for me?"

"I want to say since I was twelve." Harry shrugged at questioning eyes. He needed distance so he regained his perch on the barstool. "And if I'd had the money, I would have hired a private investigator. I did run away about ten times the first two months you were gone. I went in different directions attempting to find your trail."

The mechanic checked her finger. There was no blood so she decided to retrieve the mugs of coffee. "Black ok?" Harry nodded. "It's funny. I don't even know which way I went. I didn't even have any money. Just the clothes on my back, my driver's license and my mechanic skills."

Rocho placed the coffee on the counter in front of Harry before distancing herself once again. Hastily, she finished slicing the strawberries. Instead of bringing them to Harry, she kept the counter between them.

"Your first stop was Macon, Georgia." Rocho's azure eyes blinked several times. "I wanted to establish my law practice, far away from Mom and Dad as I could get. So I moved to Flint."

This time Rocho's large eyes grew wide. "As in, Flint, Michigan?" Harry nodded. "Not knowing I would end up here in little Portland." The mechanic couldn't help chuckling at the irony.

"Yeah. I was one of the lawyers that helped when the water crisis happened." Harry knew was ongoing. He couldn't say more. It would probably never end. Damn governments. "Anyways, I have a timeline of where you've been. But it took my PI up till now to locate you here. When she said you'd been here for nearly a year, I knew I had to reach out. And fast."

Finally, Rocho picked up the bowl of strawberries and her own coffee and sat next to her brother. "Well, you don't have to worry about me running this time. Not unless something happens and Sylvia and I both decide to move somewhere else."

"That's the other reason I chose to reach out now." Harry sipped his coffee several times. "As I said, I've been keeping up with the news since it broke Friday evening. You're finding yourself in trouble again. And by using your real name, they might spot you and seek you in Mississippi."

"Shit." Rocho became quiet after the lone curse. It wasn't for her. It was for what her past could do to Sylvia. She knew it wouldn't look good with the sexual harassment allegations. But she hadn't thought about someone coming for her from Mississippi.

The lawyer studied his older sister. "You aren't worried about yourself." Rocho wouldn't look him in the eyes. "You are worried about how all of this will reflect on Sylvia. About leaving her behind."

"I've been on my own for nearly fifteen years." Rocho continued to stare into her coffee. It was something she could focus on. "Whether I'm alone or in prison, no big deal. Even finding love that I never thought I would, I could handle it. But Sylvia begged me to never leave her. She didn't know she was doing it at the time. It goes back to her mother. I still don't know how old she was, but her momma died of cancer. And no girlfriend has remained. They've all cheated. Even her father hasn't exactly been there for her."

For a moment, there were no words. Harry could only hear what their parents had always said about Rocho. She had been selfish. She was a freak of nature. How nothing she ever did was good enough. And all she wanted to do was inflict pain.

All these years, Harry had known it wasn't true. Yet, when you are told things, over and over again, they become a part of you. And as the old saying goes, the bad stuff is easier to believe.

"Well, we can, with your permission, both be there for her." Harry attempted to take his sister's hand. It hurt when the flinch caused his grasp to loosen. "If nothing else, I'm a lawyer. Not just a lawyer, but I have partners who specialize in different areas of the law. I myself can handle corporate law. Which means I can help with the dealership. Plus, the sexual harassment lawsuit. My best friend does taxes. And my wife does criminal law, such as rape charges."

"Wife?" Though there was quite a bit to gather from what her brother had just said, Rocho focused on the latter part. "You are married?"

"Yup. For three years now." Harry retrieved his cellphone. It didn't take long for him to load his album of family pics. "This is Jessica. And this is Renee. She'll be two next week."

Rocho was speechless. First, her brother showed up at her doorstep. Second, she found out he never stopped looking for her. Third, he wanted to help with the business and her defense using his entire team.

And most importantly, Rocho discovered she had a family. A brother who loved her. She hoped a sister-in-law who would allow her to have something to do with Renee.

Tears were now at the corners of the mechanic's eyes. "I have a niece. One that's named after me." Rocho finally turned her focus fully on her brother. "I have to call Sylvia. Let her know that you are here. That you want to help. She's been calling around. No lawyer around here, including Lansing and Grand Rapids, wants to touch this with a ten-foot pole."

"One thing before you do that." Harry turned his attention back to his cellphone. With a few swipes, he had another picture up. It was an older photograph that had been restored. "Mom crumpled it up and threw it in the trash. I rescued it."

Rocho reverently acquired the cellphone. Her hand shook as she took in the picture. Had she ever been that young? Her hair was longer than it was now. Her mother had insisted it was 'girly'. Jokingly, she was leaning against Harry, who was barely up to her hip at that time.

More tears threatened as Rocho stared at the cellphone. "Sylvia will love to see this. I don't have much of a past to speak of. I lived here. There. I didn't make friends. I just worked, ate and slept. Then I moved on. I haven't spoken of life before the allegations. Not really."

Harry stood. "May I?" Rocho tipped her head as tears were falling freely. He held open his arms. The tough mechanic gratefully fell into her baby brother's arms.

Neither had realized just how much time had passed. The two were startled with a voice. "I didn't feel like cooking so I stopped at the only Chinese place in town and got your fav…"

Sylvia nearly dropped the food she was carrying. Her girlfriend was in the arms of a man. She didn't have time to register the tears that were freely flowing down the mechanic's cheeks. "What the fuck is going on in here?"

Rocho hastily placed herself between her brother and her girlfriend. "I'm sorry, Lil One. I forgot to text you. Someone finally tracked me down. The one with the initials H.M.B.

It was a moment before Sylvia realized who was standing behind her girlfriend. His height was similar, as were the eyes. The hair color was different, but even standing still there were so many similarities.

"I'm sorry for how I initially reacted." Sylvia placed the Chinese on the counter. She stood in front of her girlfriend. "Seems you two have been having some serious talk going on here." Gently, Sylvia wiped the tears from Rocho's cheeks.

"There was." Rocho didn't know where to begin. "First off, I want to officially introduce you two. Harry, this is my girlfriend Sylvia. Sylvia, this is my baby brother, Harry."

Sylvia maintained some kind of touch upon Rocho as she shook the man's hand. She had to admit he had a firm grasp. She realized her hands were probably still dirty, even after scrubbing them at work. "I'm sorry about that. We spent the day with the cleanup crew. There's hope the dealership might survive yet."

Harry looked to his sister. "Guess that part hasn't made the news. Someone trashed every vehicle, new and used, at the dealership. It didn't stop there. They also trashed every computer and anything of value inside. I know Sylvia has been on the phone, when not helping with the cleanup, with the insurance company."

"They are balking at first." Sylvia's eyes closed. She was exhausted. And itchy. She needed a shower. "Something about because the insurance had been in my father's name and the transfer not being official yet, they were not going to ok reimbursement or some bullshit like that. Sorry bout the language. Been a long day. Do you two mind if I grab a quick shower before we eat?"

"I didn't even think of that. Harry has me off my game." Rocho didn't even hesitate. She gave Sylvia a gentle kiss before watching her walk toward her bedroom. She turned to see the comical expression upon her brother's face. "What?"

"I think your girlfriend could use better insurance and representation. What do you think?" Harry was already reaching in his pocket for his business card. "If my wife and crew are willing, we could rent a place for a little while. Until things are settled."

"I'd like to get to know you, Jessica and little Renee." Rocho blushed again at the thought of a little girl out there named after her. All these years, she never thought she was good enough to have friends. Now she had family and someone she wanted to spend the rest of her life with.

"Sounds like a plan. I won't make any calls until we discuss things with Sylvia." The pair had settled on the couch. "Though there's a part of me that wants to call Jessica immediately and tell her to pack up Renee and the rest of the associates."

"Renee?" Sylvia had been true to her word when she had said a quick shower. She hadn't even bothered with blow drying her hair. The wet dark blonde locks were kicking up Rocho's libido, not that just a sexy Sylvia on her own didn't.

"My niece." Rocho could barely utter the words. Harry looked from his sister to Sylvia and back again. He understood. Though a married man and knowing Sylvia was taken, he had to admit the look was sexy and then some.

Sylvia snuggled up to her girlfriend. Though she was starving, she wanted to know what had happened while she was at work. And to get to know the one person that seemed to actually want something good for Rocho, besides herself.

"Shall we begin with family or business?" Harry leaned back. He knew he had to tread lightly. If there was one word he was forced to use to describe Sylvia it would be feisty.

"While the business is in shambles, I need some good family tones." Sylvia felt the squeeze. If they did forge a lasting relationship, Harry would become Sylvia's family.

"All right. I'll backpedal a little." Harry cleared his throat. Rocho was off like a shot. She brought back three mugs of coffee placing them on the coffee table. "Thanks, Big Sis."

Once seated next to her, Sylvia could feel it. For once, Rocho didn't stiffen when complimented. She relaxed into Sylvia's arms. It felt wonderful.

"I tried, even at twelve, to defend Rocho." Harry picked up his coffee. It was cool, but he didn't mind. He and his wife differed when it came to hot vs cold coffee. "Even before twelve. When she first came out, I was like love is love. First time I said it, Daddy backhanded me."

With the anger he spoke, Sylvia noticed for the first time how Harry's Southern drawl came out. The way Rocho spoke, she often forgot that her girlfriend had been born and raised in Mississippi. Rarely, if ever, did her mechanic's accent come to the surface.

"The bastard." It was Rocho's sultry voice that startled Sylvia. It was even deeper as her blonde head was resting comfortably on the mechanic's ample chest.

Sylvia hugged her girlfriend. The pain Rocho must be feeling having to relive some of the things her parents had done to her. Or in some cases, had not done to her.

"It never phased me. I continued to preach to him and Mom as he called it." Harry chuckled. It had taken years for him to come to terms. Years and distance.

"When I first heard of the accusations, I attempted to head down to the jail." Harry angrily shook his head as he remembered. "It took both Mom and Dad, but they locked me in my room. They didn't let me out until they had heard you'd escaped. I immediately ran away."

Sylvia was having difficulty holding her tongue. While her father was being a dick about accepting Rocho, he had never given her a difficult time before about being a lesbian. She wondered what had caused his reaction to her.

"Over the next two or three months, I ran away. I attempted to find my big sis." Harry shook his head. "After a while, I had to give up. Mom started locking me in my room at night. Dad had his cronies put an ankle monitor on me."

"What!" Sylvia hated to leave the warmth of her girlfriend's side, but she had to make certain she had heard correctly. "Was your dad a cop or something?"

"Or something." Rocho gently tugged on Sylvia until they were snuggled against one another. "Dad, when I left town, was the District Attorney."

"You mean he was the one who was going to prosecute his own daughter for rape?" Brother and sister nodded in tandem. "And he abused his power and had his own son monitored so that he couldn't help his sister?"

Once again, both siblings nodded in tandem. "And I thought my father was being an asshole by telling me not to see Rocho because she was a drifter and a pervert. And that if she's convicted, there's a clause that says he'll take the dealership back."

"I already have some ideas about that." Harry leaned forward so he could look Sylvia in the eyes. "Not that there is more to talk about with the past, but right now you and Rocho are in trouble. I can help both. I have a legal team. If I can find a place or two to rent, then we'll be all set."

In all the excitement, Sylvia had forgotten the visit she'd had just before she'd left the dealership. "Well, there might be something I can do on that end."

Rocho glanced down at her girlfriend. Her senses were tingling. While it didn't seem like it was something she would hate, it did seem like something she wouldn't be a fan of.

"I was going to tell you, Rocho, as soon as the paperwork went through." Sylvia sat up so she was looking her girlfriend in the eyes. "This all took place before the accusations took place."

The mechanic held up her hands. Sometimes one just needed to hear whatever the news was. Like when someone takes of a bandage. Just rip that sucker off, hair and all.

"Anyways, I bought a house I was going to lease to Rocho. Only I wasn't going to tell Rocho that I was the one she was renting it from." Sylvia managed to maintain the deep stare her girlfriend was sending her way.

Rocho hastily stood from the couch. "So we begin with lies. Just like mother and father." The mechanic shook her head and made her way into the spare bedroom.

Sylvia wanted to chase after Rocho. There was something informing her to remain where she was. "Well, I royally fucked that up." She turned toward Harry. "The offer still remains. At least it would be perfect for you and your wife."

"I'm going to head back to Flint in the morning. I'm staying in Lansing tonight, so I need to get going." Harry stood, as did Sylvia. "I know it's been forever since I've been around my big sister and the things she's had to deal with have changed her. But just give her time. She used to get mad easy, but forgave fast."

Not wanting to think how long Rocho would remain mad at her, Sylvia could only nod. "I'll just have to be patient. You travel safe. And I can't wait to see your little one. I love children."

It was a bit awkward, but the pair managed to hug. Sylvia realized as she walked Harry to the door. It was just like Rocho. Though she had just literally met the man, she felt as if she'd known him forever.

Harry hesitated just outside the door. "I'll call tomorrow around eight, if that's not too late. I'll have been able to get home and discuss things with the gang."

"Sounds like a plan. Just hope Rocho is speaking to me by then." Once again, Sylvia felt herself being brought into a strong hug. "Thanks. You hug like your sister."

"I'll take that as a compliment." Harry winked as he began his descent. He hoped his sister wasn't too pigheaded.

Though only spending a few hours with Sylvia, she seemed like a real keeper.

It wasn't to be that evening. Sylvia spent the evening picking at the Chinese food she had brought home. She was grateful she didn't drink as she knew she would probably have been drunk off her ass.

The night ended with Sylvia in the master bedroom. She had gained the courage to leave a note outside of Rocho's door. Her only hope was that after her girlfriend read it, she would forgive her. If not, life would become that much more complicated.

Chapter 17

It was nearly ten thirty the next morning when Rocho finally emerged from the sanctity of her bedroom. She cursed herself for not obtaining her brother's contact information before she had exited the living room.

Was she more upset that Sylvia had attempted to say goodbye before leaving? That was when Rocho heard the crinkling sound as she took a step. It was a note from her girlfriend.

Rocho made her way into the kitchen. Another sign of just how caring Sylvia was was the fact there remained a half of pot coffee, along with a breakfast burrito.

The mechanic sighed. Rocho poured herself a cup of coffee and placed the breakfast burrito in the microwave before opening the note.

There was a part of Rocho that was terrified of what the note would say. Running had been all she had known for so long. Remaining was so difficult. Having someone, anyone, believe in her was almost like a fantasy.

Finally, Rocho read the words:

Sweetheart,

I'm sorry. It was stupid not to tell you of my plans. It was simple. Tell you I bought the house. If you wanted to rent it, we'd work out the payment. I'd have a place to winter the Trans Am. We'd have a place to work on cars. If not, I'd keep it and rent it out to someone else. It was all up to what you wanted to do. If you even stayed. I was so afraid you were ready to run. I just went ahead and bought it. Now, if your brother can convince his wife, they can use it and you can stay with me. Again, if you want. I got your brother's contact information. It's on the back of this note. I just want to say, I did this without talking to you, but it wasn't to pressure you. It was just to give you an option as

I know you didn't want to stay where you were and didn't think you were ready to move in with me. That changed so fast...I can't say sorry enough.

I love you, always.

And just like that, Rocho felt like a fool. The beeping of the microwave caused the mechanic to jump. There was a part of her that wanted to forget eating and run down to the dealership. Even if she were supposed to be maintaining her distance.

"Wonder if Sylvia has any travel mugs. Today would be a good day for a walk." Rocho began searching the cupboards as she practically inhaled the burrito.

Finding what she was searching for, Rocho poured the remainder of the coffee in the mug before cleaning the kitchen and leaving for her expedition. She hadn't even discovered what was the likely outcome for the dealership the prior evening.

"I'm beginning to feel like a bigger and bigger heel." Rocho carried the travel mug in one hand and her cellphone in the other. She hoped she wasn't bothering her brother as he was driving. That was the last thing she wanted to do. Distract him while he was attempting to concentrate.

After four rings, Rocho was about to hang up. "Hey, Big Sis. Hope you don't mind. My spies, er, private investigator gave me your cellphone number. Have it programmed in. I'm just pulling into my office now."

"I was hoping I wasn't catching you while driving. And I'm grateful you have my number." Rocho took a sip of her coffee. It was a beautiful day. "I'm just sorry I acted like a two-year-old and didn't get to properly say goodbye last night. I hope to see you and your family here soon."

There was the shutting of the car door. "If I have my way, we'll be there on Thursday. Both you and Sylvia need to mount your defense. Plus, the dealership needs some financial help. From what I know of your girlfriend, she graduated top of her class. But this is not the expected, so…"

"Yeah. Speaking of Sylvia, I kinda made certain I was scarce when she left this morning." Rocho decided she had berated herself enough. "I'm taking a walk. Seeing if anything catches my eye. If not, I'll just beg on my knees."

A hearty laugh could be heard through the phone. "You won't have to, Sis. Just show her you are sorry and that you love her. Speaking of loving, I have to go. My wife is giving me eyes. Hope to see you in a couple days. Love you, Big Sis."

"Love you baby brother." Rocho disconnected the call. While grateful she and her brother had spoken, she remained concerned about her relationship with Sylvia.

The mechanic continued to walk and gaze at some of the windows downtown. Rocho loved to see what the small shops had. Something caught her eye.

Deciding, as much as she wanted to make her way directly to the dealership, Rocho had to get a closer look. Once inside, she realized how hot it was. July had hit and with it came the heat and humidity of summer.

Rocho cautiously held up the model. She couldn't believe the detail. It was nearly identical to the one that was sitting in the parking lot of the dealership. "This is so perfect, it's as if I special ordered it."

The mechanic snatched up the model and took it to the counter. The price of over a hundred only caused her to balk because she didn't carry that much cash on her. It appeared another use of her debit card would be necessary.

The only reason Rocho rarely, if ever, used the debit cards she acquired with each bank account she opened was because of how easily they could be tracked down. Harry had already done that and would stand by her side. So what did she have to lose now?

With the model safely in her bag, Rocho was on her way once again. The mechanic wondered if she should once again provide lunch for the crew. She wasn't certain how much more cleanup there was. With the size of the dealership, she was certain there was a great deal left, sadly.

The smell of baked goods caught Rocho's attention. Before the mechanic could enter the small bakery, she heard her name. When she glanced up, she cursed under her breath.

It wasn't just one person calling her name. It was several voices shouting Rocho's name. Not certain if she would be welcome or not, the mechanic chose to seek shelter inside the small bakery.

Rocho found herself leaning against the door. She was out of breath when she faced what appeared to be a mother/daughter duo. Both had sandy blonde hair and hazel eyes. One had a little grey in her hair and laugh lines around her eyes, but still looked amazing.

"That was some entrance." The younger of the two eyed the tall, raven-haired woman. "I know you." She wiped her hands on her apron. "You've been in the news. A lot." She came out from behind the counter. "What can we get for you?"

The mechanic nearly found her knees weak. Rocho had been certain that the young woman would have said something about the allegations about her, but glossed over them. "Well, I was thinking of treating the crew of the dealership. I'm technically supposed to stay away for certain reasons, but I figure they have to cleanup without me so…"

"That's quite a crew." The younger one was doing all the talking. Rocho noticed the mother was giving her what she would term the evil eye. "Don't know allergies or favorites I suppose." The mechanic shook her head. "That would make it too easy." The young woman chuckled.

With the glare Rocho was receiving, she decided to maintain her distances, unless the young woman asked her to come closer. Or the time came to pay. "I was thinking a variety pack of cookies or cupcakes. Kind of cheesy, but it's something everyone likes."

"Easy, but simple. And you're right." The young woman turned immediately back to the counter. "I think I know exactly what will fill your order. Mom, we have enough cupcakes to fill this nice lady's order?"

"Nice lady, my ass." The older woman grumbled under her breath. It wasn't quite soft enough so that Rocho couldn't hear. When their gazes met, it was azure eyes that were boring into hazel eyes.

"I'm sorry. I'm not nice. I forgot my manners." Rocho didn't move any closer. "My name is Renee Bishop. My friends call me Rocho. It's nice to meet you, Ladies."

The younger of the two women glanced from her mother to Rocho. "My name is Becky. That grumpy old cow is Jenny. Usually I'm the one upfront and dealing with the customers for just this reason. Before me, it was my grandmother. May she rest in peace."

"I'm sorry for your loss." Rocho bowed her head. When she glanced back at Jenny, the baker wasn't looking at her. She instead was busying herself with filling the order. "I haven't ever stopped in here. But then, I've only lived in Portland a year. Once I find out when my girlfriend's birthday is I'll have to get you to bake her a cake."

"See, Mom. Repeat business already. And that's with you being your grumpy ass self." Jenny grumbled under her breath which caused Becky to chuckle. "It'll only be a few more minutes." The young woman glanced out the window. "I think the ones chasing you are gone. Or they are hiding and waiting to pounce again."

Rocho glanced over her shoulder. Sure enough, there was no media waiting for her. She couldn't relax. Not until she had her treats and was out of sight of the older woman.

"At least not in sight." Rocho watched as Jenny continued to grumble as she helped her daughter finish with the treats. "I want to thank you for doing this on such short notice. And I'm sorry I never visited you kind ladies before."

Becky shrugged. "It's, unfortunately, not uncommon. Even with setting up a website and doing a little online advertising, small town businesses are slowly dying. Why come here and spend a little more money when you can shop at one of the supercenters and pay less?"

A heavy sigh escaped Rocho. "I know. That's why I initially hesitated in taking the job at the dealership. I normally look for a position at a mom and pop place as they used to call them."

Immediately, the grumbling lessened. Rocho guessed her words had some kind of effect on Jenny. "Times have changed. All the laws and tax credits go to the corporations. Used to be they went to small businesses."

Rocho was shocked when Jenny spoke. Her voice was strong. "I agree, Ma'am." The dark head bowed. "If my girlfriend can get the dealership running again, how bout we make a deal?"

Becky waited to see what her mother's reply was. Again, normally it was the younger baker who did the interacting. "What kind of a deal?"

"Well, these cookies smell delicious. What if I or someone from the dealership pick up a standing order for like three dozen cookies." Rocho wasn't certain the number. "They would be available in the waiting area. And of course, there would be a sign with the phone number, website, address and whatever else you would want."

Hazel eyes grew wide. "But the media inferred…" Jenny placed the last of the cookies in the box she had been working on and handed it to Becky.

"That I was an ogre. That I was guilty, before even having faced my accuser." Rocho watched as Jenny had the good graces to blush. "It's all right. The media has been quite convincing. They usually are."

Becky shook her head. "You shouldn't let her off that easily. She might be an old bitch, er dog, er human, but she can still learn new tricks." The younger baker dodged the plastic glove that easily flew over her head. "Luckily, she has bad aim."

While Rocho was enjoying the banter, she wanted to see Sylvia. The previous day would have been complete torture had she not had the unexpected visit of her baby brother. "I probably do too."

The young baker giggled. "If you're serious about us providing baked goods for the dealership, just call or email us. The contact info is on the boxes." Becky handed the four large boxes to Rocho. "Are you going to be able to handle them?"

"I've got it." Rocho paid for the yummy treats before nodding her appreciation. Becky held the door open. The mechanic glanced around. For now, there was no sign of the pesky vultures.

The walk to the dealership didn't take long. The sun had risen to its zenith, and with it had brought the heat and humidity. "Wish I'd brought drinks to go along with these sweet treats."

As expected, there were a handful of news crews. "Hmm, maybe the small town news has moved onto something bigger and better. One can only hope."

Rocho was surprised at the mess. She hadn't witnessed the recovery, other than what she had seen on the television. She had to keep in check what she would like to do to the son of a bitch as she knew there were microphones and ears everywhere.

"Rocho!" The deep, male voice drew the mechanic's attention. Rick sauntered up to his boss. He didn't care if she was on leave nor believed for a second the allegations leveled against her. "Let me help you with those."

Gratefully, Rocho allowed Rick to take the boxes of cookies from her. "I thought since you guys were doing different work than usual that you could use a sweet treat."

Rick slapped his boss on her broad shoulders. "You just missed that girl of yours." He leaned in closer. "Not that I blame you. If I was a little younger and of a different, um, well you know, I'd give you a run for your money."

Azure eyes blinked several times. Rocho couldn't respond. All this time, she had thought she'd remained distanced from all her coworkers. Yet, she had made friends after all.

How could she have ever thought of leaving? Rocho was blindsided by the thought. After all, she now had her baby brother in her life, as well as niece and sister-in-law.

And the most important person in Rocho's life wasn't even aware that they were walking toward her. Sylvia was acting like a general. It was the best way to describe how she was giving orders to her employees and those sent by the professional cleanup company.

Rocho placed a hand on Rick's shoulder and winked at him. Before Sylvia could issue another order, the mysterious mechanic came to stand in front of her. She saluted. "Private Rocho Bishop reporting for duty."

It took a moment for Sylvia to fully realize that her girlfriend was standing before her. She nearly knocked Rocho on her ass. Not caring that there were camera crews or strangers around, she sought out her girlfriend's lips.

Finally, when oxygen became an issue, Rocho held Sylvia tightly in her arms. She glanced up at a blushing Rick. "If I get a greeting like that just for showing up, what kind am I going to get for bringing cookies?"

The comment earned a gentle slap to her shoulder. Rocho, though she knew should be angry with the world, was happy. It wasn't something she could explain. "Let me help you up." It didn't take much to help the smaller woman to her feet.

"Cookies for the crew, huh?" Rocho shrugged. "I think they'll appreciate that. After all, you've already set them up with pizza. Now they can have dessert."

The couple was followed by Rick into what Sylvia had termed the command center. It was basically the old financial office. It was the sole room that hadn't been as damaged, for some reason.

The computers had been taken out, but the paper files had been left intact. It was suspicious, at least to Sylvia. The police didn't find it so much so. Of course, she thought the local police hadn't thought of all the angles. There might be the need of a private investigator. If she could ever afford one.

Rocho leaned into a convenient ear as Sylvia had yet to release her. "Treats for you could be provided in person. But at another time."

Sylvia swallowed hard. Was this the same woman who had insisted on taking things slowly? Was this the same woman who had not long ago wanted to run far away?

Knowing now was not the time, Sylvia leaned up and placed a gentle kiss upon her girlfriend's lips. They could discuss exactly what Rocho had been up to and why she was so chipper only four days after being accused of sexual harassment.

It wasn't long before word of mouth spread and the command center was overflowing with the dealership's employees and the cleanup crew. It didn't take long for the cookies to be wiped out. Rocho wished she had purchased more. The two crews had worked so hard.

After everyone had left, Rocho noticed Sylvia's stance. While her girlfriend was putting on a brave front in front of the rest of the others, in front of the mechanic, her defenses were down. "Come here."

It didn't take more than those two words for Sylvia to be in strong, protective arms. She managed to place just enough distance between them so she could look into azure eyes. "I don't care about the lawsuit. I need you here. Don't leave me."

There were those words, once again. A month of knowing one another and Rocho had now lost count of how many times she'd heard them from Sylvia. Of course, half the time her girlfriend hadn't even realized what she had been saying. Still…

"I'm not exactly dressed today to help." Rocho was wearing cutoff blue jeans and a sleeveless t-shirt. "But I can run home and change."

Sylvia had another idea. "There are the work overalls you used to wear." A dark eyebrow rose in question. Rocho had assumed all had been destroyed. "Your hidden stash. The ones you had for me." A petite hand waved to the ones she was wearing. "And another in my office."

Rocho watched the sway of hips. In some ways, she was kicking herself for wanting to take things slow. But she had rushed into the relationship with Juliette. Granted, they were both kids still. But it had her gun shy.

The pair were alone in what used to be Sylvia's office. Rocho shuddered at the complete destruction left behind. While she had seen it all the Sunday it had happened, she had not seen it after the debris had been cleared.

Once they were alone again, Rocho felt herself pressed against a wall. This time, there were no tears. There were only hands wandering. There were only lips seeking hers.

It wasn't surprising, not this time. While they had been lucky with no loss of life or harm to anyone, there had been destruction on an epic scale.

The mechanic could understand. This could very well be the loss of livelihood for so many people, her girlfriend included. Sylvia needed something real. She needed something to connect to. And that was their blossoming relationship.

Finally, Sylvia halted her assault. "I would say I'm sorry, but I'll never be sorry for showing my affection." Once again, a blonde head was upon a strong shoulder.

Long arms were around a petite body. They made certain the body was snug against the taller one. "Don't ever apologize for showing how much you love me." Rocho leaned her chin on the slightly sweaty blonde head.

They remained in the embrace until Sylvia's cellphone interrupted the intimate moment. "I swear if this is another fucking news reporter…" Her voice trailed off when she heard the voice on the other end of the line. "Sorry bout that, Harry. Been a day and a half."

Rocho couldn't help the warmth that must be showing on her face. She was in the arms of her girlfriend and her brother was on the other end of the phone call. At least part of her life wasn't a hundred percent chaos.

"Wow. I can't believe you guys will be here tomorrow. What happened to Thursday?" Sylvia listened to the response. "That bad that your financial guy wants to get started right away. Well, it'll be nice have family around. I have the keys so you can either come by the dealership or apartment, depending on when you get here. Though it's only big enough really for the three of you."

Rocho waited impatiently. From this side of the conversation, she gathered something was needed that they immediately take a look at the case. And that there was the need for more than just the house to accommodate everyone.

"The small hotel is the only one in town." Sylvia listened intently. "I wish I had suggestions. Outside of the years away at school, I've lived in Portland all my life. The closest place would be Lansing and that's about a fifteen-minute commute."

There was more silence as Sylvia listened to Harry. Rocho watched the expressions that crossed her girlfriend's face. She couldn't decipher what was being said as the small blonde was now beginning to pace.

"That sounds like a plan. But what about payment? I mean, it's not going to be cheap. I can let you use the house rent free…" Sylvia was obviously interrupted.

Rocho placed herself in front of her pacing girlfriend. Sylvia held up a single digit. There was more listening before the phone call ended. "Are you as stubborn as your brother is? Does it run in your family? Should I be aware of it now?"

The questions threw Rocho off. "Well, I know when it comes to the happiness and safety of the ones I love, I can be stubborn. What has baby bro done or said?"

"Well, Harry is insisting that he pay some kind of rent." The next part Sylvia couldn't look Rocho in the eyes. Her voice was barely above a whisper. It was a good thing the mechanic had better than average hearing. "He and his associates want to do this pro bono."

The news wasn't exactly a surprise. From the vibe Rocho had gained from the few hours visit with her brother, she'd been shocked had he charged full rates, if anything at all.

"Glad he did fall far from the tree then." It was a blonde eyebrow's turn to raise in question. "Daddy spent his entire career campaigning. Claiming he was about making Jasper County safe. That was a joke. He was in it for the money and the prestige. Momma was no better. She played the dutiful, stay at home wife. But if we strayed from the bible or made him look bad, it wasn't a switch she used to punish us."

Sylvia swallowed as she witnessed the transformation once again. This was the vacant mechanic. The one who would take their punishment, without thought. It begged the answer to the question of why had Rocho run?

If Rocho had endured beatings at the hands of both her parents, why would facing a prison term cause her to run? And continue to run? Was there something she and Harry had forgotten?

"I'll say it again, and I thought my father was a complete asshat." Sylvia brought her girlfriend into a hug. She kissed her gently on the lips. "Now, how bout we move on from the seriousness of this. You can get your hands dirty. I should see how the troops are doing."

"I'll be out in a few minutes." Sylvia nodded. She realized it was partially due to the emotions having been drudged up by her innocent inquiring about a stubborn streak.

When Sylvia reemerged into the daylight, she realized it wasn't daylight anymore. Time hadn't exactly escaped them.

The blasted weather forecasters had messed up once again. Yet, they somehow get to keep their jobs.

Rick was the first to notice Sylvia emerge from the building. "Where's our favorite mechanic?" His pale blue eyes were focused on where the owner had emerged from.

"She's changing into overalls I had hidden that weren't shredded." Sylvia glanced up at the sky. "Looks like we're gonna need an extra pair of hands. Did I miss this in the forecast?"

There was the softest of rumblings and it wasn't either of their stomachs. Rocho had joined the pair. "I don't like thunderstorms. The last one ended with you sick and was the beginning of Martha's accusations."

"Not a fan, either." Sylvia shook her head. "Still, if we are ever going to get this place open again, if only to be able to service cars, we need this lot cleared. Let's do what we can until the rain hits."

It was several hours later before the first sprinkles actually began to fall. It was, luckily, close to quitting time. As was habit, Sylvia and Rocho were the last to leave.

"What now?" Rocho knew they both needed to wash up and eat. But she sensed that something was weighing heavily on her girlfriend's mind.

Sylvia scanned the dealership lot. "One more day and we should have it ready for the service department to open. That means you could oversee that part. I'll have the sales' team split up. We can hit the various county auctions. At least get the previously used lot restocked. We'll have to reissue the orders for the new year models."

"Enough!" Sylvia jumped. Normally, Rocho was so quiet and gentle. In fact, she couldn't remember a time when the mechanic had raised her voice. Even when Laurie had been an ass, it was with a cool, deep voice Rocho had taunted her.

The fear in emerald eyes shown and Rocho instantly cursed herself. "I'm sorry for raising my voice. It's just that when I asked what you wanted to do, I was referring to what you wanted to eat. Who showered first. And where you wanted to place this."

Emerald eyes now had a hint of curiosity in them. Rocho shyly held out the brown paper bag. "I wish I'd had a chance to wrap it. But I guess it's what's inside, not the wrapping."

There was no tentativeness as Sylvia eagerly took the bag from her girlfriend. If there had been giftwrap, it would have been torn off. A gasp escaped Sylvia. "Where did you find this?"

Rocho's smile was shy. "I took the long walk here. I couldn't decide what I wanted to do for you and the crew. More pizza probably would have been appreciated. Then I saw that in the window of the old dime store."

The only reason Rocho even knew it had been a dime store at one time was because she was a history buff. When she first moved to any town, small or large, she would spend several weeks at the local library studying the history.

"I can't believe it was just in the window." Sylvia held up the model car. With the exception of the coloring, it was the spitting image of Sylvia's classic Trans Am. "You couldn't have planned this if you had special ordered it."

"I know." Rocho had lost count on the number of times she had found herself unexpectedly with an armful of Sylvia. She was grateful that this time she hadn't landed on her ass. "Now, shall we at least decide on something to eat, showering and then decide a plan of attack for tomorrow?"

"Sounds like a plan." Sylvia gave her girlfriend another squeeze. She was grateful she had placed old cloths over the seats as neither had a change of clothing. Even changing out of the overalls wouldn't help with the sweat stained clothing beneath.

Placing the model car with care in the trunk of her Trans Am, Sylvia decided she was too tired to drive. "Would you mind?" Rocho merely nodded as she took the keys.

As Rocho pulled out of the dealership, a thought occurred to her. "I forgot. When I picked up the cookies, I suggested partnering with the bake shop. It's the one downtown. It's owned by a mother/daughter duo."

"And just how did one come by this arrangement?" Sylvia was, grudgingly admittingly, jealous. Her eyes were just a tad greener than normal.

"Well, it was clear the mother knew who I was. The media was lurking. She didn't like me." The jealousy was rapidly leaving emerald eyes. "And when I suggested that maybe we could have the cookies each day, along with where to get them, she seemed to like me a little better."

"I bet." Sylvia couldn't help laughing at her own insecurities. Then a thought occurred to her. "And just how was the daughter toward you."

Azure eyes blinked several times as she pulled into the parking lot of the apartment complex. She'd already decided she would make a quick meal while Sylvia was taking a shower.

"She was friendly enough." Rocho readjusted the driver's seat as she always did before exiting the car. She waited as Sylvia made certain she had a certain item from the trunk of the car.

"Renee?" It was several moments before Rocho turned to face whoever was speaking to her. While all legal documents demanded she be referred to as Renee, her employers and doctor's offices, when she went, had it down to use her nickname.

"Momma?" Rocho felt the warmth of Sylvia's presence by her side. She was grateful her girlfriend had hesitated in wrapping her arm around her waist.

Standing before them was a shell of the woman Rocho remembered. Louise Bishop had once stood tall, around five-foot-eight. She now was hunched over. Her dark locks were slowly being overtaken by grey.

In her wildest dreams, Rocho never would have imagined meeting her mother like this. Her fantasies, or horror shows, always had been with the mechanic on the inside of a jailcell looking out at the beautiful woman she remembered.

"I know I have no right to ask you this." Louise turned to the young woman. She'd been informed by her husband what the headlines had said. That her daughter was in an…unbiblical relationship. "But can we talk?"

Chapter 18

This was not like sitting with Harry. That had been surreal, but in a good way. Louise sat in the lone recliner in the living room, while Rocho practically had Sylvia wrapped around her. Though they both needed to eat and clean up, neither wanted to leave the woman alone.

"You've come a long way." Rocho didn't really want to talk to the woman who had given up her right at being called momma nearly fifteen years ago.

"Your father and I divorced about four years ago." Louise spoke without emotion. "He didn't like how I had allowed my looks to go downhill. He said it was because I'd go to all sorts of rallies for anti-…"

"Let me guess?" Rocho felt her ire growing. "You marched in every anti LGBT parade. You supported every LGBT discrimination law that came along. You went from door to door to gain signatures for…"

A gentle squeeze of her leg informed Rocho she had made her point. She sighed heavily. Once again, her protective streak had reared. And the claws had come dangerously close to gouging her mother's eyes.

"All true." Louise wasn't ashamed of her past. In fact, sitting with her daughter and watching the snuggling of two perverts was nauseating. "I came for one reason and one reason only."

Louise rose from her chair. She handed Rocho a pristine appearing manila envelope. "What your father doesn't know is that it wasn't the marching or protesting that did this to me."

It took a moment for the older woman to make it back to her seat. Louise took a steadying breath. "I have Osteosarcoma. Won't bore you with the details. It's cancer of the bones. Not sure how long I have to live."

In a way, Rocho felt as if she'd been hit physically more than emotionally. She'd long ago grieved for a mother and father. In fact, she thought of this woman as nothing more than a stranger who had just informed her that she was dying. There was sympathy, but nothing more.

Silence ensued for a long time. Louise finally understood that her daughter had nothing to say to her. "I guess I've been dead to you for a long time. I hope what's in that envelope gives you some measure of comfort. I'll be heading back to Mississippi. If you see your brother…"

Louise rose from the chair. She couldn't finish the thought. Her son had made it clear. He had made it crystal clear he wanted nothing to do with her when he left Mississippi. Home was where she was headed, but it was to die alone.

Without another word, Louise made her way to the front door. Though it barely shut behind her, it was as if a strongman had slammed the door shut.

Rocho held the manila envelope in her hand. She wasn't certain she wanted to know what was inside. Yet, her mother, who had made it perfectly clear she loathed her, had made the trip from Mississippi to Michigan just to personally hand it to her.

"That was…" Sylvia was dying to know what was in the envelope. But she was more concerned with how the unexpected visit of her mother was affecting her girlfriend.

There was no response. Rocho's defense mechanism had kicked in. The young woman stared at the envelope as if it would bite her.

The only thing keeping Rocho from collapsing against the couch was the strength of the woman sitting next to her. The arm holding her upright. And the way their souls were attempting relink.

"My life has always been interesting, but since meeting you, it's hit an all new level." Still, there was no response from Rocho. Sylvia decided on another tactic.

Keeping her right arm wrapped around Rocho's waist, Sylvia used her left hand to brush back loose, long raven locks. She placed gentle kisses on the expanse of neck exposed. Her path led to a convenient earlobe to which she began to lick and nibble.

A low growl escaped Rocho as the gentle kisses began to stoke something deep within. Without a word, she turned her head so that she could seek out willing lips.

The pair held onto one another. Tongues began dueling. Before long, the manila envelope was forgotten and Rocho had pulled Sylvia onto her lap so that the young woman was straddling her.

When Sylvia began rocking against her stomach, Rocho's hands descended to her hips. Reluctantly, she broke the kiss. Out of breath, she managed to squeak out, "I don't want my mother to be the reason we make love for the first time. Not that I don't want to make love to you every second of every day."

Sylvia could barely breath. The words were having trouble penetrating. She honestly had never been as turned on as she was just from kissing and a little stroking and vice versa. She was in trouble when they finally did make love.

As Sylvia stared into nearly violet eyes, she couldn't help the words that came next. "I just hope we don't wait until next Valentine's Day before we make love."

The thought caused Rocho to growl. "The way my body is feeling at the moment, I'd say that Labor Day is waaaay too long away." Rocho winked, though it was extremely true. Her clit was throbbing quite nicely.

"Now, what say we see what's in the envelope?" Sylvia reluctantly unstraddled her girlfriend. Talk about pulsating. She realized they hadn't had their showers or meals. That could wait. She reached down and picked up the envelope.

Rocho reluctantly took purchase of what her mother had left behind. She was shocked when she revealed an eight by ten picture of the family. But instead of there being the four of them, there was another figure.

The mechanic stared at the female figure. They were nearly identical appearing. The picture had to have been taken when she was about six. In other words, it was when Henry was barely old enough to sit up on his own.

"I have a sister?" Rocho couldn't take her eyes from the picture. It was Sylvia who turned the picture over. The names etched on the back were her parents, brother, herself and Connie DeMarco. "DeMarco?"

Now, Rocho stared intently at the name, not the picture. "I think my father's sister married a man with the last name of DeMarco. But it's been so long that I can't be certain. Maybe Henry knows better than I do."

"That can wait." Sylvia tugged on her mechanic until they were both in a standing position. She wrapped her arms around Rocho's waist. "Now, I don't know about you, but I'm itchy from the sweat and grime. My stomach is irritated with me for not feeding it. So…"

Rocho inhaled deeply. It was to regain the moment. While making out with Sylvia had garnered a great deal, it was as if her mother had stolen something. And it was nearly impossible for the mechanic to retrieve it.

"Imagining you in the shower while I make dinner." Rocho tilted her head in concertation. "That could be dangerous if sharp objects are involved."

There it was. It wasn't a hundred percent, but it was close. Sylvia knew that if they spent the remainder of the night snuggled on the couch, it would return. "Sounds like you have to be careful."

Sylvia was off toward the master bedroom before Rocho could react. The mechanic shook her head as she glanced in the refrigerator to see what she had to work with. There wasn't much, but at least there was some salad mix and some left over grilled chicken slices.

Two salads were waiting by the time Sylvia had finished showering. "I don't smell anything." She made her way into the kitchen. "Except for hard work." There was a wink to show she was merely teasing.

"I do smell. I've been slacking for far too long." Rocho gently kissed Sylvia on top of the head as she passed. "I'll make it quick. I'm not bothered with what to drink."

It was Sylvia's turn to watch the sway of Rocho's overall clad hips. "We really have to revisit this taking things slow." It was an odd thought for the young woman as she poured them each a glass of white grape juice.

Sylvia was in the mood for a little music. Instead of eating in the kitchen as normal, she decided dining in the living room was in order. She placed both plates of salad on the coffee table in front of the sofa before returning with the juice.

"Now, what to listen to?" Sylvia didn't have an extensive CD collection. Most of her music was downloaded. Still, she had a few relics as Laurie had loved to refer to them.

Laurie. That was not a thought she wanted to have. Yet, the earlier thought of taking things slow was probably provoking it. In the past, especially after being cheated on by her first girlfriend, she'd instituted the two-month rule.

"Not sure that's happening with Rocho." Sylvia chose a country singer she knew had been her mother's favorite. Martina McBride had some really great songs. In fact, the CDs had belonged to her mother.

The volume of the music was perfect. Just high enough so that you could hear the words, but not loud enough so that one could not carry on a conversation. And perfect to snuggle up to, after they'd eaten and relax.

Rocho decided that casual dress was for the best. That meant worn sweats and a t-shirt. Sylvia was dressed in shorts and a sleeveless t-shirt. Those were dangerous combinations.

The song caught Rocho's attention. She hadn't heard it since she was in Mississippi. She could never refer to it as home. The closest she had was the apartment. As she sat next to her girlfriend, she was rapidly realizing it was because her home was wherever Sylvia was.

"Casual night." Sylvia nodded as she handed Rocho the salad. "Sorry I didn't go all out with the cooking. But the leftovers needed to be used up, so…"

"I don't mind leftovers. It's better than them going to waste." Sylvia couldn't help herself. She reached out and squeezed Rocho's firm thigh.

In the back of Sylvia's mind, she knew they had so much to learn about one another. Rocho was accused of sexual harassment. There were the rape charges they would have to face. There was the dealership to contend with.

But looking into azure eyes, Sylvia was having difficulty remembering all of that. Even her stomach literally growling to remind her it had been too long since she'd eaten could keep her from wanting to straddle her girlfriend once again.

Finally, it was Rocho who managed to break the spell the pair had fallen under. Her words earlier were haunting her.

She didn't want their first time to be after a visit by her mother who had thrown more uncertainty into their lives.

Was that really the reason? Rocho pushed the lettuce and chicken around her plate. She dared not glance at Sylvia. She wasn't certain she could control herself.

Would that be such a bad thing? Rocho finally took a bite of the grilled chicken. Her stomach could barely handle it. She knew now her body didn't want food. It wanted Sylvia.

Physically, that was fine. But emotionally? Once again, Rocho felt the hand upon her thigh. It caused her to swallow deeply. She reached for her grape juice. The liquid disappeared in two gulps.

Sylvia placed her plate on the coffee table. She took Rocho's barely touched one and did the same. After grasping her girlfriend's hands, she made certain she was looking deep into the depths of azure eyes. "Why are we fighting this?"

The soft music continued to play in the background as Rocho struggled. How could she put into words what she herself was struggling with?

After the fourth song began, Sylvia decided their relationship would remain the same. They would have some amazing make-out sessions. They would allow for some roaming hands, all over fully clothed bodies. But until Rocho was ready for anything more intimate, she would have to remain content with just that.

"I'm so attracted to you I'm about to explode." Rocho hadn't exactly meant to say it like that. Widened emerald eyes showed Sylvia's surprise. "When you were sick, you were insistent we, um, and I almost lost my willpower. But there's just one thing that's holding me back."

Sylvia wasn't certain which to respond to. She was just informed she had thrown herself at Rocho. And didn't remember a damn thing about it. While that was huge, and something to be discussed later, she needed to know what had held Rocho back.

"I'm extremely attracted to you, if you hadn't noticed." Sylvia gently placed a finger under Rocho's strong chin. Using as little force as necessary, she made certain her girlfriend was looking her in the eyes. "What is holding you back? Please."

Azure eyes closed. The intensity of the emerald eyes was nearly overpowering. Rocho managed to open them once again. "I've only fully shared myself with one other woman."

If a garbage truck had run her down, Sylvia didn't think she could feel as blindsided as she did at the moment. It was nearly as akin as admitting at thirty-four she was a virgin. It would have been one thing had Rocho been in a committed relationship for a decade or so. But…

It took a moment for Sylvia to form words. Words that would hopefully comfort and give a little encouragement. "A woman who betrayed you. And that you've not had closure with. And you've not had anyone else to trust in all these years since. With the most precious things in the world. Your heart and soul."

Rocho felt like a child as she nodded. She felt relief as Sylvia wrapped her in a hug. It wasn't merely the embrace of a lover, but that of a friend. Someone who she could trust. And of someone who could trust her.

It was as if Rocho was in a haze. She felt Sylvia slip away. The warmth of her body had left her. But that wasn't the only reason she knew her girlfriend had left. It was an ache deep within.

Suddenly, two hands were in her own. Rocho glanced up into understanding azure eyes. "Come with me." It was quite a few heartbeats before the mechanic was able to stand. It was even longer before she realized there were no dishes on the coffee table and the music was silenced.

Sylvia watched her girlfriend. Where a strong, independent woman should be standing was a confused young woman who had been taken advantage of. How many times had she been taken advantage of? The most painful thought of all was did Rocho even realize it?

"Come with me." It was a gentle command. Sylvia squeezed Rocho's hands until the mechanic finally found her feet moving. When the direction they were headed was revealed, there was no force on earth that could make the mechanic move once again.

There was one force. Sylvia just had to figure out the words to gently motivate her girlfriend properly. "This isn't about us being more intimate than holding one another like we would on the sofa."

A dark eyebrow rose. It was the only indication Sylvia's words had any effect on her girlfriend at all. A sigh escaped her. When Rocho froze, she froze better than anyone she knew.

"Granted, I would get to have my fully clothed body stretched against yours, with my head on your shoulder." Sylvia squeezed the hand she held. She waited to see if there was anything resembling a reaction once again.

A right eye twitched several times before a goofy smile was upon Rocho's face. "I..." She had to clear her throat before she could express what she was thinking. "I'd like that very much."

Sylvia continued to lead them into the master bedroom. In the back of her mind, she would love to spend every night snuggled up to her girlfriend. First, they would have to see how this one night transpired.

"I just hope that this night ends better than the last time." Rocho had just settled under the sheets. Though it was summer, she normally liked to have something covering her. She also liked to have the fan on for white noise.

The mechanic smiled as Sylvia turned on the small fan before settling next to the long, lean body. "And what was so bad about last time?" Her mind was about feeling Rocho next to her the entire night.

"Your father." Sylvia's body stiffened at the memory. Not being caught in what could be considered a compromising position. It was how Rocho refused to protect herself. "Though we don't have to worry about that again."

Sylvia nodded. "Unless someone I don't know about has keys." Emerald locked with azure for a moment. "I'll be right back. I'm going to lodge a chair beneath the door and doublecheck the sliding glass door."

Rocho softly chuckled, but understood. She stared at the ceiling. Triggers. Hang-ups. She really needed to find a way to fight them so that she could move on. So that she could be ravishing a certain petite blonde, instead of merely holding her all night.

As Sylvia returned, Rocho's breath caught. There was nothing wrong with merely holding her girlfriend. It was just that both their libidos and souls craved more. Kissing. Hugging. Snuggling. And now holding one another all night long were amazing, but one day they would need that physical connection. But when would that one day be?

Chapter 19

The service department was open. Rocho was back in her element. A new secretary had been hired with both she and Sylvia interviewing the young lady.

If Rocho was honest with herself, there was something vaguely familiar about Kaz Livington. Her hair was a light brown compared to Sylvia's silky blonde. But the pair shared radiant emerald eyes.

Rocho shook her head as she directed the next vehicle into the bay. So far, the customers didn't seem to care that she was accused of sexual harassment. Or were they sympathetic because someone had done such damage to the dealership? Whatever it was, the moment their website had advertised the service and parts department was open for business, it had been nonstop.

The only thing missing was Sylvia. Rocho took the keys from the owner of the vehicle. "If you'll just see the newest member of our team, she'll get you fully checked in. And you'll find some sweet treats in the waiting room."

The dark head nodded in the direction of the young woman who waved her hand. Kaz had said she'd heard about the allegations, but was comfortable. She just wanted to prove she could do the job. To herself and to her mother who was almost always belittling her.

Kaz hastily filled out the paperwork with the customer and directed the older lady to the waiting area. It still required a little work, but was safe for the customers. And there were the nearly addictive cookies waiting for them.

The secretary easily fielded calls while keeping an eye on the mechanic. It had nothing to do with sexual attraction. Kaz had never found someone, male or female, that stirred her. Well, she did crave intimacy, but not of a sexual manner.

For the secretary, it was like watching a graceful panther. It was obvious who was in charge. It was obvious Rocho knew what she was doing. It was obvious everyone turned to her if there was even a slight question. All of those things were what Kaz aspired to.

"She is something else." Kaz jumped at the unexpected sound. She turned and found herself looking into green eyes. They were similar to her own, but were closer to the sea. "But you do know she's taken."

Not able to find her voice, Kaz merely nodded. "Sorry to have startled you, but Sylvia asked me to check on you throughout the day to see if you had any questions. You do know who I am and at what extension I'm at."

It took a moment for Kaz to find her voice. "Your Miss Ranch. You are Miss Reed's personal Secretary. She pointed you out when I first arrived and gave me your extension number in case I had any questions."

"Miss Ranch?" Elizabeth shook her head. "Miss Reed?" Kaz found herself squirming wishing for the phone to ring. "You'll find, for the most part, Sylvia and Rocho are pretty informal, as am I. I'm Elizabeth."

"Thanks." The phone ringing immediately had Kaz's attention. But, she had to admit, it didn't have her full attention. The beautiful redhead who stood glancing over her shoulder easily had captured her attention.

Elizabeth watched the young woman. Their system was one of the easiest to come by. Frank had been an idiot so he'd insisted that his secretary had researched something that even he could use.

"Ladies." Rocho bowed her head. Elizabeth had noticed how the mechanic had changed since returning. Not that she had ever been close to anyone but Sylvia, but Rocho maintained an extremely respectful distance when she could at all times. "Sorry to interrupt, especially if this is a teaching session, but Mr. Montgomery's Cadillac is ready. Would you mind taking care of him, Kaz?"

"No problem, Rocho." Kaz couldn't help the warmth she felt when their fingers accidentally touched. Her mother hadn't been into hugging. The closest she had been to any kind of physical contact was spanking her daughter. If not worse.

Elizabeth watched as Kaz made her way into the waiting room. Rocho, not well known for reading people, had been watching how Elizabeth had been studying the newest member of the team.

"You know, you might want to learn from my situation." The redhead's attention finally turned from where Kaz had disappeared. "I'm not saying you shouldn't be friendly. Nor am I saying you shouldn't seek something more than friendship. But be careful how you go about it."

Instantly, Elizabeth's cheeks felt like they were on fire. She couldn't form a complete sentence. She couldn't even form a complete word. She kept stuttering.

"Relax." Rocho noticed Kaz was returning from the waiting area. "I don't think your interest would be unwelcome. Just be cautious. And take your time."

The secretary blew out a breath. She hoped her cheeks had returned to some sort of normal coloring. "Your phone never rang once. But Rocho here was lazying around when I'm certain there's more work to do."

Rocho allowed for herself to be the scapegoat. "We're still running on time. But I best check with Rick to make certain. You ladies don't work too hard. And Kaz, let me know if any emergencies come in."

"Will do, Rocho." Once again, Kaz watched the mechanic as she confidently went about her job. "I hope this place makes a full recovery." Her eyes finally found similar green ones. "Everyone is so nice and helpful here."

"We are like a family." Elizabeth could see the flinch. She wondered if there was something in Kaz's family background that caused the reaction. "To me, it's the family you choose that is the most amazing family."

The sentiment brought a megawatt smile upon Kaz's face. "I've heard that sentiment many times. Family isn't always the ones you are born into, but the ones you make. I'm hoping to make it here." Their gazes continued.

The phone ringing brought the pair out of their haze. "Thank you for calling Portland Auto Center. Kaz from service department. How can I help you?"

Elizabeth made an eating motion to which Kaz nodded before turning toward her computer screen. Lunch was another hour or so away, depending on how busy they both were.

Reluctantly, Elizabeth made her way back to her side of the dealership and to where Sylvia was. Her boss was on the phone, nearly constantly, in an attempt to replace their stock.

The secretary waited outside of the office. Elizabeth wanted to see if Sylvia needed anything before returning to her desk. She knew both her boss and Rocho were expecting a call from the mechanic's brother.

Sylvia waved a hand indicating she wanted to speak with Elizabeth. "That's excellent. We'll be ready for them on Monday. You'll have payment by the end of Friday. Just give me the account numbers and my secretary will be happy to have the money transferred."

Green eyes rolled. Elizabeth waited until Sylvia had ended the call before speaking. "My secretary will be happy to. Willing, but is she really happy to?"

"If we turn the dealership around, you all will be happy. Unlike my father, I'll be giving generous year-end bonuses." Sylvia knew Elizabeth well enough by now that she had known there was only teasing behind it. Still, she couldn't help the comment.

"Boss, I…" Sylvia stuck her tongue out at her secretary. "Careful, Boss. Rocho probably doesn't want you using that on anyone but her."

Something about the way Sylvia turned her full attention back to the computer screen had Elizabeth wondering if there wasn't trouble in paradise. "Is everything all right, Boss? I don't want to pry. And you can tell me it's none of my business and to get my ass back to work."

"We've become friends." Sylvia nodded toward the door. Elizabeth hastily closed it behind her. "I'm not going to give away anything. Let's just say jokes like that, especially around Rocho, need to be curbed. We haven't made love. Yet."

The emphasis on the word 'yet' was loud and clear. Sylvia was frustrated. Not so much with Rocho, perhaps. It was the body that was physically frustrated.

"Sylvia, I'm sensing a little physical frustration." Sylvia's cheeks were beyond red now. "We've all been there. I've been with a woman who wasn't interested in the physical side of a relationship. There are ways of relieving yourself. Besides…" She held up her hand and wiggled her fingers.

The blush grew even brighter, if that was possible. "Knowing myself hasn't exactly been a problem. There are some nights we are making out and things get touchy/feely. I need the release." Sylvia shrugged as if it was no big deal. And to her, it wasn't. "I just want to keep the jokes to a minimal."

"Yet, if we stop them, Rocho might think you've told a huge secret." Elizabeth saw the light flickering in emerald eyes. "Don't worry. I know how sensitive things are around here. But it's because of the lawsuit, not because of other facts."

Sylvia felt a small weight had been lifted from her shoulders. "Thanks. Now, you need to get those transfers taken care of. And I need to speak with Marvin about whether or not he was successful at his auctions. I want to have lunch with Rocho before two today."

Elizabeth giggled. "I'm having lunch with the new girl. She's adorable. And don't worry. Rocho already gave me the motherly warning. Friends and mentor. If something more develops along the way…"

"Just be careful." Elizabeth nodded on her way out the door. "Oh and get a hold of Marvin." She heard the giggle just as the door closed.

It was only a moment later when the door opened. Sylvia didn't even glance up. "Marvin, I'm hoping you did well yesterday. If you did, we could have this lot at half capacity with used vehicles while we wait for the new models to come in."

"I told you not to go in there." Sylvia's head whipped up at the panicked sound of Elizabeth's voice. "I'm sorry, Boss. I tried to stop him. I was on the phone with Marvin and he just walked on by."

"It's all right. I know you did your best." Sylvia hastily stood. "Wait until you see the trash taken out before you send Marvin in."

Elizabeth hesitated before she left father and daughter alone. Her gut was churning. She figured Sylvia could handle herself, but there was something in the way Frank was eyeing his daughter. Plus, Sylvia and Rocho had made it clear the former owner was not welcomed.

"Frank. What do you want?" Sylvia decided to play it relaxed and cool. She seated herself in her father's old leather seat. For some reason, it had been spared the destruction.

"Don't you mean, Daddy?" Sylvia leaned further back. Her arms casually crossed over her chest. "Very well. Miss Reed, I'm here because I wanted to personally serve you these papers. My lawyer advised against it, but I wanted to see your face when you read what they are about."

The chair squeaked annoyingly as Sylvia leaned forward to inspect the papers her father had placed upon the abused desk. Frank was suing her for ownership of the dealership. Not on grounds of perversion, but because she was about to go bankrupt.

Sylvia glanced up from speed reading the papers. She understood the gist of it. Harry would be able to fully decipher it all. Her expression never changed as she placed the paperwork upon the desk.

"It's very interesting." Sylvia tipped her head. "I think my lawyer will be extremely interested in this. He'll be here sometime today or tomorrow. And then we'll see who has the last laugh."

Instantly, Sylvia knew her words had aggravated her father. There was a vein that was pulsating at the temple. "Why do you keep trying to take this away from me? Is it because I was doing so much better at it than you?"

Frank wanted to strike out at something. The words were hitting far too close to home. Still, he wouldn't allow for her to see that she had guessed the truth. "You know why. Rocho isn't fit to be around anyone. You or children. How many children come in here?"

The powerful, confident male voice caused Frank to turn on his heels. "I'll bring my daughter here anytime I can. Course, I've come all the way from Flint to represent this fine lady so I might not make it all that often."

Brown eyes blinked several times in an attempt to understand what was happening. Sylvia rose from behind the desk. She didn't hesitate in hugging her, she hoped, future brother-in-law.

"Didn't expect you until this afternoon." Sylvia wanted to add insult to her father. She hoped Harry would understand. A gentle kiss was placed upon the lawyer's cheek.

Both of Frank's hands were now balled into fists. "Who the fuck are you and why the fuck is my daughter kissing you?" His anger grew when he noticed the smirk upon Sylvia's face.

"My manners are horrible. But then, you raised me, not my mother." Wow. Sylvia was mentally chastising herself. She was goading her father. Maybe a little too well. "Father, this handsome young man is my attorney. And as irony would have it, he's Rocho's baby brother."

"What…" Frank eyed the way his daughter's arm remained wrapped around the tall man's waist. "And are you enjoying your perverted lifestyle with him? Maybe a three-way?"

All of the joy and cockiness Sylvia had been feeling instantly drained from her body. In fact, Harry found he was having to hold her up. "Would you kindly move. You've upset my sister-in-law."

What had caused Harry to refer to Sylvia in that manner, he was uncertain. He knew part of the tension in the room was because of the relationship between Sylvia and his sister. Someone he was extremely protective of.

None in the room had heard the mechanic's entrance. Rocho saw who remained standing in front of Sylvia's desk and could surmise what had transpired, at least minimally.

Rocho could also surmise why her girlfriend was clinging so tightly to her brother. "I'll take her, Harry." The mechanic easily lifted Sylvia into her arms. She brought her girlfriend to the couch.

Sensing the arrival of his sister could actually cause the situation to become worse, Harry placed himself between the elder and the two women. "I didn't catch your name. My full name is Harry Mason Bishop. I'm indeed one of several lawyers happy to represent Rocho, Sylvia and the dealership."

The mechanic couldn't help smirking at the order her brother chose to list his clients. While in Rocho's mind, Sylvia was the most important person, she understood that listing her first would irritate Frank even further.

"I'm Frank Reed. Only a month ago, I stupidly signed the dealership over to my daughter." Frank lunged for the legal paper left on the desk by Sylvia. He shoved it into Harry's capable hands. "You can read this and contact my lawyer. I won't be allowing these two perverts to destroy what I built up."

Harry calmly glanced at the now crumpled papers. He hadn't heard of the law firm Mr. Reed had hired. From the wording, it was as if a first-year lawyer had written the paperwork. Still, he wasn't about to take anything for granted.

"You've served the paperwork, which should have been served by a third party. Someone that has nothing to do with the case." Harry carefully folded the papers and placed them in the inside pocket of his business jacket. "I'm certain your lawyers informed you of this or they aren't worth the money you are paying them."

For some reason, that was the last straw. Frank lunged at Harry. If Sylvia hadn't been weighing her down, Rocho would have launched herself in defense of her brother. The mechanic watched in awe as Harry deftly sidestepped the man.

Frank's head found purchase with the brick wall. It was with enough force that he slumped to the ground. It took a moment for Frank to rise to his feet. Even when he stood, he swayed ever so slightly.

"Mr. Reed, you might want to be cautious. It appears you might just have a mild concussion." Harry stood his ground as it appeared Frank was ready to charge again.

By this time, Elizabeth was watching from the doorway. She wasn't alone. Marvin had arrived for his meeting with Sylvia to go over the previously owned vehicles he'd acquired. There was another figure. One that was the newest member to what most who worked for the dealership referred to as a family.

It was several heartbeats before Frank realized the true nature of the situation. Rocho remained holding Sylvia upon the couch, though her appearance was much healthier. Three people were at the door watching, along with his daughter's lawyer. Now was not the time to push things.

"I'll let my lawyer do the talking." Frank made certain to brush the young man as he walked past him. As the trio at the door parted, he paused.

Were his eyes deceiving him? Frank swallowed hard. He hoped no one noticed his reaction when he saw Kaz. In a million years, he never thought he'd see the young woman. After all, to his knowledge, she and her mother were supposed to be living in Ohio somewhere. At least, that's where the payments were sent.

"IF you'll excuse me." Frank purposely shoved past the young woman. He had to distance himself from the dealership. He had some phone calls to make.

Sylvia shook her head. "Well, that was an interesting end to the morning." She glanced around the room and took in the concern in each person's eyes. Even the two newest members of her family. "I'm all right. He, as my father, just knows what buttons to push."

Gently, Sylvia squeezed Rocho's hand. She hastily rose from her seated position. She felt the lean body mimic her movements so that it was standing behind her. "I know we are all busy in our different departments and lunch will be difficult to coordinate so how bout we meet at Fabiana's? Elizabeth, could you take a count and give them a head's up? Maybe around seven thirty?"

"You got it, Boss." Elizabeth winked. She was growing fonder and fonder of Sylvia. The woman continued to grow and mature before her very eyes. Granted, they were only a couple years difference in age. "Kaz, you want to see who wants to join the fun." She turned toward Sylvia. "Or just the big wigs, Boss?"

Sylvia's eyes rolled playfully before answering. "It's for whoever wants to show up. Kaz, you see who wants to from the service and parts departments. Elizabeth, you handle the sales and financial. Coordinate between you. Count me and Rocho in. What about you, Harry?"

"I'd love to meet the crew." Harry tapped his chin. "Unfortunately, little Renee had a cold so that excludes Jessica. And my associates won't be here until morning as their accommodations won't be ready until then."

"You heard the man." Elizabeth nodded before shutting the door, leaving Harry, Marvin, Rocho and Sylvia alone. "I hope Renee's cold doesn't last long. Can't wait to meet my little niece. And sorry to do this, Rocho and Harry, but I have to finish up with Marvin before I can do anything else. You two have lunch if you can."

Rocho held up a finger as Harry already had made his way to the doorway. He nodded in understanding. Apparently, Marvin did as well. The office manager pretended to be busy by Sylvia's desk.

"Are you really all right?" Rocho placed a gentle kiss upon Sylvia's forehead. There remained a strain in her girlfriend's body.

"As all right as I can be after one of daddy's spectacular visits." Sylvia closed the distance and placed a gentle kiss upon Rocho's lips. "You go. Enjoy lunch with your brother. Don't be afraid to bring me back something." She winked.

There remained a dullness Rocho didn't like in those emerald eyes she loved so much. She knew better than to argue with Sylvia. Not only would she bring lunch back for her girlfriend, she would snuggle in bed tonight with her.

In fact, Rocho had a suggestion to make. But later, when they were alone. It would be a huge step for the mechanic. One she fully hoped she was ready for.

The brother/sister duo exited from Sylvia's office. Elizabeth winked at Rocho. It was something the mechanic was becoming accustomed to. It was Elizabeth's natural tendency to flirt and make everyone smile.

"So, do you want the full tour or would you like lunch?" Rocho hesitated. If they continued forward, they would head to the parking lot, where there remained some workers cleaning up some of the damage.

If they turned to the left, they would be in Rocho's element. While things were busy, she had checked before leaving to make certain an extended absence wouldn't be missed.

"Why don't we wait until after hours." A dark eyebrow rose in question. Harry couldn't help shaking his head. "Lawyer.

I know the OSHA rules about customers in the back of shops like this, at least during operating hours."

"That's true." Rocho had to admit to be extremely disappointed. Yet, she knew her baby brother was watching out for her. "So, something to eat it is. What about Jessica? Will she and Renee be all right?"

"Renee brought some of the things we had at the house." Harry guided his sister to his sedan. "Almost wished I'd bought an SUV or minivan. Even with only one child still in diapers and eating mostly baby food, it takes up a lot of space packing all she needs."

"I wouldn't know." There was an emptiness inside Rocho. If she was honest with herself, there was also a bitterness as well. It was something she had never considered.

Harry hesitated with his hand on the key with it inserted into the ignition. Azure eyes met azure ones. "You've lost out on a great deal of things because of Mom and Dad, haven't you?"

Rocho sighed heavily. There was an ache forming. Suddenly, she wasn't so hungry. Suddenly, she smacked her forehead with the palm of her hand. "I forgot. Mom paid me and Sylvia a visit. She gave me a picture."

"What?" Harry sat back the key forgotten. "Last time I heard from either Mom or Dad was when he wanted me to return home to help him win his unprecedented tenth time in a row. I not so politely turned him down."

"All I know is that we had just locked up the place and she was waiting for us." Rocho couldn't maintain her brother's gaze. The blasted triggers were coming back to her. Even after spending a glorious night in her girlfriend's arms. "I didn't even recognize her."

"Hmm." Harry was intrigued. He'd given up any feelings towards his parents a long time ago, as had Rocho. But to suddenly have one or the other show up on one's doorstep was beyond intriguing. Especially with the allegations upon her…

"I think she returned to Mississippi to…" Rocho swallowed. Her appetite definitely having disappeared. "Die. She did look like she was sick. But I don't know for certain."

"Do you have this picture with you?" Rocho shook her head. "I hate to say it, but Mom dying alone or with Dad doesn't concern me. What does concern me is what she left for you. I assume it's at your apartment."

Rocho managed to nod. "If I get turned around, just give me directions." Harry could tell his sister was becoming defeated. He hated seeing her like this. Yet, having her back in his life under nearly any circumstances was nearly heaven.

It didn't take long to navigate across the small town. It wasn't long until Rocho was handing him the envelope that contained the picture.

At first, Harry couldn't contain the grin. The joy he felt at the memory of once being in his sister's life. But then he spied the woman next to Rocho. "What the fuck?"

It was the first time Rocho had heard her composed brother curse. She had distanced herself, not wanting to see the picture again. "What?"

"I'd forgotten all about cousin Connie." Harry examined the picture even closer. "And I forgot how close she resembled you. One thing I never forgot was how she wanted everything that was yours. Including your girlfriend."

Chapter 20

The employee dinner had been interesting, to say the least. It had also been quite a bit more expensive than Sylvia had expected. She would have to begin watching her spending, whether it was for personal or business expenditures.

Sylvia had noticed how Rocho had hardly touched her dinner. Harry had managed to isolate her and mentioned what the siblings had discovered about the picture. It was something the lovers to be would have to discuss once they were safe in their apartment.

With the weather remaining mostly sunny, Sylvia was insisting they mostly use the classic motorcycle. They would have to seek different modes of transportation once winter struck.

Rocho was sitting on the couch. Her head was resting against the back with her eyes closed. To most, she would appear to be sleeping, but Sylvia knew better.

Most likely, Rocho was processing everything that had transpired today. There was what had happened with Frank. Sylvia shivered at the thought of her father. Then there was the realization of a possible coverup. The finality would be overwhelming, at least for the mechanic, when it came to the number that was at dinner.

It was time. Rocho needed to relax. After all, there was still one more day of work. Then they could spend the weekend with Harry and his associates. Hopefully little Renee would be over the cold enough so they could spend time with her and Jessica.

Stealthily, Sylvia slid next to her girlfriend. She kissed Rocho gently on the ear. The unexpected touch caused the mechanic to jump. "Sorry. Didn't mean to disturb you or your thoughts."

Rocho's smile was, at best, forced. Azure eyes immediately closed. "Just thinking about the what ifs. What if Harry had been older. What if my parents hadn't been homophobes. What if I hadn't forgotten about my cousin who had a tendency to want to be like me a little too much."

"Then we'd never have met." Sylvia never forced eye contact. She merely allowed her words to sink in. Patience wasn't her greatest virtue, but for Rocho, she would wait an eternity if she had to.

A sad smile was on Rocho's face as she understood. "I know. There's that theory. For every choice, there are exponential outcomes. I just can't help wondering about the what ifs." Finally, Rocho turned to face her girlfriend. "Even with being able to work with you all day long and come home with you each and every night."

"Sweet talker." Sylvia had to hold her libido in check once again. "I know what you mean. Even with the lawsuit, rebuilding the dealership and my father showing up from time to time, the only thing I'd change is how long we've known one another."

It was Rocho's turn to tease. "You are just aching to be beyond the two month rule." Sylvia blushed. If possible, it made the young woman even more desirable than before.

Without thought, Rocho leaned in. She placed a chaste kiss upon Sylvia's lips. It was merely in thanks for everything she had done for her.

While it had been Frank who had given Rocho a chance when she'd first come to Portland, it was Sylvia who had remained by her side. She had been the one who received as much pleasure as Rocho did in restoring things. To building them up.

And when someone came along and attempted to destroy what they both, in only a month's time, had attempted to build, Sylvia decided to stand by her. It was nearly blinding the unwavering faith the young woman had in her.

In that moment, Rocho couldn't hold back any longer. It wasn't her libido that was her undoing. After all, she had tamed that, with only her own touches for the past decade and a half. It was knowing that she had someone who believed in her, without physical proof.

The thought of such unconditional support did something to Rocho. After a decade and a half of suppressing her libido, it was suddenly springing to life with a vengeance. She knew if she were to begin something, Sylvia wouldn't stop her.

"Sylvia, are you certain that I'm the one you want?" Rocho couldn't help feeling like a frightened virgin. It was as if she was trying out for the basketball team and afraid of being picked last. Or worse, not being picked at all.

Sylvia merely shook her head. Was this the life she would lead? Having to reassure Rocho from time to time? As she stared into azure eyes, she really didn't care if she had to or not.

Everyone had their baggage. Sylvia was terrified of being abandoned. It wasn't because of past girlfriends so much, though most had cheated on her. It was because of her mother's death at such a young age.

"I have a song or two going through my head." Sylvia placed a hand on each of Rocho's cheeks. "But I'll say this. When I saw you working on the Bel Air the first day I walked in the service department, I knew there was something about you."

Azure eyes had trouble not looking away for once. "I remember that day. It was over a month ago. I glanced up and was lost in emerald eyes. I think I even scratched the paint and had to do a repair job." Rocho chuckled embarrassedly.

Moments between them began flashing through Sylvia's mind. Nearly every moment the pair had spent together, whether as boss or friends, there had been some kind of connection. It had been leading up to this moment.

"And now I want to do a repair job of sorts." It sounded so cheesy the moment it left Sylvia's mouth. It wasn't her best moment. But, for some reason, it just seemed to fit.

After all, Rocho had been a mechanic and fixing things since before she was eighteen. Sylvia had grown up in her father's dealership. He had wanted her out front, but she had spent a majority of her time in the mechanic bay.

Azure eyes darkened to a level that caused Sylvia to swallow. The shade was similar to when Rocho had been defending Sylvia to Laurie. But there was something different, as well.

Without warning, Rocho swooped Sylvia in her arms. The smaller body was cradled against the slightly solider one. While Sylvia was far from out of shape, Rocho's heavy lifting throughout the day added to her general workout.

"Tell me now." Rocho could feel her need growing by leaps and bounds. Already her inner thighs were coated with her desire for the woman who had her arms loosely wrapped around her neck. "I'm reaching the point of no return."

Sylvia maintained her grasp on Rocho's neck with her left hand. She ran her right hand through black locks. With just a little bit of pressure, she caused Rocho's head to be guided toward hers. "I've been at the point of no return for a long time. But for you, I would have stopped. Remember, I love you. I'd do anything for you."

It didn't take much for the millimeters between them to be closed. This kiss was beyond what they'd shared up to this point. It was definitely a promise to something more. Rocho's knees were growing weak. She had to break the kiss so that she could finish carrying her girlfriend to the master bedroom.

With reverence, Rocho placed Sylvia on the edge of the bed. She took a few steps back. Jade eyes watched as the mechanic deliberately unbuttoned each button. With purpose, strong hands eased each piece of clothing from the long, lean, muscular body.

Sylvia swallowed. Wearing shorts and a sleeveless t-shirt really hadn't revealed much. And then there was the revelation of abundant moisture between Rocho's legs. This just from kissing and holding.

Without a word, Sylvia rose from the bed. Unlike Rocho's deliberateness, the clothes were practically torn from Sylvia's overheated body. Her breasts were heaving as her breathing was already nearly out of control.

It was Sylvia who held out a hand in invitation. It didn't take Rocho the beat of a heart to grasp the hand. The younger woman pulled their naked bodies together. A gasp escaped from both women. This was what both had been dreaming of.

Had it only been just over a month since they had met? Had it only been a couple weeks since Rocho had been accused of sexual harassment? Had it only been a week since her brother had arrived in her life and was now here to defend her?

Rocho was overwhelmed with all these thoughts. While there was the physical connection between them as their overheated bodies touched and desires mixed, it was the emotional connection they shared that was overpowering the mechanic.

A stray tear escaped Rocho's right eye. Sylvia hated releasing her grasp on the woman she loved, so instead she leaned on her tiptoes to kiss the tear away. In doing so, she caused their breasts to rub together.

Both women groaned. Sylvia knew she was still the one who would have to make the first move. While Rocho had been the one to pick her up, she had questioned Sylvia. The mechanic had to ensure herself, as much as Sylvia, that this was what they both wanted.

The kiss strayed from one cheek to the other, before Sylvia found Rocho's lips. It was a passionate kiss, but it was as if the mechanic was holding something back.

Mentally, Sylvia was shaking her head. Internally, she was crying for what one woman could do to another. If she ever came face to face with Juliette, she would use her particular skills with words and let her know what an idiot she had been. And if that didn't work, perhaps allow for some of the self-defense classes The University of Michigan offers freshman.

Rocho moaned as an insistent tongue wasn't just asking for entrance. The tongue was making it known, loud and clear, that it would be allowed its entrance. Soon, tongues were dueling and the mechanic found her legs growing weak.

Gratefully, Rocho found herself being led to the bed. She was aware enough to attempt to catch the weight of her body on her elbows. While Sylvia wasn't fragile, she was precious to Rocho. She didn't want to do anything to harm her lover.

The groan that escaped her was nearly embarrassing when Sylvia opened her legs and wrapped them around her waist. She could feel the golden curls, along with desire, rubbing against her stomach. "Gods! That feels…"

Rocho couldn't find the words. Azure eyes closed. Her dreams of making love with Sylvia paled with the real thing. She knew they would, but she was on sensory overload.

Sylvia was struggling with tears of her own. While her physical reactions were unlike with any woman she had ever been with, that wasn't the reason. It was because of how Rocho was reacting.

Whether it was a simple kiss, touch and now just the first step in making love, Rocho was overwhelmed. Sylvia's lip quirked into a sneer. This was to be one long night of lovemaking. They would be in for a long day at work. But she wasn't about to complain. Not for a millisecond.

Slowly, Sylvia began rocking her hips against that flat stomach. The kiss deepened until oxygen definitely became an issue. As they continued to stare into one another's eyes, Sylvia witnessed it again. It was fear.

Was it fear of doing something wrong? Sylvia placed a hand upon Rocho's cheek. She rubbed a thumb against a swollen lower lip. "No fear when you are with me. Only love and acceptance. Remember that."

Suddenly, Sylvia found her neck being attacked. There was sure to be a mark. And perhaps, this wouldn't be as long a night as she had thought. She smirked. It would be if she had anything to say about it.

A majority of her thoughts were lost as Sylvia felt the mouth trail from her neck to her right breast. She felt the weight of her lover shift. It wasn't long before her left breast was enjoying being massaged.

Gods! It had been so long since Sylvia had been made love to like this. Laurie had been rather physical in her lovemaking. If one could call it lovemaking. It was more like wham bam thank you ma'am.

Rocho hadn't touched a woman like this since Juliette. In fact, Juliette was the only woman who she had truly made love with. There had been a couple others before the one who had accused her of rape. But those couplings had been between awkward teenagers. At best, groping or pawing would be the best way to describe those times.

Now, Rocho was with an experienced, mature woman. But it wasn't those things that was making this time so amazing for Rocho. It was the love. Gods! How had she been so lucky in wandering into the small dealership in a small town in Michigan?

The legs wrapped around her tightened and Rocho knew she was doing something right. She couldn't help grinning as she enjoyed suckling on each breast. Gods how she had missed this. Even if she didn't taste another part of Sylvia's body, she could die a very happy woman.

The way Sylvia was thrusting against her informed Rocho her lover needed more. There was a part of her that remained afraid. Forever would she curse Juliette for causing her to be able to fully revel in making love to her soulmate.

Soulmate. The thought was startling. But not enough for Rocho to stop her slow, intentional descent. "Gods, you taste amazing." Rocho wasn't certain if it was the already salty flesh or Sylvia's natural taste. But it was causing her arousal to become nearly painful.

The thought caused her to pause, momentarily. Rocho knew she was being trusted. There was no way she could ever break Sylvia's trust. Her tongue swirled around a perfect naval. The brushing of the amazing body had caused Rocho's nipples to harden.

Sylvia jumping nearly caused Rocho to dislodge from her perch. She hadn't been prepared for the nipple of Rocho's right breast to graze against her throbbing clit. Once Rocho settled once again, the nipple was pressed even firmer against the nerve bundle.

Strong thighs opened fully as heels dug into the bed. Sylvia found her hips thrusting against the pointed pearl in an attempt to gain some release from the maddening sensations Rocho's kisses, touches and licks were doing on her stomach.

"You have amazing abs." Rocho's voice was gravelly. Sylvia wondered if it was from restraint. She understood. She was having to restrain herself from turning the tables and dive fully into those liquid dark curls.

Rocho couldn't resist rubbing her cheek on those abs. The contrast of soft skin to rock hard abs was one of those unique sensations. One she didn't think she would ever become accustomed to.

There was a pull. Something Rocho needed to do. Slowly, she continued her way down. Every inch she kissed, touched and licked. She was determined to memorize every moment of this coupling. For the cynic inside wouldn't let go of how this could be the only time they would be together.

Sylvia was writhing. She didn't know what to do with her hands. When she felt the sucking on first one thigh and then the other, she groaned. There was another burst of moisture that instantly coated her golden curls.

Before Sylvia knew what was happening, her legs were hanging over strong shoulders. Her breasts were being massaged by two strong hands. Her head was moving back and forth in anticipation. It had been so long since someone who truly loved her had touched her like this.

Rocho already had Sylvia's essence upon her lips from the tender kisses she had placed upon those golden curls. It was time for more than just an inkling. It was time to devour what was hers to take.

The thought caused Rocho to once again hesitate. There was such a primal state to the mechanic. It was there before

Juliette. It had been there when she had defended Sylvia from both her father and ex-girlfriend.

It's not the side Rocho wanted to show Sylvia. At least not the very first time they made love. If after they had been together and her lover wanted something more aggressive, but not this time. Not until she could be certain she wouldn't go too far.

"Don't stop now." Rocho was once again brought out of her inner musings and fear. The timber of Sylvia's voice caused her to shudder.

After placing another gentle kiss upon the blonde patch, Rocho ran her tongue the entire length of Sylvia's sex. It caused her lover to attempt to thrust against her face. A smile formed on the mechanic's face at the power she held.

After distancing herself ever so slightly, Rocho glanced up at her lover's face. Sylvia's expression was a combination of euphoric and frustration. It was a catalyst for what the mechanic was about to do.

The thrust of Rocho's tongue was timed perfectly with the squeezing of both of Sylvia's nipples. Two hands flew to cover the larger ones upon the perfect breasts.

Sylvia couldn't even begin to explain what all she was experiencing. She knew she wanted Rocho's hands to continue their manipulations of her breasts and she wanted the strong muscle that was now lapping up her abundance of juices to begin stroking her nerve bundle.

But if Rocho concentrated on her clit, Sylvia knew she would find her release. While that was the end result both wanted, both wanted this first time to last, to be savored.

"I…" Sylvia wanted to say what she needed and that was for Rocho to devour her clit. To suck it like there was no tomorrow. But this delicious teasing could go on all night.

Rocho held the tip of her tongue against the throbbing nerve bundle. She placed just the barest of pressure upon Sylvia's clit enjoying the pulses.

"Please…" Sylvia could no longer wait. She was so ready to find her release. Strong hands would not allow her to thrust against the strong muscle. Her hands could only barely reach the dark head that was nestled between her legs. It wasn't her short arms. It was because they were already feeling like rubber from the strain.

There was a war within Rocho. It was wanting to continue to feel and taste Sylvia. It wasn't about prolonging her lover's release, though there was a little of that mixed in.

Finally, Rocho began flicking her tongue continuously over the hypersensitive nub. Her thumb and index finger gently squeezed Sylvia's nipples in rhythm with her tongue. It wasn't long before Sylvia's velvety walls were beginning to tighten around Rocho's tongue.

Once again, Sylvia was writhing on the bed. "Oh Gods Oh Gods." Not only did she feel the explosion that led to the stars behind her eyelids, she felt the explosion of more warm liquid that was attempting to escape Rocho's tongue.

Rocho would have none of it. She lapped every single drop of Sylvia's nectar as fast as it was expelled from her body. The mechanic was in heaven. She hadn't tasted a woman in so long and never one so sweet.

Finally, Rocho felt the gentle touch in her hair. She knew it meant Sylvia could take no more of her gentle touches. Reluctantly, she lowered Sylvia's legs to the bed. She slid her sweat drenched body along the equally sweat drenched body.

Reverently, Rocho drew Sylvia to her. She positioned the blonde head against her shoulder. Her own clit was pulsating with need, but she wanted to make certain Sylvia was all right.

In a voice so soft, Rocho had difficult hearing the words, Sylvia mumbled, "That was the most amazing thing I've ever experienced." A deep breath was expelled causing Rocho's nipple to harden even more. "Just give me a moment and I'll show you exactly what I've been fantasizing about since we met."

Rocho kissed the drenched blonde head. "I can't say I'm not more than ready for you to return the favor or that I've not fantasized about you touching me. But I do understand. I attempted to take my time. So that you'd know exactly how much I love you. So that I could prove…"

Though still rather spent, Sylvia managed to prop herself on her right elbow. She used her free hand to force Rocho to look her in the eyes. "To prove that you weren't an animal?" The way azure avoided looking into emerald informed Sylvia of the answer.

A heavy sigh escaped Sylvia. "I'm not going to lie to you." She wished with her entire being that she could take Rocho's hurts away. "There will be times when I appreciate aggressive lovemaking. It will be mutual. It will be consensual. And if it's ever too much, for either of us, we'll make certain to say so."

Finally, azure eyes were able to maintain the loving gaze directed at them by emerald ones. Once again, a tear strolled down Rocho's cheek. For some reason, the sight of it, caused a surge in Sylvia.

The floodgates were open once again as Sylvia continued to kiss Rocho's face. Her lips found her lover's once again. Before she knew what was happening, she was straddling Rocho's stomach.

Sylvia leaned down so that once again their breasts were brushing. She continued exploring her soulmate's mouth with her tongue. The feel of her own need against the soft tightness of Rocho's stomach caused her to groan.

Finally, reluctantly, Sylvia released Rocho's lips. She placed gentle kisses on each corner. "You are so gorgeous. And your hands. I'm so lucky you are so good with your hands." She winked before taking one hand and placing it between their bodies."

Rocho groaned as she felt the renewed wetness. She wanted to slide her lover to her mouth so she could lap each and every drop once again. But she knew that this was Sylvia's show. She would allow her girlfriend free rein.

Azure eyes grew wide when her hand, drenched with Sylvia's desire, was slowly raised toward the young woman's lips. Each and every drop was licked and then sucked from each digit.

A matching flooding was achieved. Rocho having watched Sylvia taste herself and Sylvia having witnessed Rocho's reaction to the maneuver.

Once again, Rocho couldn't believe when her hand was placed between them. She whimpered when she felt Sylvia jump when her finger brushed the younger woman's clit. She whimpered even louder when the hand was brought to her own lips. She didn't hesitate for a second in sucking every last drop of her soulmate's desire from her fingers.

Sylvia's emerald eyes darkened. Rocho responded to her like no other lover ever had. She was repeating but she couldn't help herself. This woman was truly the other half of her soul. It had to be why they were so connected to one another.

It took everything in Sylvia's power not to ground her mound onto Rocho's flat stomach. She allowed for large hands to begin massaging her breasts. Even though it was heavenly for

Sylvia to feel those large hands upon her breasts, she knew the pleasure Rocho gained from touching her.

Gifts. Every touch, taste and movement Rocho experienced was just that. They were a gift from the woman she loved. From the woman she hoped was the one. The one who could look past all of her shortcomings and be there forever.

A gasp escaped Rocho as she felt Sylvia slide once again down her body. There was ample lubrication between their sweat covered bodies and Sylvia's desire. Their breasts were pressed together as the young woman nibbled on Rocho's earlobe.

The nibbling led to Rocho's neck. She knew there would be a mark. In a way, she was glad. It meant that everyone would know, at least for a day or two, that she belonged, body, heart and soul to Sylvia.

"Mmm." Sylvia couldn't help it. She enjoyed the sensations of Rocho's skin beneath her lips and tongue. The deep valley between her soulmate's breasts was where she could become lost forever.

In fact, Sylvia inched her body downward so that she could use her hands to manipulate each breast as she continued to suckle the skin between those luscious breasts. The addition of Rocho's hands on either shoulder only enhanced the sensations Sylvia was enjoying.

Slow. Sylvia had to remind herself that she wanted to take all night long to explore the woman beneath her. And yet, she wanted to taste the ample offering she knew was waiting for her. There was one solution. Reluctantly she released the left breast and trailed down the curvaceous side until she found what she was looking for. It took moving ever so slightly, but Sylvia found what she was looking for. And she brought the treasure back to her lips to sample.

Rocho watched as emerald eyes closed. The reaction upon Sylvia's face could only be described as if the young woman had tasted ambrosia. It was something the mechanic could fully relate to, as that was how she felt the first time she had even caught the scent of her lover's desire.

Azure eyes once again grew wide when Sylvia reached around herself. Instead of tasting the ambrosia immediately, she generously coated each nipple with the goodness. Rocho knew what was to happen and she still found herself exclaiming, "Sweet Jesus."

There was the sign of enjoyment on Sylvia's face as she bent down to take one nipple into her mouth. After making certain each and every drop was removed, she made a feast of the other nipple. Each suckle caused a very significant throbbing of Rocho's clit.

Sylvia slowly moved downward again. This time, she halted so that her heated mound hovered over Rocho's. She reached between them. She allowed for both of their clits to merely touch. It was an interesting sensation as their clits beat as one. It was as if their heartbeats were synced. It was as if their souls were reconnecting with every touch and kiss.

Forgetting this was solely for Rocho's pleasure, Sylvia began rocking. Their erect clits rubbing against one another was nearly more than the young woman could handle. As she glanced into azure eyes, she realized how close her soulmate was to finding her release.

It was too soon for that. Reluctantly, Sylvia slid down until she was nestled between two extremely long legs. She inhaled and couldn't think of a more intoxicating scent than the one being offered before her.

Rocho was near tears once again. The tenderness to which her body was being treated was something she didn't think she deserved. And yet, she knew Sylvia would disagree. In fact, her soulmate would most likely continue to show her just how much she disagreed with that thought. For a very long time, and not just the immediate future.

Instead of a tongue, Rocho felt a finger playing in her soaked folds. It caused her hips to involuntarily jump. The mere touch of her soulmate was truly doing more to her than she thought possible.

Slowly, the single digit entered Rocho. Azure eyes closed. In all the times she had been with a woman, which weren't many, she had never been fully penetrated. "I've never..." She trailed off when surprised emerald eyes glanced up at her.

Sometimes, Sylvia forgot just how inexperienced Rocho was. They spoke of it, but not in detail. It was because of the blasted assault charges. "I don't have to. I can't just..." She playfully circled her tongue around her lips tasting the combination of herself and her lover upon them.

The movements caused Rocho to groan. To some, she was a thirty-something virgin. All because she hadn't been fully penetrated. She didn't think that way. "I'm not certain. But I trust you. I love you."

The words brought a beaming smile upon Sylvia's face. Trust. It was the one thing she knew was at a premium for Rocho. To trust someone with her classic motorcycle was one thing. But to trust someone with their body, heart and soul was a level that caused her to halt her breathing momentarily.

Rocho watched as Sylvia once again lowered her head. She wasn't certain what to expect. She'd heard stories of the pain. Mostly that was with women being penetrated by men. Still, she wasn't certain if she was ready for what Sylvia had in mind.

When the insistent tongue began encircling her clit, Rocho groaned quite vocally. This continued for so long that the mechanic thought she would find her sought after release. That's when Sylvia began to use a single digit once again.

The index finger followed the entire path of Rocho's sex while the amazing tongue continued to encircle her pulsating nerve bundle. It was becoming too many sensations at once. Her walls were beginning to tighten.

The tightening of Rocho's walls were the signal Sylvia had been waiting for. She made certain her finger was well lubricated before she slowly began to enter her lover's core. When she felt resistance, she halted her forward movement.

The entire time, Sylvia continued to encircle Rocho's clit with her tongue. When the walls around her finger began to relax, Sylvia once again began to slowly penetrate her soulmate. She continued the process until with one final slow thrust, the veil of the mechanic's womanhood had been fully broken.

"Oh my sweet Lil One." Rocho didn't know where the words came from. All she knew was she had just experienced the most amazing orgasm of her life. Yes, there had been a little discomfort when Sylvia had broken her womanhood. But she had done it in a way that had concentrated solely on the amazing sensations. "Come here. Please."

It was several moments before Sylvia was able to make her body move. She had experienced a small release of her own when she had heard Rocho refer to her as Lil One. Finally, she was once again being held by the woman she loved.

Rocho found herself kissing the top of her girlfriend's head. She glanced at the clock on the nightstand. When they had arrived home, it was nearly nine. It was now nearly one in the morning. "That was amazing. But we're going to be exhausted. It's nearly one."

Sylvia was drawing lazy eights upon Rocho's stomach. "Frankly, I would love to spend each night similarly and be exhausted. You, my lover, were simply amazing. Tender. Loving."

"So, no regrets?" Though Rocho didn't have any regrets, she couldn't bring herself to believe that Sylvia didn't. She knew it was silly. But it was her insecurities.

"The only thing I regret…" Sylvia was suddenly straddling her soulmate. "Is that we won't have more time to explore each other's bodies. We really should attempt to sleep. So much going on." Her hand strayed to a suddenly erect and convenient nipple. "Still, there's always caffeine…"

Azure eyes blinked. Rocho could see the fire in emerald eyes. There was also love. She swallowed hard. There was no time to prepare herself for the attack on her lips. The only thing she could do was make certain she wasn't left out of the fun.

Hands began to duel. It was clear this was not about going slow or making certain each knew how much they loved one another. This was about the fire of desire each felt for the other.

Finally, after tongues had dueled for what seemed like an eternity, hands shifted lower as if synchronized. In fact, both fingers entered the other at the exact same time.

Rocho was leaning against the headboard. She leaned back so that she could give Sylvia more access. Their fingers sought out clits. In a way, it reminded the mechanic of the scene they had walked into the first time she had visited the apartment.

There was a part of her that remembered Sylvia's reaction. And the words that were exchanged. But this was different. They weren't just fucking one another. They were kissing. They were touching. They were taking one another to the heights of ecstasy.

Sylvia remembered as well the scene that they had walked into. She remembered well the words that had been said. This was so different than that. And it wasn't just because they had spent how long making love. It was because this was between two women who were giving and taking. Not just one taking and not caring about the other.

Their mouths practically smashed together as their fingers found one another's clits. Stroking each other's tongues in rhythm with the stroking of their clits continued until both were calling out into one another's mouths.

Rocho held tight to the body that had collapsed against her. If it weren't for the headboard, she'd be flat on her back. "I don't think I can have another orgasm. Not tonight. And I so want to continue this."

The sentiment caused Sylvia to chuckle. "And who was just mentioning the time and how late it was." She kissed Rocho's convenient cheek. "I know what you mean. Normally I can handle more than that. But you make me feel more."

Sylvia moved her head from Rocho's shoulder. She wanted to make certain her lover understood. "You make everything feel magnified. I want a repeat of this as often as we can. But for the rest of the night…can you just hold me?"

"I second the motion to repeat often." Rocho chuckled as she sounded like what she thought her brother might sound like. "And there's nothing more than I'd love than to hold you. In fact, if that's all I get to do…"

A finger smelling of their combined essence hushed Rocho. "As much of a snuggler as I can be, I want us to make love. If we don't each night or even go without for a month or two, I'm fine with that. But now that I have a taste of you, literally, I'm not giving that up."

Rocho wanted to believe. She needed to believe. But she'd been blindsided before. This time, she had found the real deal. She couldn't lose this. It would literally kill her if she were to lose what she and Sylvia had already built and would continue building.

Chapter 21

The next two weeks seemed to return to a sort of normal. Whatever that was. For Sylvia, it meant being able to restock most of the lot with perused vehicles and ready for the new model ones to arrive. For Rocho, it was to maintain the service and parts department, which were running smooth as ever.

When they weren't working on the dealership, they were meeting with Harry. It wasn't merely about building cases against both the sexual harassment lawsuit and Frank attempting to regain the dealership.

The one thing, besides the times of making love, that were making a difference for Rocho in believing perhaps she truly did deserve love and happiness were the Sundays she spent with Harry's family.

The very first time Rocho had held her namesake had left her nearly breathless. It had also left her with an aching she truly had never thought she would ever feel. She only wondered if Sylvia would feel the same.

"Are you ok?" Sylvia brought their drinks from the kitchen to the patio. The sun was slowly setting. The young couple were enjoying the cool evening late July air. She couldn't believe that August was just around the corner.

Rocho glanced up at the woman she loved. Was she all right? "I'm more than all right. But there is something I've been thinking about since seeing a picture of Renee."

Sylvia placed the drinks upon the table between the two lawn chairs. Instead of returning to her own chair, the young woman sat in her soulmate's lap. "And what is that?"

Having an inkling of what Rocho was thinking, Sylvia wasn't certain she was ready for the conversation. Was that why she had chosen to sit in her girlfriend's lap instead of her own chair?

"Children." Rocho couldn't look Sylvia in the eyes. While they had made strides in their relationship, somethings remained a struggle for the mechanic. Instead, she stared into the sunset. It wasn't even as beautiful as the woman in her lap.

So, they were thinking along the same lines. "I have to admit, that little cutie has me thinking as well." The comment caused azure eyes to finally meet with emerald ones. "I'm not saying I think I'm ready now. But I'm not opposed to it."

"We have too much happening at the moment." Rocho leaned in and kissed Sylvia's sweet lips. "But I wanted to discuss it with you. I just didn't know how to bring it up."

Sylvia caressed Rocho's cheek. In other circumstances, this would easily lead to a round of lovemaking. "Communication is something that doesn't come easily for you. We'll have to work on that."

The cheek beneath Sylvia's hand warmed considerably from the slight blush. "You're not the only one. As it turns out, Daddy and I didn't exactly have the best communication, either. I'm just wondering what else he lied or didn't tell me about."

It was Rocho's turn to caress her girlfriend's cheek. "Here we both go again with our triggers or past coming back to haunt us. For me, it's finally trusting someone enough to consider being good enough to be a parent to a child."

"Co-parent." Sylvia winked at her lover to take the sting out of her words. She knew it was a slip of the tongue. She shivered at the thought of what Rocho's tongue was truly capable of.

"That's the thing. I never even thought I'd find someone who would trust me." Rocho swallowed. Carefully, she sought out her cola and took a generous swallow. An impressive belch followed. "Pardon me."

"And now that you know I trust you with my body and business, is it too early to think of us co-parenting?" Sylvia was generally curious what her soulmate thought. She was questioning as much as Rocho was, now that the subject had been brought up.

When Rocho didn't answer, but stared where the sun had nearly finished its descent, Sylvia knew she had to clarify. "This isn't just a question you have to answer. It's something we have to answer. We both have to think about it. Are either of us ready? If we are, do either of us want to carry a child? Do we want to adopt? If we adopt, do we want an infant or an older child?"

The body beneath Sylvia stiffened. She realized that she had pushed too far too fast. Gently, she forced Rocho so her soulmate was looking into her eyes. "Sorry. That was the businesswoman in me. I plan. I think of all the contingencies. What I want for the immediate future is to continue to get to know you. For us to just become accustomed to one another. And unfortunately, we have to plan with the cases upcoming. Ours is first up on Monday."

Sylvia was grateful Marvin had pretty much learned running the dealership. There were things she would have to oversee and sign for. But overall, he could handle a majority of the day to day running of the business.

There was always Elizabeth. Sylvia knew her secretary knew as much as she did about running the business. And if there was a question, her secretary would place a hold on anything she felt uncomfortable about for Sylvia to take a look at.

When Rocho refused to relax, Sylvia knew drastic measures were required. "So, I know it's late. But I bet the ice cream place is still open." There was a definite shift in the body beneath her. "And we could always take The Fuzz out for a spin. It's been a little bit with work and all."

Rocho couldn't help the smile. She knew she was like a kid in a candy store when it came to her favorite motorcycle. For some reason, perhaps because Sylvia had helped restore The Fuzz, she had an unnatural attachment to the motorcycle. "And then maybe we can cruise the backroads?"

"You read my mind, hot stuff." Sylvia reluctantly rose from the warmth and safety of her seat. She retrieved the glasses of cola. Last time they had become distracted and left the pop on the patio there had been a swarm of bees to contend with.

The pair dressed for the slightly cooler night with windbreakers. Sylvia hated it as she preferred to feel the warmth of her soulmate through as little clothing as possible. The thought caused her to swallow as memories of their lovemaking entered her mind.

It was a quiet walk to their assigned parking spot. Rocho uncovered the classic carefully, as always. She was grateful when the machine appeared untouched. After encounters with Frank, Martha and Derek, she was always thinking the worst was possible. And did they know if her mother had actually returned to Mississippi?

The keys were dangled before Sylvia. It was the usual dilemma. Did she want to feel her breasts pressed against Rocho's back or vice versa? There was also the power one felt being in control of such a machine as the police special.

"I think I want your arms wrapped around me." Sylvia winked. There was that double meaning their coupling had caused. Before they had become more than employee/employer, they had had to be cautious. But now, flirting could be more than fun. And it was quite addictive.

Rocho swallowed. It wasn't from the thought of her arms wrapped around Sylvia as they weaved through the backroads. It was from something she had never attempted. Not exactly an avid reader, she did read romance novels on occasions.

There was one in particular that came to mind with Rocho's arms wrapped around Sylvia this way. In fact, if they weren't overly tired from cruising around, she would have to see if her soulmate was interested.

All thoughts of making love momentarily vanished. It was the way it was when the motorcycle vibrated beneath Rocho and the wind caressed her face. Freedom. It was why, whenever she moved to another town, she had normally chosen a motorcycle.

Rocho loved nearly any classic vehicle, but she had a soft spot for motorcycles. They could go where four-wheeled vehicles could not. Feeling trapped within her own mind, not being able to share who she was, that freedom meant so much to the mechanic.

Now, Sylvia knew nearly everything there was to know about her. Rocho knew there were things she probably had forgotten over the years. Things she would rather not remember. Sadly, like having a younger brother. But she had been as honest with her soulmate as she could with anyone ever in her life.

Sylvia could sense some pretty intense emotions running through her girlfriend's mind. Normally, Rocho would completely relax as they rode the motorcycle. It was better if they were headed out of town, but still this was unusual for her soulmate.

The motorcycle eased into one of the parking spots furthest from the ice cream shop. They normally parked a distance from wherever it was so it was less likely anyone would come close to damaging the classic.

It was with regret, each time, that Sylvia waited for Rocho to ease her body from the motorcycle. There was always a loss of warmth. Since they had made love, there was a loss more profound. She couldn't quite explain it.

"So, have you decided what you are treating yourself with?" Sylvia grasped Rocho's hand without thought. While Portland was progressing, it remained a small town with some religious beliefs. "I think I'm going to have that brownie earthquake thingy."

Rocho shook her head and smiled knowingly. Sylvia had a thing for sweets. But more so, she had a weakness for chocolate. "I'm in the mood for…" She turned suddenly and kissed her girlfriend gently on the lips. The mechanic ran her tongue over her own lips. "Don't think they have that particular flavor."

Sylvia giggled. It felt amazing to see Rocho relaxed and acting like a kid. After their serious conversation earlier, she knew her soulmate needed a distraction. "I bet you're glad I'm not on the menu."

The mechanic leaned down so she could whisper into a convenient ear. "Not here, you're not. But when we get home." When Rocho stood upright, she winked at her girlfriend. "I think I'll have a rich, thick strawberry mocha shake."

The pair continued giggling, hand in hand toward the ordering window. Directly in front of them, also holding hands, was the secretary for the service department and Sylvia's personal secretary.

When Elizabeth turned around holding an ice cream cone, she couldn't help smirking. "Well, hello Boss. Looks like great minds think alike."

Kaz, being the shy young woman she was, hid slightly behind the slightly older woman. She wasn't comfortable with everyone knowing that she and Elizabeth were slowly becoming more than mere friends and coworkers.

A blonde eyebrow rose. When she felt a hand to her back, Sylvia wondered if Rocho had an inkling in regards to the nature of the relationship between the two valued secretaries. "Looks like. We thought a frozen treat and a ride on Rocho's classic motorcycle would be a good idea."

"Would you like to sit for a bit or take a walk with us?" Elizabeth felt the body behind her stiffen. She and Kaz hadn't really spoken about their growing friendship and what they would tell others.

"You don't get enough of me at work?" Sylvia noticed Kaz's posture. Her understudy at college had been psychology. It helped to be able to understand and read people when dealing with the business world.

"Maybe you're right, Boss." Elizabeth made a mental note, while she and her 'friend' were snuggled on the couch tonight, to speak with Kaz. See how far she wanted this relationship to go. Who she wanted to know. "Besides, Monday is a big day for us all. We have to cover your butts at work."

The wink caused Sylvia to chuckle. The words also seemed to cause Kaz to relax. "We'll be counting on all of you answering the phones and staring at computer screens all day long. The real front-line workers." She returned the wink.

"Our ice cream is melting. So, we'll let you order yours." Without thought, Elizabeth grasped Kaz's hand. "See you briefly on Monday. Enjoy your sweet treats." Once again, the secretary winked before leading her friend toward the back of the ice cream parlor. It was built to overlook The Grand River.

Sylvia shook her head. "I used to think Elizabeth wanted a relationship with me. She's just naturally flirty." She turned toward her lover whose face was nearly that of a ghost. "Are you all right?"

Rocho managed to shake her head. She didn't care who was watching. Without thought, she brought Sylvia flush to her body. Luckily, the younger woman went willingly and wrapped her arms around the mechanic.

It was a moment before Rocho managed words. "I'm sorry. It was just how close Elizabeth and Kaz seemed. I know nothing like that ever happened between Martha and myself, but it makes me wonder if I did anything that ever construed feelings that weren't there?"

"Trigger." It was one word that they were both sadly accustomed to. And both were working on overcoming. Together. "Let's get that sweet treat and take a walk. Then you owe me a ride on The Fuzz."

Swallowing a couple times helped the bile to sink. Rocho wondered if it was merely because it was her two coworkers that had been so friendly toward one another. Had that been the trigger?

It was something to think about. For now, Rocho needed this weekend with her soulmate. She needed whatever treats, be they sweet confections or sweet kisses or lovemaking. "Sounds good to me."

It was after midnight when the pair finally returned to their apartment. Sylvia wanted to speak with Rocho about something. It wasn't about children, though it was something that wouldn't leave the back of her mind.

Rocho had other ideas. After the run-in with their friends, she couldn't let go of her insecurities. Even with the freedom of the road and having her arms around Sylvia, she couldn't release the negativity she was feeling.

Their earlier conversation was actually a plus in Rocho's mind. It had been overwhelming the thought of the two of them raising a child. It had just not been something the mechanic had thought Sylvia had wanted to speak of so soon.

When Sylvia turned around, she found herself pressed against the wall. She found her arms pinned loosely above her head as Rocho's right hand began to unzip her jacket.

Rocho's lips were demanding, as was her tongue. The grasp on Sylvia's wrists diminished some, but remained commanding. Finally, the mechanic had to come up for air.

Sylvia knew that look in her lover's eyes. Permission. "Why don't we take this to the shower?" Cobalt eyes darkened. In the midnight hour, they were nearly violet.

All Rocho could do was smile. She was relieved that her advances were not overly aggressive. Yet, she wondered. As she was certain Sylvia was. When would she stop second guessing herself when it came to making love with her soulmate?

Clothes were shed as they slowly made their way to the bathroom. It was Sylvia who made certain the water temperature was just right. The entire time, they traded soft caresses and kisses.

Finally, Sylvia grasped Rocho's hand and led her into the shower. As the spray hit them, it awakened something in the mechanic once again.

It was as if they were under a waterfall. It felt familiar as Rocho gently backed her lover against the cool tiles. The kisses they shared were not animalistic. They were tame, nearly.

Sylvia gasped as Rocho was now marking her neck. This was a different Rocho. This was the lover that came alive after having been given permission to make love. To be as gentle or as aggressive as the mechanic's inner warrior became.

The kisses trailed to her collar bone. Sylvia knew where this was headed. There was a part of her that wanted to urge

Rocho to hurry. But she wanted her lover to know that she trusted her. That she was in complete control.

And that control was leading to what Rocho considered perfect breasts. The water caused the soft skin to be slippery. The warmth of the mechanic's mouth mixed with the warmth of the spray.

Another warmth flooded Sylvia as her wetness began to paint her thighs. Never before had she ever become so ready so instantly than when she did with Rocho. Even the thought of her soulmate touching her caused a flood. Sometimes at the most inopportune times.

Sylvia's legs were already beginning to weaken as Rocho's hands had replaced her mouth. Rocho was taking her time. She was enjoying the abs her girlfriend maintained with the workouts they enjoyed together.

Finally, Rocho was on her knees. Her hands were on Sylvia's hips. She felt a hand on either shoulder. Though leaning against the wall, she could imagine how difficult it was to remain standing.

It would become even more difficult with what Rocho had in mind. With ease, she lifted Sylvia's right leg over her left shoulder. There wasn't any preamble. Her tongue dove in deep into the hot, wet treasure that was awaiting her.

"Fucking Hell!" Sylvia hadn't been made love to like this…Ever. It was becoming something she repeated often she was realizing. Her fears were attempting to fight through the pleasure she was feeling.

No. Rocho would never leave her. Sylvia gasped as one hand slid down the outside of her body. She knew where it was heading. It wasn't long before a single digit was thrusting alongside the strong muscle already thrusting against her clit.

"I'm gonna fall." Sylvia meant it in more ways than one. There was no way she could support her weight once she fell over the cliff. Once she found that ultimate release.

Rocho wanted to tell Sylvia she had her, but couldn't stop tasting. She couldn't stop bringing her soulmate to the ultimate release. Instead, she wrapped her free arm around Sylvia's waist.

Even after Sylvia screamed her name and the flood of juices nearly drown Rocho, she couldn't stop her tongue. The sensitive bundle of nerves throbbing against her tongue was driving her nearly insane.

It was petite hands running through her wet, dark locks that finally caused Rocho to reluctantly cease her tasting of her soulmate. She swallowed before she was able to look into emerald eyes.

Sylvia managed to shake her head. She crooked her finger. If she'd had the strength, she would have helped Rocho in standing. As it was, her soulmate didn't have the strength either. Their wet bodies slid delightfully against one another.

"You are as talented with your tongue as you are with your hands." Sylvia kissed Rocho's eyes. Fear had returned. It was amazing how quickly it could come and go. "Give me a moment and I will wash your back." She winked.

Rocho relaxed as she leaned on her arms to keep her weight from crushing her soulmate. Emerald captured azure for the longest of moments.

No matter if they were to ever find more than what they had now, Rocho would be the happiest woman in the world. All they had to do was to deal with the two trials. Once they were over, they could discuss children. They could discuss where they wanted to live. They could discuss…

All thought was lost as their positions were soon reversed. "I guess I'll start with the front." And boy did Sylvia ever start with the front. Nibbling on a convenient earlobe as a finger grazed Rocho's heated opening.

The tables had turned. It was Rocho's turn to nearly not be able to stand. "Sweet tongues on fire." Sylvia hesitated for a moment in her attack on her soulmate's body. A blonde eyebrow rose in question. Rocho managed to shrug.

Sylvia giggled as she nibbled the chin in front of her. She nibbled down the collarbone until she was taking turns sucking on one nipple and then the other. Never did the single digit actually enter Rocho. It continued to just barely touch the heated opening.

Their eyes met just before Sylvia thrust her fingers inside. They could feel the spray of water rush over them as Sylvia continued to thrust in and out. Her thumb began caressing Rocho's clit.

Rocho's hips began moving in pace with Sylvia's movements. It wasn't long until Rocho called out Sylvia's named repeatedly. It was her turn to be held up. "Now, we should wash up and take this show to the bedroom."

It was a long Saturday night and Sunday morning. It was interrupted Sunday evening when Harry and his family arrived for a late supper. He had an ulterior motive in wanting to speak to them about the next move. Monday was to be one long day.

Chapter 22

Courtroom. Rocho had never been in one. Even with her father as an attorney/District attorney. She had had several nightmares in regards to them. Ever since she had been on the run since she was eighteen, she had one nightmare after another.

Those nightmares had pretty much disappeared since sleeping in the same bed snuggled next to Sylvia. Rocho was certain her soulmate had suffered from nightmares of abandonment and her body next to her had aided with lessoning those as well.

Rocho was sat between her brother and lover. While knowing she had family that believed in her, she remained worried about her chances of proving that she was innocent. This wasn't a criminal proceeding, but still. It was about her guilt or innocence.

Worst of all, if Rocho was to be found guilty, so would Sylvia by association. It wasn't merely the mechanic that was named in the lawsuit. It was her employer, as well.

A hand upon Rocho's forearm caused her to jump. She turned to look into the gentle emerald eyes. "Sorry. I just wanted to do this real quick before the judge entered."

The kiss was gentle. It was sweet. Yet, it wasn't chaste. A clearing of a throat caused Rocho to turn toward her brother. He wasn't looking at her, but she could see his cheek was an interesting shade of pink.

"None of that when the judge is in here." Harry managed to look his sister in the eyes. He winked before turning back to his paperwork. His private investigators had given him some unsettling information. He only hoped his opponent hadn't gotten his hands upon it.

Before either of the ladies could respond, the court was being called to order. Rocho felt uncomfortable. It wasn't just being in the courtroom. It was the conservative monkey-suit as Sylvia termed it that felt so constricting.

Before Rocho or Sylvia could respond, the call to rise came. Rocho felt her hand being grasped and being given a squeeze as her eyes watched the figure in the black robe enter through the hidden door to the left of the bench.

The judge was male, nearing his sixties. He wore wire-rimmed glasses. His eyes were dark. They found her azure ones. For some reason, she felt as if he had already judged her guilty. She was grateful there were six people they had to convince of her innocence and not just the angry appearing man.

"I'm Judge Gibbons. I've been judge in the county of Ionia, Michigan for nearly a decade." The judge shuffled a few papers. "Before I bring in the jury, I have to say something."

Rocho stiffened. Usually by now she thought a judge would allow those in attendance to be seated. "In all my years as a lawyer and judge, I have never seen such an overwhelming case against a defendant. I suggest that a plea-bargain be met."

Harry stiffened beside her. "Your Honor, with all due respect, do I have to ask for a mistrial or a new judge before we even begin?"

Judge Gibbons leaned forward. "You might want to rethink your entire case. Unless you have something hidden that you've not shared."

The tapping of the judge's fingers was annoying Rocho. Once again, a gentle squeeze was given to her hand before it was released. They had to be cautious with showing too much affection, even though their relationship wasn't supposed to be on trial.

Harry straightened to his full height. He'd dealt with small town judges. He'd dealt with big city ones. He'd dealt with ones that thought they were the law. This one seemed to encompass all those traits. And worse, he was antifemale.

"Again, with all due respect, I will present my case. And I will prove my clients' innocence." Harry maintained steady eye contact with the judge.

"Very well. But I believe you are mistaken." The judge turned to the plaintiff. His eyes widened slightly. "Everyone may be seated." He waited until quiet had once again settled over the small courtroom. "Let's get on with this. Bring in the jurors."

The case Martha's attorneys unfolded caused Rocho to cringe. The first three hours caused her to even begin to wonder if she wasn't guilty. She was grateful for the hand upon her leg, gently squeezing every so often, especially when there were blatant lies being told.

"Before we break for lunch, I urge the defendant to once again consider my earlier suggestion." Judge Gibbons didn't say more as he didn't want to influence the jury. "With that said, we'll reconvene at one-thirty."

The banging of the gavel caused Rocho to jump. She waited until she felt Sylvia take her hand before she even began to breathe. She was guided to outside the small courthouse and finally into The Trans Am.

Harry leaned into the open passenger window to speak with his sister. "I know it doesn't sound good. It's the plaintiff. It won't. We'll get our say. My advice, please try to eat something."

Instead of answering, Rocho managed to shrug. Sylvia managed not to sigh. She knew this would be difficult on her soulmate. But seeing it as it unfolded was nearly too much. "I'm just going to take her for a drive. We'll be back in time."

The attorney knew his sister, but not as well as her girlfriend. "Be safe." Harry stood back and watched as the sports car took off. "It's a good thing you have her, Big Sis. You're gonna need it."

Sensing a presence, Harry turned around. He froze in place. Two figures he hadn't seen since he had left Mississippi were on the steps speaking with his counterparts. "Shit."

OOOOOOOOOOOO

The Trans Am purred as Sylvia waited for the milkshakes. They wouldn't be as good as the ones from the local ice cream place, but it was faster. And they could sip them while they sat overlooking the local park.

"Things are going to be all right." Sylvia turned to see what she expected. Rocho was staring out the window. There was nothing really to see. Just more restaurants, a grocery store and cars moving about.

The line moved slowly. They were next in line. "Rocho, you do have faith in us, right?" There was a deep pleading in Sylvia's voice.

It was enough to force Rocho's attention to her soulmate. "I believe in us. I believe in Harry. I just don't believe in the system. I don't believe in things always working out the way that it's supposed to."

Sylvia had to wait to answer as their small milkshakes were ready. She knew that Rocho wouldn't be able to eat much, but hopefully the ice cream treat would be enough.

After paying, Sylvia handed both drinks to her soulmate. She slowly pulled into traffic before heading to the local park. She was grateful the temperatures were turning cooler, especially with them both dressed for court.

"Things don't always turn out the way they are supposed to or the way you want them to." Sylvia managed to sip on her shake before continuing. "After all, if things had turned out the way I wanted I'd have my mom beside me rooting us both on."

Rocho sighed. She knew she was being selfish. She wasn't the only one who was being dragged through the ringer. "I'm sorry. I guess this is worse than I thought it would be on me. It can't be easy for you or the publicity for the dealership."

Finally, Rocho managed a sip of her milkshake. Jamocha. It was her favorite, when not purchased at the local ice cream place in Portland. "Gods that's good."

Sylvia swallowed at the near moan Rocho emitted. She remembered the moans that had escaped her soulmate when they had made love the previous night as neither had been able to sleep a wink.

"I could joke and say any publicity is good publicity." Sylvia shrugged as she sipped her milkshake. "I'm not worried about the business. We have backup plans."

Rocho hastily finished her milkshake. If her stomach wasn't so queasy, she would have wished for a larger sized one. "You are the planner. I'm the drifter."

"And together, we make an excellent team." Sylvia finished her milkshake. She turned toward her soulmate. "We best get back. Before we do, we are the perfect team. I can plan long-term and for nearly any contingency. You can plan for emergencies and by the seat of your pants. Just remember that as the trial continues."

For the first time that day, Rocho actually felt like they could beat this. She leaned across the gearshift and gently kissed her soulmate. "I can't wait until this is over with. And your father goes away. Then we can start our life together."

"I like the sounds of that." Sylvia licked her lips. "And I love the taste of that." She winked before making certain Rocho was wearing her seatbelt again.

As always, Sylvia drove her baby with care. She would have held hands with her lover if the car was not a manual. The drive to the courthouse didn't take long as the city of Ionia wasn't much bigger than their small town of Portland.

The two were forced to release one another's hands before entering the courtroom. Until their relationship was brought up by Martha's attorneys, they would be forced to hide their relationship.

Sylvia was several paces ahead when she realized Rocho wasn't walking beside her. Hastily, she returned to her lover's side. Instead of asking, she followed the path of azure eyes.

There was an older man. One who was definitely related to Rocho's brother. Sylvia could only surmise that it was their father. The other person was a sandy blonde woman with hazel eyes. The pair were speaking with Martha's attorneys.

Though several inches shorter, Sylvia managed to block Rocho's line of sight. It brought her soulmate's attention to her. She grasped both of her lover's hands before leading her to the defendant's table where Harry was waiting for them.

Both Harry and Sylvia blocked Rocho's vision of the strangers. At least they were strangers to Sylvia. "Would either of you care to tell me who those two are and why Rocho has gone from actually slightly smiling to appearing to have seen a ghost?"

Harry waited several heartbeats. There wasn't much time left before the judge would begin the afternoon session. "The tall, distinguished looking man is our father."

The attorney knew that he should inform Rocho that he knew their father would most likely be testifying. As would the woman he hated most in the world. "And the woman with him is the infamous Juliette."

It was only Harry restraining Sylvia to keep her from beating the shit out of Juliette. A gentle touch on her lower back caused her to calm enough to regain her courtroom etiquette. "I'm sorry." She nodded to Harry before turning toward her soulmate. "And thank you."

"We'll both need restraining if she's allowed to testify." Sylvia nodded her head in agreement. Rocho tugged gently and the pair kissed.

Harry cleared his throat. Only because it was time for the judge to begin the afternoon session. They all rose and were seated. None of the three were shocked when Harry, Sr. was the first to be called to the stand.

After being sworn in, the attorney for the plaintiff didn't waste any time. "As the father of the main defendant in this case, Renee Bishop, do you have any information that would show as to the lack of character of Miss Bishop?"

Even before he said it, Harry knew what would happen. He was right as the judge immediately overruled his objection. If this were a criminal case, he would have grounds for appeal.

Hands clasped tightly as Harry, Sr. told the tale. "My daughter was always trouble. I can't tell you how many times she was sent home from school. She barely passed any of her classes. We tried to set an example, as I am influential."

Harry, Jr. wanted to object, but he knew any objections would be overruled. He wished he'd asked for a change of venue. Or that he'd studied this particular judge's past record better.

"The real trouble began when Renee was in high school. She wanted to be a mechanic. Not that there's anything wrong with working with one's hands, it's just not what we wanted for her." Harry, Sr. looked at his hands. "It's what being with those in the classes led to."

There was a pause before the male attorney urged him to continue. "One day, Renee came home. She claimed she had an attraction to girls. There was one in particular. We didn't raise our daughter to be…" There was an effort before Henry, Sr. continued. "Different."

There was murmuring from those in attendance. So much so that it caused the judge to bang his gavel several times. "I will clear this courtroom if y'all cannot behave." Finally, the judge motioned to the plaintiff. "Get on with it."

The attorney nodded and motioned to Henry, Sr. "We weren't at all surprised when the authorities came to the door one day. They had an arrest warrant for my daughter. The chargers were raping a young woman."

"I object strenuously once again." Harry, Jr. was now on his feet. "There is no proof of these past accusations. And even if there were, the defendant is accused of sexual harassment. Unless there have been changes in the charge that I'm not aware of."

"Sit down before I find you in contempt of court." Judge Gibbons pointed his gavel threateningly at Harry, Jr. "Even if Miss Bishop were merely accused of rape, it shows prior inappropriate behavior. Now, is there anything further from this witness."

Harry, Jr.'s hands clenched and unclenched. He wanted to say more. He was being denied even cross examining his father. It would take some legal maneuvering indeed to prove his sister's innocence.

"Actually, we've only one more witness." The attorney waited until Harry, Sr. was seated in the gallery. "The plaintiff calls Juliette Beacher to the stand."

Rocho wanted to bolt from the courtroom. If it hadn't been for the nearly painful grasp of Sylvia's hand upon her own, she just might have. She could almost hear her soulmate's plea of don't leave me screaming from sultry lips.

When Rocho turned to look at her soulmate, she saw the fire in emerald eyes. If looks could kill, Juliette would be dead. With each strut taken by the sandy blonde, Sylvia's grasp tightened on Rocho's hand.

The mechanic leaned in and whispered into Sylvia's ear. "You're gonna break my hand if you're not careful." The words caused the grip to finally not be deathlike.

Sylvia exhaled deeply. She knew if she ever saw the woman who had accused her soulmate of rape, she would have difficulty in restraining herself. A courtroom was not the place or the time. Perhaps there never would be.

Rocho had barely heard what her father had said. With Juliette, it transported her to another time, another place. She was eighteen again. She had just graduated from high school.

The young woman was excited. Not only had Rocho just graduated, she had found someone she wanted to start her life with. When they had driven off that day in her most recent remodel, Rocho had thought they would make love and then hit the road.

But that wasn't what had happened. Oh they had made love. Or at least for Rocho it had been making love. Juliette had insisted she be taken home. So, instead of leaving that night, the mechanic had chosen to leave the next morning.

The next morning had led to handcuffs. Rocho had been processed like she was a common criminal. How she had been given bail and who had paid, she had no clue. All she knew was with the way her parents had never accepted her lifestyle, they would never defend her. They would prosecute her. In fact, she had no one to help her. There was only one thing to do.

Instead of driving away in the vehicle she'd remodeled, Rocho had decided she could use the money. Before she had left town, she had sold it for far less than it was worth. But the bus took her two states away. And when she felt like someone was becoming too close, she would do the same. Sell everything and move two states away. She would run. Run until she could run no more.

It brought Rocho here to the state of Michigan. She had allowed someone close. And now she sat in a courtroom. But she was far from alone. On one side was her soulmate. On the other was her brother.

"And that woman raped me. Repeatedly." The statement brought Rocho from memory lane. She managed to focus on the witness stand. Juliette was pointing a shaking finger accusingly toward her.

Once again, the gallery erupted. The gavel pounded several times. Judge Gibbons' face was now a dark red and there was a vein pulsating dangerously on his forehead. "That's it. Clear the courtroom. And you all will be lucky if I allow anyone in tomorrow."

It took several minutes before the small gallery was cleared. Judge Gibbons took a moment to calm himself. "I had hoped this trial would have some semblance of dignity, but I guess that's out of the question. If this continues, I'll bar media and spectators from being in attendance."

Judge Gibbons glanced at his watch. "I see that it is nearly three. Does the plaintiff have any more witnesses to call?"

"We have one more witness. We call to the stand the plaintiff, Martha Neilsen." The attorney helped the young woman from her seat and waited for her to be sworn in. "I'm only going to ask you what happened and what you did to rectify the situation you found yourself in."

More lies. How Rocho brushed up against Martha nearly every day. How she finally asked her out to dinner. When she spoke to Sylvia in regards to the ongoing harassment, she was fired on the spot. Shortly thereafter, a relationship between the business owner and mechanic developed.

The gavel pounded. Court was adjourned for the day. Harry was saying something, but Rocho couldn't hear the words. She could feel Sylvia holding her hand. She felt when she leaned in and kissed her gently on the cheek.

Sylvia knew Rocho wasn't hearing a word her brother was saying. She turned to Harry. "If there is anything important that needs to be done before tomorrow, please call me tonight. I need to get Rocho home. We need to snuggle. She's…"

Harry nodded. He couldn't even begin to imagine what Rocho was feeling at the moment. While their parents hadn't loved any of their children, he had at least earned some affection from them. It hadn't been until they had shunned Rocho that he had turned his back on them.

"Just take care of her. Try and get her to eat something." Harry squeezed Rocho's shoulder. "I'm sorry I didn't warn you that Juliette might testify. We'd located her, but didn't know if they had. But Dad being here blew my mind. I have a few tricks up my sleeve. If that judge will start actually being a judge and allow a fair trial."

Rocho managed to nod. She didn't blame her brother. In fact, she had thought in her gut that Juliette would somehow show up in her life one day. Now was the perfect time.

As for their so-called father, he would pick now to return. Rocho was at her lowest. He wanted his revenge. And he wanted to look good to his colleagues back in Mississippi.

"Come on, Hot Stuff." Sylvia, as always, was attempting to use humor to defuse the situation better. "We've got a date with a salad and a couch. Then a nice soft bed."

Sylvia winked at Harry before making certain Rocho walked beside her. It wasn't long before they were in the small public parking lot. She turned toward her soulmate. "We got through day one. We'll get through day two. I think this will be over tomorrow."

Rocho nodded. She wanted to say something. But she just couldn't find her voice. Or was it she couldn't find the words? Either way, she remained silent the entire fifteen-minute drive home.

Once settled on the couch, Rocho stared at the blank television screen. They rarely watched television, but it gave her something to stare at.

The mechanic didn't even notice the plate being placed in front of her. Rocho barely noticed when Sylvia sat next to her. The cool plate was placed in her lap. "Thank you."

Sylvia watched as the food on the plate was pushed around. Every so often, it made it into Rocho's mouth. At least her soulmate was eating something.

"All right. Enough of this." Sylvia retrieved their dinner plates to take them to the kitchen. When she returned to the kitchen, instead of sitting next to Rocho, she made her way to the CD player.

The music was soft and had a slow beat. Sylvia held out her hand palm up. She crooked her finger at her lover. "Would you do me the honor?"

The love shining in those eyes and the softness of the voice finally had Rocho smiling again. She relaxed as she rose to her feet. And when their arms wrapped around one another…

The next two hours were spent slow dancing around the living room. There would be no lovemaking tonight. There would only be holding one another. Until they faced the next challenge. Until they faced the next round.

Chapter 23

Round two. That's how Rocho was looking at it. They arrived early at the courthouse. She didn't want any more surprises. Plus, she didn't want the chance to accidentally run into Juliette or her father. Hopefully both had returned to Mississippi, but most likely had stayed for the attention.

Rocho knew her father was attempting for a way to be reelected. If he could testify against his queer daughter, it would appeal to the conservatives back in her home state.

Harry was shuffling through paperwork next to her while Sylvia had an arm wrapped around her waist. There was no use in denying their relationship. Whether it was the sexual harassment trial or for the ownership of the dealership, they were to be open and honest about their relationship.

"Renee." Rocho jumped at the familiar voice. A voice until the day before, she hadn't heard in a decade and a half. She turned to see her father standing there. "You haven't changed. You are still shaming your family."

Before Harry, Jr. or Rocho could respond, Sylvia rose from her seated position. She held out her hand. "Hi. My name is Sylvia Reed. I own the dealership up on the hill. Your daughter, my lover, is the head mechanic. It's nice to meet Rocho's father. I've already met your wife and your youngest child."

The district attorney looked at the hand as if it would burn him if he touched it. "If you don't mind, I was attempting to have a conversation with my daughter."

Sylvia made certain she was standing between Rocho and her lover's father. "If I may show my disrespect to an elder, what you were really doing was attempting to further shame Rocho for being who she is. When the shame is upon you and your wife for turning your backs on your child when she needed you most. And now for showing up in a small town which remains conservative and caters to your kind of thinking."

"Look here, young lady." Harry, Sr. would have taken a threatening step toward Sylvia had there not been the wall that separated the gallery from those involved with the trial. "This is family business. Stay out of it."

Finally, Rocho rose to her feet. It was her turn to place herself between her lover and her father. "Daddy. I see you haven't changed any. You are about your image. About what you think those so-called family values are all about. Do you know how I've spent my life since leaving Mississippi?"

When her father would have responded, Rocho continued. "That was a rhetorical question. You've never been a family-oriented person in your life. Mother certainly never has been with the way she has worked with all those organizations. So leave me and my lover alone."

Harry, Jr. decided it was time for him to speak up as well. He knew it was close to time for court to begin. But he needed to support his sister and her soulmate.

"Because of the way you treated Rocho, you've missed out on me." Harry, Jr. placed a hand upon his sister's shoulder. "Not only me, but my wife and your granddaughter. And you'll miss out seeing what Rocho and Sylvia do with their life. Just leave us all alone."

Once again, anything Harry, Sr. would retaliate with was cut short by the call for everyone to stand. Hastily, Rocho was sandwiched between her brother and soulmate. This time the judge didn't take too long in having everyone being seated.

Once again, Rocho wasn't wholeheartedly listening to the proceedings. Harry was calling her co-workers. She knew that everyone that worked in the bay with her would have her back. She knew that Elizabeth would as well.

For some reason, Rocho was worried about what her brother had up his sleeve. While it was in her and Sylvia's best interest, she wondered who would be called to the stand next.

"If it pleases the court, the defense calls Louise Bishop to the stand." Rocho turned toward her brother so fast she nearly strained her neck. Harry felt his sister's eyes upon him, but refused to look at him.

It was several moments before Louise managed to stagger to the witness stand. In the short time since she'd seen her daughter, her health had taken a drastic turn for the worse. She now only had a few weeks left to live.

After being sworn in, Harry approached his mother. He hadn't seen her since he'd left home. The pictures his private investigator had shown him hadn't prepared him for the sight of how far her health was failing.

After clearing his throat several times, Harry managed to begin the questioning. "For the record, state your name and relationship to Renee Bishop. And tell us what you know of the past accusations against her."

Louise couldn't look either of her children in the eyes. She focused, instead, on her husband. She wondered why she had stood by him, even after they were divorced. Their marriage had never been about love. It had been about power.

"I was raised in a strict, Baptist upbringing, as was my ex-husband." Louise was surprised when Harry, Sr. couldn't maintain her gaze. "We attempted to raise our children that way. But our eldest, Renee, had this stubborn streak. But it was more than that."

"Objection, your honor." Harry, Jr. turned and glared at the plaintiff's attorney. How many times had he objected, only to have them overruled? It had caused him to stop objecting when he normally would during a trial.

"I allowed a great deal of leeway." Judge Gibbons hated to admit how harsh he'd been. But he had read the online comments and the headlines of the local newspaper. "I think it's only fair the defendant enjoys some latitude as well. Overruled. For now."

Harry, Jr. attempted to hide his surprise by turning back to his mother. "Please, go on with your story." He attempted to not hate the woman sitting before him. But he couldn't stop himself. Not the way she had treated his sister.

"Renee simply knew herself. Even when we attempted to tell her to hide that part of herself." Louise sat back. It wasn't in defeat. She was exhausted. She only hoped she would be able to finish before she would exhaust herself fully.

"When she came to us, we tried everything to make certain she hid herself. That she wouldn't shame us." Louise sighed heavily. "But she was her own woman. Even as young as fourteen, she was her own person."

There was a pause. Louise was so tired. It felt as if her life was slipping from her body. Or was it her soul? She had to hurry and be concise.

"Then she began dating Juliette Beacher." Louise finally managed to glance at her daughter. She was shocked to see azure eyes staring at her. "I knew the girl wasn't any good. And when Juliette started taking up with my niece, Renee's cousin, that just confirmed it."

"I want to reiterate my objection." The middle-aged attorney hastily rose from his seated position. He knew where this testimony was leading. If Louise was allowed to finish her story, there would be no winning.

"And I want to see where this is leading." The judge glared at the attorney. He realized he had been played when at first he had been told this was an open and shut case that would be good for his reelection campaign.

"The night of the rape accusation, I had followed Renee. I watched as she was lost in fixing her cars." Louise sighed heavily. "I didn't have the guts to admit to her that she was being true to herself. That she was good at fixing herself. If I'd just come forward back then, my daughter never would have felt like she'd done something wrong. That she was less than she was. Or that she'd have to run and hide from anyone."

By the time her words had finished echoing, there were tears trickling down Rocho's cheeks. Never in a million years had she thought her mother would say anything that would clear her name. And what's more, there even felt as if there was an ounce of love in her voice.

Before anyone could say or do anything, Louise Bishop slumped in the witness stand. The bailiff was the first to the stand. The older woman hastily felt for a pulse. "We need an ambulance. There's only a faint pulse."

It was a whirl of activity. Rocho held onto Sylvia as she watched the paramedics work on her mother before she was carted off. The mechanic wasn't certain which was overwhelming her more; her mother testifying on her behalf or her being rushed out of the courtroom.

Judge Gibbons waited until things had settled down. "Settle down. Even though there's still three more hours left in the day, I suggest we adjourn for the day. And Miss Bishop, I send my sympathies."

Rocho managed to nod in appreciation. She turned to her brother. "This may sound insane, but I want to see Mom. I want to be at the hospital."

Harry nodded in agreement. "From what my PI informed me, she was lucky to be here. The pictures I was shown hadn't prepared me for this."

Sylvia was speechless. And it was bringing back memories. She wasn't certain if she could… "I'm sorry." Rocho turned her attention toward her lover. Emerald eyes showed something they never had before. Fear.

"Sylvia?" Rocho reached toward her soulmate. Sylvia couldn't help taking a step back. "What's wrong?"

"I can't. Not right now. I'm sorry." Sylvia leaned forward. She kissed Rocho gently on the lips. "I'll see you at home. I just need…" She shrugged. She didn't know what she needed. But she did know why she was reacting this way.

Rocho reached out but Sylvia was already halfway toward the exit. "What the Hell?" The mechanic shook her head. For a moment, she wanted to chase after Sylvia.

"Is she all right?" Harry was staring at his sister. While they had pretty much won their case, he was beginning to wonder at what cost.

"I'm not certain." Rocho finally turned toward her brother. "Do you know where they took Mom?" She needed to do something. If not chase after Sylvia, she needed something to do.

Harry stood straight. He looked directly into azure eyes. "I'll check on Mother. You check on Sylvia." Would there be an argument?

"But what about Mom?" Rocho was torn. The woman who loved her unconditionally or the woman who had only shown her hate her entire life, until she faced her mortality.

"I'll deal with our mother." Harry pulled a resisting Rocho into his arms. "Don't let our mother come between the best thing that has ever happened to you. I'll drive you to the apartment. If Sylvia isn't there, you can do a search for her. Please. For me."

A deep breath was expelled before Rocho reluctantly agreed by shaking her head. She wasn't prepared for the small group of reporters. Harry attempted to shield his sister from the vultures, but they were quite persistent.

The drive to the apartment complex was made in silence. Rocho wasn't certain what to say to Sylvia. Why had her soulmate run out after the mechanic's mother had been taken away in an ambulance?

The Trans Am was not in its parking spot. "Looks like she hasn't been here. I'm heading up to the apartment. See if she was there. Then I'll make some calls. Once I've found her and know what's going on, I'll call you."

Harry's smile was sad. "And once I find out Mom's condition, I'll call you. I won't worry if you don't answer. I'll leave a message."

"Thanks." Rocho watched as her brother left the parking lot. Harry having brought her home meant a great deal of driving. It was something she owed Harry for.

Rocho took the steps three at a time. She was grateful for her long strides. The moment the door was opened she knew that she was alone and that Sylvia had not returned to the apartment.

Just to make certain, Rocho hastily scoured the apartment for a note. There was nothing. She retrieved her cellphone and dialed her soulmate's number first. There was no answer.

"Sylvia, Sweetie, please call me and let me know how you are." Rocho hesitated before hanging up. "I don't know what has triggered this. I'm sorry my brain isn't working to see it. Call me. I'm heading out on The Fuzz. I'll check my phone often. I love you. More than anything."

After hanging up, Rocho hastily changed out of her courtroom clothing. The weather was cool so she decided on her leather motorcycle pants, sleeveless t-shirt and black leatherjacket. Something she hadn't worn since the early spring.

Once again, Rocho took the stairs three at a time. Before causing The Fuzz to roar to life, Rocho checked her cellphone. She made certain it was charged and tried Sylvia's number once again.

The motorcycle roared to life. Where to look? There weren't many places Sylvia would go. Since she had nothing to do with her father, that was not an option. The only other friends or family her soulmate had would be Harry and his family or those at the dealership.

Rocho was racking her brain in an attempt to decipher why Sylvia wouldn't want to accompany her to the hospital. And then it dawned on her. So much so that Rocho nearly missed her turned and spilled.

"How could I be so stupid and inconsiderate?" Rocho continued to mentally berate herself as she made her way to the dealership. In her heart, she knew Sylvia wasn't there. But she hadn't a clue as to where her soulmate was. Perhaps Elizabeth would.

After ignoring quite a few inquiries, Rocho made a beeline for Sylvia's office. She was grateful when Elizabeth was sitting behind her desk. "Have you heard from Sylvia?"

"Well hello to you too, tall, dark and handsome." Elizabeth could see the danger in azure eyes and knew that now was not the time for teasing. Nor was it the time for questions.

Everyone had heard what had happened in the courtroom. And she was dying to know. Still, Rocho was dying to know where Sylvia was. "Boss Lady hasn't called in, which is quite unusual."

"Damn." Rocho leaned against Elizabeth's desk. "I was stupid. After my mother shockingly testified for me, she collapsed and was taken away in an ambulance. My first instinct was to head there. I forgot about Sylvia's mother and how she battled cancer."

"And lost." Elizabeth nodded. While she wasn't around when it was taking place, she remembered how Frank had been for the first few years she'd worked for him. And Sylvia would not be the woman she was today without her mother's death.

"I wish I'd been here." Rocho began pacing. "And I wish I'd remembered. In my defense, my brain hasn't exactly been functioning the last couple days. Still, I should have thought of it when I saw the expression on Sylvia's face."

"Stop. You both are stressed." Elizabeth stood and made it so she stopped the pacing mechanic. "Who wouldn't be? The dealership was nearly destroyed. You were accused of sexual harassment. You were just raked through the coals in court and will be again when Frank gets through with you."

Rocho peered down into understanding eyes. "Thanks. I just want to find her. I really don't know. We really only go for walks and the ice cream place. It's here or home, otherwise."

"Hmm." Elizabeth thought what she might do. "This might sound a bit off, but what about visiting her mother's grave? I've not lost my parents, thankfully, but I did my grandmother. I used to visit her grave often."

"Thanks!" Rocho hesitated. "Of course, I don't know where her mother was interned."

Elizabeth rolled her eyes. "That should be easy to look up. Give me a moment." The secretary resumed her seat at the computer. "Here it is. It's the Portland Cemetery. Do you know where that is?"

"I do. Might sound creepy to you, but when I first moved here, I used to take walks there." Rocho shrugged. "It's peaceful and people leave you alone."

The secretary couldn't help the laughter that bubbled forth. "You are too much sometimes. You and Boss Lady. I hope you two remain my bosses for a long time."

"I'm not your boss." Rocho held up her hands. "Don't have time to argue. But thanks for being a good friend. Sorry if I don't call and give you the juicy details."

"Just go get Boss Lady." Elizabeth winked. She watched as Rocho tore out of the dealership. She felt the presence before Kaz cleared her throat. "I have no idea what's going on. Just what they reported on the news. Only thing to add was Boss Lady took off and Hunky Mechanic had no idea where she was."

Kaz smirked. Her friend had some colorful nicknames. And she had an interesting way of describing things. "I just hope Sylvia will be ok. Rocho seemed to be dealing with everything somewhat well."

Elizabeth looked into emerald eyes. She still felt they reminded her of Boss Lady's. "As long as they aren't stupid enough to forsake one another, they'll be fine. Now, how are you doing? I know you prefer things quiet and having to testify couldn't have been easy."

The younger secretary merely shrugged. "It wasn't easy. But Mr. Bishop was nice to me, as was the other attorney. Working here is actually not too much with the public so I can deal easily. And there's you."

"Ah, now we know why you are doing ok." Elizabeth winked. "If you're up to it, we can get together this weekend. I know of this great movie. We can snuggle on the couch. And maybe, if you're ready for it, snuggle in bed."

Kaz swallowed. They'd spoken at great length how her body didn't crave sex. That all she wanted was snuggling. Maybe a chaste kiss here and there. And definitely hugging.

But Elizabeth was a sexual being. How could she ever be happy and content with someone like Kaz who could never give her what she truly needed?

OOOOOOOOOOOO

Sylvia could feel the chill in the air. The tears that had fallen were now slowly drying. "Oh, Momma. I wish you were here. Daddy never would have treated me like this. And I never would have run out on Rocho when she needed me."

The young woman sat cross legged upon her mother's grave. It had been too long since she had visited. With Laurie cheating on her when she first returned and everything in between, she had not visited as she should have.

"At least someone has been taking care of you." Sylvia made certain the few weeds attempting to take hold were removed. "The way I should be there for Rocho."

The sun was now setting on the day. Sylvia didn't even know how long she had been in the cemetery. She barely even remembered the drive from Ionia to Portland. At least nothing had happened to her or the Trans Am.

Sylvia thought she heard footsteps. She froze. Normally, no one was out and about in the cemetery. With the sun beginning to set, she wondered who on earth it could be.

When the shadow fell across her, Sylvia just knew. Without turning around, she spoke. "I thought you'd be at the hospital with your mother."

Rocho shifted her weight nervously. "At first, I didn't understand what had upset you so. I mean, seeing anyone collapse like that is shocking. I have to admit, sadly, that I'd forgotten how your own mother must have suffered."

Now Sylvia did turn to see her soulmate. The remorse in Rocho's eyes was beyond anything she had ever seen. Before she even knew it, she was on her feet.

There were tears trailing down the tanned skin of her soulmate's face. Sylvia gently wiped the tears from Rocho's cheeks. "It's not sad at all. We've had an extremely emotional two days. Seeing your accuser and mother. Having your mother testify in your favor. And then her being taken away."

Rocho couldn't resist tugging on Sylvia until she was holding her snuggly against her. "And you seeing Louise taken away was a trigger for you."

The mechanic felt the movement against her shoulder. Rocho closed her eyes. "I'm sorry I was too preoccupied. I know I don't have to apologize. I just wanted to say it. Now, how about you introduce me to your mother?"

Sylvia remained with her arms around Rocho, but made it so they were looking into one another's eyes. "Are you serious?" The mechanic nodded.

A small chuckle escaped Sylvia. "A parent I'm glad I can introduce you to." They turned toward the headstone. "Mom, this gorgeous mechanic is Rocho. She's my soulmate. If I have my way, she's gonna marry me and we'll live happily ever after."

Rocho wobbled slightly. It was another day of being blindsided. While they had both expressed wanting to spend the rest of their lives together, the talk of marriage hadn't exactly been broached.

"Well, I not only get the privilege of meeting your mother, where you get your good looks and charm, I am proposed to." Rocho spun Sylvia around so that they were looking into one another's eyes. "Did you mean it?"

A blonde head nodded vigorously as emerald eyes twinkled. "I had wanted to do it before Harry and his family left. That way we can hopefully celebrate the dismissal of the sexual harassment suit, have the ownership decided in our favor and most importantly begin planning a wedding."

"Wow." Rocho leaned in and gently kissed her fiancée. "I have to say yes to it all." She picked up Sylvia in her arms and began spinning around. They were dizzy by the time she stopped. They collapsed to the ground in a heap.

"I'm sorry about that, Mrs. Reed." Rocho made it so Sylvia was in her lap. "I should have more respect for you. It's just your daughter sometimes causes me to get carried away. Plus, we do have a lot to celebrate."

Sylvia placed her head on Rocho's strong shoulder once again. "She's right, Momma. I've never met anyone like Rocho. She's stirred me from the very beginning. Not just my hormones, either."

There was a definite warmth underneath Sylvia's ear. "We have so much in common. We just connect. And she's been a protector. You'd love her, Momma. You'd have hated to see what's become of Dad. Or maybe you knew."

"Unfortunately, we will probably never know." Rocho kissed Sylvia's temple. "The most important thing to know is that I'm here. I'm not leaving you. And that I say yes to your proposal. I expect a big fancy wedding. Not!"

Sylvia chuckled. "Knowing us, we'll take a couple hours off work and stand in front of The Justice of The Peace. We'll need witnesses. But other than that, I'll be happy."

"I'm happy." Rocho's cellphone chose that moment to ring. "I have a feeling I know what this is about." Careful not to release her hold on Sylvia or dislodge her from her lap, Rocho retrieved her phone. "Hello?"

"It's me, Sis." Harry ran his fingers through his hair. "Mom is in intensive care. She's not expected to make it till morning. She's not conscious and not expected to wake up. Dad's here for whatever reason."

"I don't know if I'll come." Sylvia shifted so that she could look into azure eyes. "I found Sylvia. She's doing all right. In fact, you'll be the first to know that we're officially engaged. I think I want to spend the night with my fiancée."

"Well I'll be damned." Harry was nearly bursting with relief. He had been worried the way that Sylvia had run out of the courtroom and the way Rocho had hesitated in following her that the two would have issues. "I hope my family is invited to the wedding."

"Well, we don't know if we'll have anything more than a trip to The Justice of The Peace. We'll need witnesses." Rocho heard the laughter from the other end of the phone. She also heard her father's gruff voice. "Sounds like I'm getting you in trouble with Dad."

"Dad can stuff it. While this is a somber time, I need something to celebrate. Most likely you'll be acquitted tomorrow, but we can hold onto the marriage of two soulmates." Harry felt some of the guilt he had felt throughout the years fading some.

"Well, we'll celebrate this weekend. Once all court is finished up." Rocho didn't want to mention that Harry and his family would be moving back to Flint. They would be separated by a couple hours once again.

"Sounds like a plan." Harry could hear the change in his sister's voice. He understood. He was feeling it as well. "I'll let you go. I best see to Dad. Love you."

"Love you too." Rocho placed her phone back in its pocket. "And I love you." She kissed Sylvia on the cheek. "Now, let's go home and snuggle. We still have one more day of court this week. You lead. I'll follow."

Sylvia reluctantly rose to her feet. She took a moment to stare at her mother's headstone. "I hope you approve, Momma. Watch over her. Please."

There was a gentle squeeze on her shoulder. The soulmates walked hand in hand to their respective modes of transportations wishing they could ride together, whether it be side by side or one in front of the other.

Chapter 24

Case dismissed. Rocho felt like celebrating. But not only because she had been cleared of sexual harassment, but also because she had been cleared of rape. That meant no more running. She could settle down. Finally.

Now, they had to face Frank in court. Once that was done, they could plan their nuptials and the rest of their lives. Would that include a child?

Rocho was finishing with her last oil change for the day. It felt amazing to do something as routine as an oil change. While the mechanic loved restoring old cars or discovering the allusive reason behind a faulty engine, anything to do with cars and she was in heaven.

It was time to clean up and then rescue Sylvia from the mounds of paperwork her fiancée had. Rocho smirked at the thought. It was something she was still becoming accustomed to.

It wasn't long before Rocho was dressed casually in her motorcycle outfit. It had been such a turn-on for Sylvia that she had decided to begin wearing it more often.

Kaz waved at Rocho as she walked by causing the mechanic to stop and say hi. "How are things going with my favorite secretary?"

The young woman giggled. "I don't think Elizabeth would like to know that she has been demoted." Rocho couldn't help the grin. Kaz was teasing easily. "I'm bout finished here. Busy day tomorrow. I'll have the work orders on Rick's desk. Good luck to you and Sylvia tomorrow."

"First off, I think Elizabeth can give as good as good she gets." Rocho wanted to tease the secretary, but didn't want to embarrass her. "And thank you. We know the place is in good shape when we aren't here."

"Thanks." There was the faintest of blushes upon Kaz's face. "We all defer mostly to Elizabeth until Marvin really understands the ins and outs."

"Elizabeth is amazing." Rocho leaned a little closer. "If you don't mind me saying so, I hope you and she become good friends. She's been there for me over the year plus that I've worked here. And even longer for Sylvia."

"I don't have many friends." Kaz couldn't maintain Rocho's gaze. "I'm just grateful you, Sylvia and especially Elizabeth consider me friends."

"And we're just as grateful." Rocho knew she didn't sound exactly like herself. In fact, she sounded more like Sylvia. She knew why. It was the weight that was finally lifted from her broad shoulders.

With the cheeks of the secretary reddening just a tiny bit more, Rocho decided it was time to take her leave. "I best see how Sylvia has survived her day. I'll see you on Monday, if not tomorrow afternoon."

With a wave of her hand, Rocho was off once more. When she was nearly to Sylvia's office, she heard raised voices. One, she was certain, belonged to Elizabeth. The other, she wasn't certain who it belonged to.

Rocho's pace hastened as she wondered if there was trouble. She paused as soon as she saw the wink Elizabeth gave her. As casually as she could, she came to stand behind the older gentleman.

"As I've told you three times already. My name is Elizabeth. I work for Sylvia Reed. If you want, I can deliver that letter to her." Elizabeth expelled a breath. There wasn't trouble, exactly. It was the fact the man was in need of new batteries in his hearing aids.

"And I've told you, I need to personally see Miss Reed." The gentleman held out the clipboard. "I'm from the law firm of Peterson and Everett."

The door to Sylvia's office suddenly opened and the blonde appeared. "What in the name of peace is going on out here?" Sylvia was in mid-step when emerald eyes grew wide. "Uncle Ethan?"

"Finally!" The old man used his cane to slowly close the distance to Sylvia. Cautiously, Sylvia hugged the older man. "I know this is the computer age and anyone can sign for things, but this was supposed to be delivered directly to your hands once your father retired."

"What is it?" Sylvia took the clipboard from the man she had referred to as uncle. There was a line that required her signature so she easily signed it.

"You'll have to read the contents, Darlin." Ethan patted the young woman's cheek. He knew the next part wouldn't be easy. "Your mother wanted this delivered when she knew you'd be old enough to handle it. And hopefully when you'd have someone in your life to help you through it."

Those words spurred Rocho into action. She was by Sylvia's side instantly. "I'm sorry to barge in. My name is Rocho. I'm Sylvia's fiancée."

"I'm a very old friend of Sylvia's Momma's family. I'm not really her uncle." Ethan saw the argument in emerald eyes. "We used to be that close. I'm sorry we've drifted apart since you've been at school, Darlin."

"That's all right. It's as much my fault as yours." Sylvia gently kissed Ethan on the cheek. "Hopefully, we can get together soon. And maybe you can come to our ceremony. It's gonna be at The Justice of the Peace."

"I'd love that." Ethan didn't hesitate in pulling his niece into a hug. "And if you need me after reading that, let me know." He glanced at the woman he had graciously allowed him to hug his niece. "But by the looks of it, you are in good hands."

"She most certainly is." Ethan reluctantly took his eyes from his niece and focused on the young lady he vaguely remembered as Frank's secretary. "And not just tall and dark here." Elizabeth winked at the older man. "That's why I was a bit overzealous. Sorry bout that."

"No problem, young lady." Ethan winked at the young woman. "Now if you all will excuse this old man, I have to maintain a schedule or my wife will give me a difficult time. Ladies." The old man bowed at the waist before taking his leave.

"That was interesting." Sylvia weighed the package in her hand. It was a rather thick manilla envelope. "For some reason, I don't think we should open this at work." She turned toward her secretary. "No offense, Elizabeth."

Elizabeth burst into laughter. "None taken, Boss Lady. Just let me know what's in that envelope." She took a half step toward her favorite couple, besides herself and Kaz. "When you are ready, of course."

The phone rang. Elizabeth glanced at her watch. "Looks like the last call of the day. You two behave. Only one more day in court is all we need to deal with."

"Very true. You make sure everything is ready for the morning without me and Rocho." Sylvia shook her head as Elizabeth merely waved her hand. "You, come with me."

Rocho felt herself pulled and then forced against the door. There were no complaints when she felt an insistent tongue inside her mouth. It wasn't long before hands had found her cloth covered breasts.

As good as it felt, Rocho didn't want her fantasy of making love in Sylvia's office to come true. At least not today when there were still so many people at the dealership and there was the pressing matter of whatever it was her fiancée's mother wanted Sylvia to know.

"Down, Girl." Rocho managed to break the lip lock. "As much as I'd love to strip you naked…" When her leg shifted slightly, the mechanic realized her fiancée was wearing the rare business skirt. "Though with what you are wearing…"

"I'll wear this on a Friday when we won't have to worry." Sylvia gave her lover one more kiss before reluctantly walking to her desk. She needed the buffer. It was her fault, but her body was completely on fire.

Rocho had to take several deep breaths before she bent down to retrieve the envelope that Sylvia had dropped when she had pinned the mechanic to the door. "I'm certain Elizabeth got quite a thrill out of it."

Sylvia's laughter was cut short when she caught sight of the envelope. She motioned to the envelope before turning to her computer. "I just have a couple things to sign off on before we can do our usual routine."

There was a part of Rocho that wanted to push. But after finding Sylvia vulnerable in the cemetery, she knew anything to do with her lover's mother could be a trigger.

The mechanic watched as Sylvia did what she had trained for. It wasn't what her soulmate enjoyed, but she was good at. Perhaps in the future, Sylvia could turn over running the dealership to Marvin.

"All set." Sylvia turned her computer off before retrieving the business jacket that matched the skirt. Instead of putting it on, she slung it over her shoulder. "You take care of that until we get home."

"Will do, Boss Lady." For her comment, Rocho received a swat to her stomach. After leaving the office and making certain it was locked, they walked hand in hand around the dealership. They were impressed with how everything had been cleaned and secured already.

"We've got a good crew." Sylvia nodded absently at her lover's comment. Her mind wouldn't leave what could possibly be in the thick envelope.

Finally, the pair had finished their rounds and had made it to the apartment safely. Rocho still clutched the envelope tightly as they entered the living room. "Do you want to attempt to eat anything? Or do you want to just open the mystery envelope?"

"Envelope." Sylvia didn't hesitate in making her way to the couch. She slowly lowered herself. "I'd hate to have either of us clean up anything if I couldn't keep down our wonderful lunch we shared."

"I enjoyed the five minutes of dessert." The darkening of emerald eyes informed Rocho that Sylvia remembered the make-out session they had enjoyed.

"Thank you." Sylvia kissed Rocho on the cheek before reluctantly taking the envelope. "Here goes nothing." The ripping of the envelope seemed to echo throughout the silent apartment.

There were three more envelopes inside. One was marked with Sylvia's name. The second was marked with her father's. The third was the curious one.

"What the Hell?" Sylvia stared at the envelope in shock. She handed it to Rocho to study. How had their newest employee's name come to be written on the envelope? And by her own mother?

"Kaz Livingston?" Rocho shook her head. "Should we give Elizabeth and Kaz a call? I mean, we should at least let Kaz know she is mentioned in this."

"I want to see what this other paperwork says, first." Sylvia hastily read through the paperwork. Once the businesswoman read everything but the sealed envelopes, she came across a DVD. It was labeled with her and Kaz's name. "I guess we should get Kaz and Elizabeth over here before we go any further."

Rocho was dying to know what was in the paperwork. She had attempted to read some of it, but it made little sense. "I'll call Elizabeth. Would you like something to drink? Cola? Ice coffee?"

"I think it's going to be a long night." Rocho nodded in understanding. Sylvia watched her soulmate walk toward the kitchen with her cellphone to her ear.

Sylvia rubbed her finger repeatedly over the envelope with her name upon it. "Oh, Momma. What did you do? Is this something I'm going to need help with? Is this something that will change my life?"

The case that contained the DVD caught Sylvia's attention. Would there be video of her mother? She hadn't seen her mother or heard her voice since she had lost her nearly fifteen years ago.

The soft footsteps alerted Sylvia to Rocho's immediate return. Emerald sought out azure. She could see the answer in those loving eyes. "When will they be here?"

Rocho chuckled. "They were having dinner at Fabiano's." Hastily, she seated herself next to her lover. "Until then, do you want to tell me what all that mumbo jumbo meant?"

It was Sylvia's turn to chuckle. "I'm not a lawyer. We'll have to have Harry look at some of this, but from my business classes, it looks like Dad never really owned the business. It was in a trust, I guess is the right term, until I was ready to take over."

It took a moment for the information to sink in. "If this is legal, that means the lawsuit your father filed means nothing." Rocho didn't hesitate in kissing her fiancée soundly. She was cautious of the paperwork that remained on Sylvia's lap.

The buzzing of the intercom alerted them to the arrival of their friends. "I'll let them in. Why don't you warm up the television we hardly use?"

Sylvia nodded as she swallowed. Seeing her mother wasn't something she was certain she wanted to share with anyone, besides Rocho. But if there was anyone else, it would be Kaz and Elizabeth.

"Welcome, ladies. I use that term loosely when it comes to you, Elizabeth." The secretary in question merely rolled her eyes. "Did the big lugnut tell you what this is about?"

As usual, it was Elizabeth who did the speaking and Kaz who hid slightly behind the slightly older woman. "She only said that there was a mystery envelope that had Kaz's name on it that involved you, Sylvia."

"It's from my mother." Sylvia shifted so that there was plenty of room on the couch for all four of them. "I'm not certain what you want to address first. There is an envelope with each of our names on it, plus my father's. Then there's the DVD."

Kaz stared at the envelope Sylvia handed her. She had a mother. She wasn't the nicest of mothers, but still she had a mother. What was it that her boss' mother wanted from her?

"I…" Kaz picked up the envelope. "Perhaps we should read our…notes or letters or whatever these are." She glanced up into eerily similar emerald eyes. "Maybe these will give us an idea of what to expect from the DVD."

"Sounds like a plan." Sylvia held her envelope in a shaky hand. "Before we do this, is there anything we can get you guys? We don't have anything with alcohol."

Elizabeth shook her head. "I'm good." She moved closer to Kaz. "What about you? You didn't eat or drink much." Without thought, she wrapped her arm around Kaz's waist.

Kaz was startled at first. When she looked up, she saw a pair of understanding eyes. "Guess we haven't been hiding our relationship. And no, I'm good for now."

Sylvia chuckled. "I think it's adorable. Elizabeth has flirted with everyone under the sun. It's past time she finally settled for the sweetest girl around."

Both women blushed. It caused another minor bout of giggles for Sylvia before the envelope in her hand and the sound of the low buzz of the television caused her to sober once again. "Well, I guess there's no time like the present."

Elizabeth had Kaz fully embraced against her, while Rocho was doing the same with Sylvia. The sound of tearing envelopes was nearly louder than the thundering of twin hearts.

The wording was quite different, but it amounted to the same thing. Frank had had several affairs during his marriage to Sylvia's mother. She had known of each and every one. The only one that had produced a child was one.

"Wow." Sylvia glanced up as Kaz uttered the lone word. Check that. Her half-sister.

Their identical emerald eyes met. Sylvia could see the tears forming in Kaz's eyes. She didn't know much about her sister's childhood. Her own had been lonely, after her mother's death.

"Well, I guess this means you are half owner in the dealership." When Kaz would have objected, Sylvia hastily continued. "There's generic paperwork here. It, if I interpret it correctly, says that I've always owned the dealership. And before that, it was my mother's. I know it's technically our father that binds us by blood, I think Mom would want this."

There was silence as Elizabeth held Kaz. She rubbed her girlfriend's shoulders, careful to keep from touching too intimate of areas. A gentle kiss was placed on Kaz's temple.

Something similar was transpiring on the other end of the couch. Rocho was now perched on the arm. She was rubbing Sylvia's neck. She was proud of her fiancée's suggestion that the siblings co-own the dealership. The mechanic would be happy to continue to be just that…a mechanic.

"Why don't we watch the DVD." It was Elizabeth's voice. Normally so boisterous, it was the most subdued Sylvia had ever witnessed. Even the devastation of the dealership hadn't caused this level of quiet.

"Allow me." Rocho retrieved the remote for the DVD. She squeezed Sylvia's shoulder before pressing the play button. She held the remote in one hand and Sylvia's hand in the other.

The face that appeared on the screen was beautiful. Rocho would have sworn it was Sylvia's sister upon the screen. Yet, the woman was ravaged. It was the only word she could think of. The poor woman had to have gone through Hell on earth having fought cancer and lost.

"I wish I was there to see you, my Angel." The grasp upon Rocho's hand tightened. "I wanted to call you that, but your father wanted to name you after his mother. Your father often got his own way. Too often. If you've read the letter I've written you and Kaz, then you'll understand. If you haven't, please pause this before continuing."

There was a pause before the DVD continued. "There was one way I never let your father get his way. The dealership.

It's in my name. I allowed him to change the name to his, why I don't know. But I made certain it was yours once you were ready. So if you are watching this, then you are. And you can finally give that man what he deserves. Nothing."

The outright bitterness in her mother's voice shocked Sylvia. From her standpoint, she had always thought her mother had loved her father. Or perhaps for her mother it was merely the façade a wonderful mother puts on so that a daughter can have the illusion of a happy childhood.

"Now for you, Kaz. I hope you don't mind me being so personable." Sylvia glanced at her sister. There were tears now slowly sliding down her cheeks. "I'm sorry that I wasn't able to provide you with a stable childhood. I hope you can find happiness now that you have found your sister. And I hope that Sylvia is more like me than her father and does the right thing."

Sylvia swallowed. Was she like her mother? She had been so young when she had passed away. Rocho sensed the change in her fiancée. Hastily, she squeezed her soulmate's hand before bringing to her lips and gently kissing it.

"I attempted to keep track of you, Kaz. And after I passed, I made sure my good friend Ethan kept track of you." There was a pause before she continued. "I wish I could be there with you. I'd help you with Frank. I don't know if I'd have remained with him had I not become so ill. But I did. And you both deserved better. I just hope you've found love. And I hope that, no matter your age, that you've found one another and that you'll become the sisters I've always wanted you to be."

There was a coughing fit. Someone off camera handed Sylvia's mother a glass of water. "I'm going to have cut this a great deal shorter than I had wanted. I'm sorry my darlings. And yes, I do consider you both my daughters. Just not the best mother. Though part of that is the cruel twist of nature. I love you my lovelies. Have a long and happy life. And give me grandchildren." With that, she winked.

After the screen had turned blue, Rocho turned the television off. There was only silence for the longest of moments. Talk about being blindsided. No one could have seen this coming in a million years.

"Well that's more unexpected than me falling in love with someone." Everyone turned toward Elizabeth who merely shrugged. "What? I'm good at being a flirt. Never thought someone could steal my heart."

The blush on Kaz's face was more than adorable. But the one on Elizabeth's face caused Sylvia to chuckle. "My secretary has finally grown up."

The comment caused a chorus of chuckles. Once they quieted down, Sylvia was the first to speak. "I'm serious about what I said, Kaz. I want you to think about having a percentage, if not half ownership in the dealership."

Kaz sighed heavily. "I never wanted this." She finally managed to look her sister in the eyes. "I mean, I wanted a better life than I had before. But it wasn't a monetary one. It was to have friends. To have family and to have love."

Sylvia leaned a little closer. "Well, if you allow it, you can have it. I mean, the dealership is just now out of the red. But Rocho and I are more than happy to share." Her gaze met with her secretary's. "And if there's anyone special in your life, I'm certain we can make it a four-way interest."

"Hold up." Kaz hastily rose from the couch. She nearly dislodged Elizabeth from her seated position. "This is a bit too much. I mean, I'm happy we're sisters. But the rest…" She shook her head. "It's too much."

Without another word, Kaz was running toward the door. "That's my cue. We'll see you tomorrow. If not, I'll call you. Let you know how she is."

Sylvia was kicking herself as she watched her secretary run after Kaz. She turned toward Rocho. "Guess I pushed a little too hard on that one part."

Rocho slid so that she was now sitting next to her fiancée. "It's understandable. You want to share. Everything. And you want to be the daughter your mother envisioned having."

That was the rub. The biggest thing of all now wasn't even about sharing. Sylvia was pushing so hard because she wanted to be the daughter her mother had hoped she'd grow into.

"Yeah." Sylvia sighed heavily. She returned her attention toward the envelope. She had missed the last part of the package. "There's some pictures."

Carefully, Sylvia slid through the pictures. They were of herself during different ages of her childhood up until just before her mother passed away.

More than that, there were pictures of Kaz. Sylvia wondered if Kaz had any pictures such as these. These weren't the kind that were taken for school. These were caring and loving ones.

"I wish I'd known about Kaz." Sylvia sighed as she snuggled closer to her fiancée. "In a way, I'm now looking forward to court."

"We have to let Harry in on this." Rocho didn't want to let Sylvia go, but they had to let their lawyer, who just happened to be her brother, in on what should win them the case.

"It's getting late, but we definitely have to." Sylvia kissed her fiancée soundly. "Feel like a drive?" As she rose to her feet, she brought Rocho with her.

"I'll get the DVD." Rocho hastily followed up on her promise. It wasn't long before the pair were safely tucked in the

Trans Am. "I'm going to miss this. The weather is already beginning to change. We're going to need a place to store this and the motorcycle."

"That depends on your brother." Sylvia watched traffic carefully. Though it was later, there was a great deal of it for a Thursday evening. "If he decides to head back to Flint, which I hate, then we can move into the house. If not and business continues like it has been, we can look into getting a house of our own."

"A house big enough for at least one child?" Rocho watched Sylvia's reaction closely. It wasn't fair to spring it on her while driving. But the mechanic had been thinking a great deal, nearly nonstop, since her fiancée had first mentioned the idea of adopting or having children.

There, of course, was an exception to the rule. The fact Rocho had been on trial and had her mother testify on her behalf. The fact her mother was still alive was shocking, if not miraculous. She really should visit her.

"I see you watching me." The clicking sound of the blinker was the only sound momentarily as Sylvia pulled into the house she had fallen in love with. "I do want to have a child. And it's not just what Mom said. I'm still not certain about having a child or adopting."

Rocho grasped Sylvia's hand as soon as her fiancée had parked the classic car. "Well, we can think about the logistics. I just wanted to tell you it's not shocking me anymore. And I definitely want to raise a child with you."

Sylvia swallowed. Today had been such a normal day, as far as work had been concerned. But just as the day had ended, her old family friend had handed her some paperwork. Paperwork that would forever change her life, as well as Kaz's.

"Sweet talker." Sylvia brought the hand in her grasp to her lips so that she could kiss it gently. "But not as sweet as I was when I proposed."

The laughter echoed momentarily before Rocho could follow after Sylvia. The pair were met at the front door by a sleepy appearing Jessica. "Wasn't expecting a visit from Renee's favorite aunts."

"We're her only aunts." Sylvia chuckled. "How are you doing? I never get to speak with you. It's always Harry. And tonight, unfortunately, it's who we need to see."

"Renee is one energetic young lady." Jessica looked her sister-in-law up and down. "I think she's living up to her namesake. As for Harry, he's in what he terms the office. Your niece is supposed to be asleep. Sorry."

"Hopefully, we'll get a chance to see her this weekend." Sylvia led the way. While this was technically Rocho's family, they had accepted her as their own and felt comfortable in their house.

"Knock, knock." Harry glanced up from the computer screen and motioned them in. "Hey, you. We have some really interesting information for you." Sylvia made her way to her brother-in-law.

Rocho handed her brother the thick envelope. The one that had Frank's name upon it was attached to the outside of the large envelope. "Sylvia was given these today. They came from a law firm that was friendly with her mother, apparently."

"Oh, really?" Harry's dark eyebrow rose at the name on the outer envelope. "And this? Did this come with the rest of the information?"

Sylvia leaned against the desk Harry was using. "An old lawyer friend, Ethan, had me sign for this. He said he was under orders to give it to me when I was ready to take over the dealership. There was an envelope like that…" She pointed to the one with her father's name upon it. "On the inside with my name on it, but also one of my employees. Who turns out to be my half-sister via good ole daddy."

Harry held up his hands. "Wait. You're telling me that Frank never owned the dealership and that he had a daughter outside the marriage to your mother?" Sylvia nodded. "Well, then. And the DVD?"

"The DVD is more of a personal note from my mother stating what I just said." Sylvia pointed to the envelope. "And from what I could gather from the legalese in there, she put it in simple terms."

"But you didn't open the one addressed to your father." Sylvia shook her head. "Good. Well, the judge is going to love us. Actually, I'm going to call Frank's attorney right now. Let him know what we've discovered. If this is true, could save the taxpayers some money."

"I hope it is." Sylvia shoved off from the desk and leaned into her fiancée. "We have a ceremony to plan. And I'm certain you and your wife are anxious to return to Flint."

Harry played with the paperwork in his hand for a moment before looking the women in the eyes. "Actually, Jackie and I have been speaking. We thought about moving a little closer. Portland wouldn't keep us busy, but with the money we have saved, we could live easily for a little while. Plus, we have our eye on a house that could serve as a business."

A blonde eyebrow rose. "You mean you don't love this place?" Harry shrugged. "I'm teasing. I get it. A place has to be perfect for you. Especially if you want to work out of it. We're just beyond thrilled you'll be close by."

"And maybe there'll be someone that Renee can play with." Rocho felt two sets of eyes upon her. She inwardly cursed. They hadn't discussed if they were to announce their tentative plans.

"Have you knocked up my sister?" Harry stood to his full height. To some, it would be intimidating. For Sylvia, it caused her to chuckle. Or was it his tease?

"We haven't decided on adoption or natural, but we are wanting to raise a child together." Rocho hugged Sylvia to her body. "But first, we have to make honest women out of each other."

The trio laughed. The sound brought Jessica into the room. After hastily explaining, the young woman insisted that they plan a party for Saturday. After all, if everything went smoothly the next day, they would have so much to celebrate.

Chapter 25

Instead of a courtroom, Rocho and Sylvia found themselves in their apartment. They never would have thought they would have allowed Frank in in a million years. It was Harry who suggested they meet there.

The tension was palpable as Sylvia, Rocho, Harry, Frank and his attorney stood in the kitchen. It was one time Sylvia wished that she had invested in a kitchen table instead of just using the barstools at the kitchen counter.

"Let's get this over with." Hank Greyson, Frank's attorney, hated losing. And he'd lost this lawsuit before it even began. "You have a letter for my client and some paperwork for me to look over."

Harry handed over the respective envelopes to the proper person. Hank was the only one of the two to actually begin reading what was given them.

Frank stared at the envelope. Though it had been forever, he would recognize his wife's handwriting anywhere. Yet, he couldn't bring himself to believe that it was his dead wife who had somehow kept this hidden for how many years from him.

"How do I know this is actually from your mother?" Frank glared at his daughter. It was as if he didn't know his own daughter. As if he had never known her.

Sylvia shook her head. How sad. Her father was showing his true colors. In a way, he was like a cartoon representative of used car salespersons.

"You can speak to Uncle Ethan." Sylvia watched as her father stiffened. "You remember him, don't you? He was mom's family's lawyer for at least three generations."

Frank swallowed before opening the envelope. The words were something he'd never thought he'd hear from his sweet Rose.

At first, Rose had ignored her family's objections to their union. She had truly been in love. And when she had given birth to Sylvia, it had changed everything. It had caused her to be more aware.

More aware of the affairs Frank had had. More aware of how he had turned the dealership from something that was morally rated to a charlatan status. And how he had fathered Kaz Livingston.

By the time Frank had finished reading Rose's letter, he was quite pale. "She knew." It was all Frank could manage. He slumped back against the counter, nearly falling from the bar stool.

"What do you want from me?" Frank stared into emerald eyes. They were daggers. He had never witnessed such hatred in them. Even when he'd basically attacked Sylvia's playmate, she had never looked at him with such malice.

Sylvia couldn't help the laughter that bubbled forth. "That's all you have to say?" The young woman shook her head. "And isn't that supposed to be my line? You're the one suing me for the dealership you signed over to me. That you never actually owned, as it turns out."

Frank's face was bright red. So red that Sylvia was ready to call an ambulance. "That bitch." He didn't hesitate in tearing his letter to shreds. "I had her fooled. She couldn't have known I was a broke bum who needed her money. And that bastard daughter. She won't get a red cent."

"That's not your decision." Sylvia turned away from him, not father, but sperm donor. She fixed her gaze on Hank.

"Have you read over the documents? Can we settle this and get this man out of my place? For good, I might add."

The movement was a blur. Sylvia was suddenly pressed against the counter. There were two hands around her neck. It wasn't long before she was seeing darkness at the outer edges of her eyes. It wouldn't be long before the darkness would completely take over.

Rocho saw red just as readily as Frank had attacked. Because of the adrenaline both the mechanic and Frank were experiencing, it required more strength than usual for Rocho to pry Frank from her soulmate.

Once Frank was forced to release his grip, he was slammed with all the force Rocho could muster to the floor. She easily pinned his arms to the ground by sitting on his chest and placing a majority of her weight on his biceps.

It was a trigger, Rocho knew. Sylvia had been in real danger. The mechanic had felt a surge of anger like she'd never felt before. More than the anger, there had been real terror that she could lose her soulmate. Yet, she merely had Frank pinned beneath her.

How was Rocho merely restraining the man who had very nearly choked her soulmate to death? Why was she not pummeling Frank senseless?

From behind her, Rocho heard the sound of choking and someone gasping for breath. Her eyes were nothing but menacing when she sought out Frank's. "You are lucky she's breathing. Because if you'd done her any harm, you wouldn't be breathing now."

A warm hand upon her shoulder caused Rocho to relax. Azure eyes closed. She heard Harry's voice. She could have sworn he mentioned the police. Hopefully that meant her brother had called nine-one-one.

Sylvia swallowed hard against her sore throat. Her voice was raspy. "Are you all right?" She helped ease Rocho from her father, well aware that Henry and Hank were watching them.

"Am I all right?" Rocho pulled Sylvia tightly against her body. "I'm supposed to be asking you that question, now aren't I?"

It was a forced smile that graced Sylvia's lips. They were covered, ever so gently, by Rocho's. There was a clearing of the throat. "The police are on the way."

At the words, Frank scrambled to his feet. Harry immediately blocked his path. "If you run, it'll look bad. Your lawyer will tell you the same thing. You are now guilty of assault. Plus, there are documents your wife left behind that show a trail of some extremely shady business dealings."

"Don't say a word and don't run." Hank knew there was no money to be had. This was merely one he'd have to place in his loss column. But he would defend his client to the best of his abilities.

There was a charged silence in the room until the buzzer caused both women to jump. "I'll let them in." Sylvia made certain that her father would remain where he was.

Rocho blocked what little escaped path there was. It wasn't fear of Frank running. It was fear for what a trapped man might do. Even to the daughter he supposedly loved.

After the police arrived, it was a blur. Harry was by Sylvia and Rocho's sides while they were interviewed by the police after they were taken down to the small police station. He was the one to inform them it was Frank who had paid to have the dealership ruined. He wanted to be the savior when his daughter failed.

The fact Frank never owned the dealership was the ironic thing. He would spend a great deal of time in jail. And he would never have a relationship with his child ever again.

They returned to the apartment, not wanting to face the dealership just yet. Harry stood to the entrance of the living room. He watched as his sister and her fiancée held one another. He wanted to do more, but knew that they, emotionally, had everything they needed with one another.

"I'll leave you two alone. You shouldn't have to testify against Frank." Harry already knew to stop referring to Sylvia's father by anything other than by his name. "I'll make certain the necessary paperwork is filed so that you and Kaz share ownership of the dealership."

Absently, Sylvia nodded. Just when she thought she couldn't be more emotionally overloaded, her sperm donor had to strike out physically at her.

Rocho forced her gaze from her fiancée. She was more than worried about Sylvia. "Thank you. If we need anything more, we'll call you. And of course, we still have a ceremony to plan."

Harry nodded. "I expect to be best man. And I know a certain someone who wants to be flower girl. Or at least an honorary one." He mouthed, "Take care of her." Aloud, he said, "Love you both. Call me."

A dark head nodded before Rocho hesitantly came up from behind Sylvia. Slowly, so as not to startle her fiancée too badly, she snaked her arms around Sylvia's waist.

A sigh escaped Sylvia as she felt the arms tighten around her. Her body responded easily to the loving touch and leaned into the strong body behind her.

"We'll get through this." Rocho nibbled on a convenient earlobe, but hastily stopped. This wasn't the time for making love. This was the time for holding her fiancée and comforting her.

Another sigh escaped Sylvia. Just that tiny bit of nibbling had stirred something. But she wasn't ready to do more than snuggle.

Or better yet, Sylvia wanted to do what they did best. "How about we take The Fuzz out?" She turned around in her fiancée's arms. "I know snuggling is the best for us, but I want to feel the wind against my skin. And if we have time, I want to work on a car. I don't care if it's just an oil change."

Rocho chuckled. "Whatever you want. You know I will rarely, if ever, turn down a ride on The Fuzz. And I don't care if I'm in front or back."

Sylvia swallowed as Rocho's eyes darkened. She understood the double meaning. When they made love, it didn't matter who was dominated. Who was on top or bottom. As long as it was about love, that was what mattered.

The distance between them closed hastily. Hungry lips met. Reluctantly, Rocho released her hungry grasp on Sylvia's lips. "We better stop if we're going to follow through with our plan."

Easily, Sylvia fell against Rocho's body. "You are so right. Wow." The body holding her chuckled. Sylvia took a step back. She slapped her fiancée on the arm. "Last one down the stairs rides in back."

It took Rocho a moment to begin the chase. It wasn't long before she was behind Sylvia and they were cruising the backroads. It just felt right to be like this with her fiancée.

After cruising for nearly an hour, they decided it was time for lunch. They stopped by the local Chinese buffet and ordered enough takeout for the entire dealership. It was a little interesting juggling the packages, but they managed.

Sylvia exhaled as she parked near what was considered the employee parking. She eased off the motorcycle before relieving Rocho of the delightful smelling food.

"I wonder if anyone has eaten or if we'll have leftovers for a few days." Rocho chuckled at her soulmate's question. Sylvia held the door open for her fiancée.

They found themselves inside the showroom. Sylvia couldn't help smiling. It was busier than she had seen it in a long time. It did her heart good to see it, if only to help continue her mother's legacy and to help Kaz and herself build their own.

"Wonder where Elizabeth and Kaz are?" Rocho nodded at one of the customers she had often helped with certain vehicle maintenance over the past year. She wondered if it was finally time for an upgrade.

"Probably laying claim to my office." Sylvia, while still reeling both mentally and physically from her father's reaction, was feeling so much better.

As they slowly avoided customers and salespersons, Sylvia noticed that Elizabeth wasn't at her desk. She wondered if her joke hadn't been spot on. Should they knock before they entered? What would the fun in that be?

When they burst into the office, a couple did part hastily. But they weren't doing anything but snuggling. Sylvia was beginning to understand. She had had one girlfriend in college who wasn't highly sexual. In fact, they'd never slept together.

"What have we here?" Sylvia made her way to the small table. She placed her packages on the table and moved out of the way so that Rocho could place hers on them.

Kaz was beyond red. In fact, Sylvia was worried her sister was about to pass out. Taking pity on her, she turned her back on the happy couple. "If you two can tear yourselves away from one another, we brought Chinese."

Rocho was smirking. Though she knew part of it was all an act, it was still good to see Sylvia teasing her sister and their good friend. "Better get some before Sylvia eats it all."

"The only thing I have trouble stopping myself from eating is you…" Sylvia and Rocho stared at one another. Both their faces turned red before bursting into laughter.

"TMI." Kaz finally found her voice. It had been an interesting twelve plus hours. She continued to adjust to the fact she had a sister and a woman who considered her a mother.

"Not for me. I love to live vicariously." Elizabeth rose, taking her girlfriend with her. "Now, let's grab some lunch, like we were supposed to before someone came in here tempting me with a much needed snuggle."

The four settled themselves around the small table. Since Sylvia's return from college, it had already seen some interesting things. She wondered how many other interesting situations.

As they ate, Sylvia explained what had transpired, including why her voice wasn't exactly hers and the bruising upon her neck. Most importantly, she explained her plans for the dealership.

"But I'm not blood related to your mother." Kaz took a moment to sip on her water. Some days, like today, she wished she hadn't given up caffeine.

"But Mom wanted you to have a part of it." Sylvia reached across the table. "She wanted me to do the right thing. In my mind, I want to be joint owner with you. Rocho is happy with being a mechanic. You can remain in the position you are very good at."

Sylvia hadn't the time to speak with Rocho in regards to opening a joint account together. As soon as they were married, she was going to do just that.

"Honestly, all I would want as far as compensation would be enough to live comfortably." Kaz turned toward Elizabeth. "I'd want to be able to actually take a vacation. Travel, maybe. Anything else, we could put back into the dealership. Charities. Maybe start up a scholarship."

Impressed. Sylvia didn't impress easily and with those few words, she was more than impressed. Of course, Kaz as an employee had been quite impressive. That's why she had gratefully hired her.

"Sounds impressive." Sylvia tilted her head as she sipped on her cola. "We might have to hire someone to handle all that. It would create another job. Always a plus for the economy."

"I like my job here." Kaz could feel her cheeks. They were warm. She wasn't accustomed to speaking so much. It wasn't that long ago that Elizabeth had made it so they could spend the evening alone. "And it's all I want to do. Not that I won't give input, when needed."

"If anyone is interested, I like my job." Elizabeth kissed Kaz on the cheek. "It comes with certain perks. Amazing how both sisters have jobs that have those perks."

Rocho couldn't believe this was happening to her. Literally only a couple months ago she had been planning on where to run to next. Now, she was sitting with her fiancée, future sister-in-law and good friend.

Lunch seemed to fly by, as did the afternoon. Rocho found she enjoyed working next to Sylvia. It reminded her of the first few meetings outside of work that she and her fiancée enjoyed. Either they had worked on the classic motorcycle or Trans Am.

Though it was later, it was a Friday night. The pair decided on another drive. It led them to their favorite ice cream place, just before it closed for the evening.

"We have to get back to walking or working out." Sylvia used her tongue to catch a runaway streak of strawberry ice cream.

It was a moment before Rocho was able to answer. Just the sight of Sylvia's tongue had the mechanic on fire. "We'll probably have to settle for working out. Soon, the weather will change. And there will be snow."

"Ugh. I might be a Michigander, but I have to say I'm not a fan of snow." Sylvia reached out. Rocho took the hint and grasped her fiancée's hand.

The pair walked along as they enjoyed their small ice cream cones. Soon, they would head back as they didn't want to leave their classic motorcycle unattended in the dark for too long.

A scream caught Rocho's attention. She didn't know if it was instincts or what, but she was suddenly running at full speed toward the sound.

"Help!" Rocho found a gear she didn't even know she had. The voice was that of a child. She was certain the closer she came and the more the voice cried for help.

Rocho met with the edge to The Grand River. It was nearly a straight drop-off into the river. A river that was not to be swam or fished in.

There was a figure bobbing up and down in the fast-moving water, just barely able to fight against the current. Rocho wasn't certain how deep the river was, but had to do something.

Hesitating only momentarily, Rocho jumped off the edge. She heard her named screamed as Sylvia caught up with her and witnessed her plummeting into the river.

The water was surprisingly not frigid. It wasn't warm, either. Rocho managed to surface not far from the small figure that's head was plummeting beneath the surface of the water once again.

How had the young child been able to fight the current? Rocho was barely able to swim the short distance to the small figure. "I'm here. Let go and come to me. I'll save you."

"Don't leave me." Sylvia's voice echoed loudly in Rocho's mind. While she needed to save this innocent child, she also couldn't leave her soulmate behind.

Before Rocho knew it, she was holding the small form in her arms. When she finally took in who it was, her heart nearly broke. It was a tiny version of her soulmate. Though the locks were wet, it was obvious they were blonde. And those terrified emerald eyes were haunting.

"Rocho!" The shout caused the mechanic to realize she was in a precarious situation. There was no way to emerge from the river. "I'm calling nine-one-one. Hold on!"

"We will, won't we sweetheart?" Rocho held the young, crying girl tightly to her body. She managed to make certain that neither was dragged too far down river. From where they were, there was the old train track bridge that had been converted into a walk trail.

There was only a muffled sound of crying from the small bundle held tightly against Rocho's chest. The head was held against her shoulder. The water seemed to becoming icier by the moment. Or was it her imagination.

Sylvia watched with horror as Rocho seemed to be losing her grasp upon the small girl. There were already rescue crews at the bridge that crossed over the blasted river that was attempting to take her soulmate from her.

The blasted flashing red and blue nights never seemed to move. Sylvia's attention returned to her soulmate. "Don't you dare fucking leave me!"

When Rocho's head submerged, Sylvia fell to her knees once again. She screamed again. "Don't you dear leave me. I can't live without you!"

"Goddamned sonofabitch." Sylvia watched in horror as Rocho was struggled to resurface. She was about to take the plunge herself, when finally she heard the sirens.

Sylvia rose to her feet. She couldn't keep her eyes from the spot where her soulmate kept failing to keep herself above water. The slamming of car doors followed by footsteps didn't even cause her focus to turn from Rocho. "Ma'am?"

"My fiancée and a child are in the river." Sylvia managed to tear her eyes from her soulmate. "Rocho, my girlfriend, didn't even think. We heard the screams for help. She jumped in without thought. But there's no way for her or the child to get back."

"Greg, it's the girl!" The female officer shouted over her shoulder. "Get the rig! We need to get them out of the water. Now!"

Sylvia watched as the whirl of activity unfolded around her. Her eyes never strayed far from where Rocho was now allowing herself to be taken away with the current.

The further Rocho was taken from her, the more Sylvia's heart ached. Her mind was screaming. But the worst thing was that her soul was screaming.

"Rocho!" Sylvia watched as the crews moved away from her. She knew it was because their best chance of saving her soulmate now was the walking trail and the bridge that crossed over it. But still, seeing her drift further and further away was heart wrenching.

Time stood still as Sylvia watched. Two officers jumped into the river. They had life preservers. As they caught up with Rocho and the child, Sylvia began to run. She didn't want to be in the way, but she had to be there when Rocho was finally safe and sound.

The pull was too great. It reminded Sylvia of the first time she had walked into the mechanic bay. Rocho had been working on a classic car. Her eyes had to focus on the tall, dark stranger. She'd nearly tripped when she'd seen the woman.

And now, Sylvia nearly tripped as she tore toward the bridge. It was nearly a half mile to the bridge. It was another quarter mile to where the fire rescuers were already hanging climbing ropes over the side and slowly descending.

Breathing out of control, Sylvia found herself being held back. She knew, in the back of her mind, that she could be more in the way. But she just had to be close, to witness Rocho being pulled to safety.

"Ma'am, calm down." Gina, the young officer who had most recently been overseeing the horrific three car accident on the bridge, spoke firmly but understandingly. One car had been hanging over the side and there had been an empty booster seat. "We're doing all we can do."

"But that's my soulmate." Sylvia finally calmed a little when she witnessed the netting that had been loosely strung. "I'm sorry."

Gina nodded in understanding before turning her back toward the scene that continued to unfold. The child with the blonde woman's soulmate was most likely the only survivor of the pile-up caused because someone couldn't watch out for a motorcycle.

Sylvia watched over the police officer's shoulder as the fire rescuers did their jobs. It was a surreal experience, to say the least, as she watched Rocho and the child being pulled from the river.

Two stretchers were brought to where Sylvia was standing on the trail. With Rocho's size, it took two firefighters to carry the mechanic to the stretcher. Of course, Rocho wasn't being carried alone. The little girl was wrapped securely in her arms.

There was shallow breathing or was that Sylvia's imagination? She watched as the EMTs attempted to disengage the young girl from Rocho's arms.

The sight of Rocho holding the young girl caused something unexpected to flow through Sylvia. While seeing young Renee had caused emotions she had never thought she would ever feel, seeing her soulmate holding a girl who depended solely on her were enough to overwhelm her, momentarily.

"Ma'am, we need to check your vitals, as well as the girl's." Sylvia slowly approached her soulmate. She didn't want to be in the way. The young man who was attempting to treat Rocho, turned toward Sylvia. "You know either?"

"Rocho is the clinging adult." Sylvia took another tentative step forward. "As for why she's holding onto the girl, she has a protective streak a mile wide. Allow me?"

The sandy blond man nodded his head. Sylvia immediately was by the stretcher. "Rocho." The mechanic's breathing was shallow at best. "You have to allow these nice people to help you. And the little one. Remember what we talked about?"

Azure eyes blinked several times. Rocho wasn't certain what was happening. She remembered jumping into the water. But the rest was a bit of a haze. The moving body against her reminded her why she had taken the plunge into the water.

Sylvia relaxed slightly as she watched those strong arms slowly ease her grasp on the child. "That's it. These experts will take care of the wee one. And they'll take care of you."

Rocho managed to nod. She was too tired to even begin to think of verbalizing how she was feeling, even when the EMT continued to ask her questions.

"What hospital are you taking them to?" Sylvia knew both her fiancée and the girl needed more attention than what could be given by EMTs.

"We'll be taking them to Sparrow in Lansing." The paramedic loaded both patients in the back of the ambulance.

Sylvia watched only for a moment before taking off. She didn't bother when the nice police officer called after her. She retrieved her cellphone and texted Harry. While calling would have been better, she knew he would understand that she wanted to be on the road immediately.

Thankfully, the motorcycle was where they had left it. Sylvia didn't hesitate in placing her helmet on. As she straddled the motorcycle, she immediately missed Rocho's arms around her. "Don't you leave me."

It took every ounce of willpower for Sylvia not to cry. The motorcycle roaring to life eased some of the strain to constrain her tears. The powerful machine would take her to her soulmate.

The trip that would normally take twenty minutes, depending on traffic, only required ten. Sylvia was grateful she had not come across any speed traps.

As it was, Sylvia arrived just as the ambulance arrived. She waited patiently at the ER desk for someone to actually realize she was standing there. "May I help you, Miss?"

"I'm here to see how Renee Bishop is." Sylvia waited, now impatiently, for any information. She felt her cellphone vibrate and knew it was most likely Harry.

"Are you family?" The woman behind the desk waited for the answer as the phones continued to ring and more people lined up behind Sylvia.

"My name is Sylvia Reed. I'm Miss Bishop's fiancée. Her brother is on the way from Portland." Sylvia leaned forward. Her emerald eyes ablaze. "Please don't make me wait until he's here."

The middle-aged woman smiled knowingly. She hastily typed in a few key words before retrieving the information she needed. "Give me your contact info. Miss Bishop is still being seen by the ER doctor. Once she's ready for visitors, someone will contact you."

"Is she at least stable?" Sylvia hastily wrote down her cellphone number. She hated hospitals. Ever since her mother had passed away in one, she had hated even the thought of one.

"I wish I had an update." The woman's voice was genuine. She hastily typed away. "Please take a seat in the waiting area. And thank you for giving me Mr. Bishop's information."

Sylvia nodded. She knew the drill. Though she was family by engagement, most hospitals still respected blood relations first and foremost.

Time once again seemed to stand still. Sylvia wasn't certain how long she paced back and forth when a familiar figure stood near the entrance. Long arms opened and she fell into the embrace without thought. "I haven't heard anything about her, yet."

"Do you want me to check? Little brother and lawyer here." Harry winked. Sylvia nodded. "Jessica is manning the phones at home with the baby. We think we might get a call about Mom in the next day or two."

Sylvia swallowed. Another person, sick as she was, being admitted to the hospital and leaving in a body bag. She couldn't think about that. After all, Rocho was in one of the emergency rooms.

It wasn't too long before Harry had both hands on Sylvia's shoulders. "The good news is Rocho is breathing on her own. The bad news is she swallowed a lot of the water. And we all know how bad the Grand River water can be."

The businesswoman inhaled deeply before exhaling slowly. Sylvia was well aware of what could happen to a healthy body. After all, she'd grown up in Portland. Her classmate had fallen in. The fall hadn't harmed him. It was the chemicals and waste that was dumped into the river that had caused him to become nearly deathly ill. Thankfully, he had fully recovered.

"They are ready to admit Rocho for further testing and observations." Harry made certain emerald eyes were holding his azure ones. "She's already showing a rash on her chest and stomach. Her temperature has spiked a little. They are coming to get me when she's assigned a room."

Harry was grateful for his reflexes as Sylvia slumped against him. The tears flowed freely. "I'm sorry." The muffled apology felt weak. "It's just that my mother passed away in a hospital. Breast cancer."

The attorney held Sylvia even tighter against him. Harry realized the trauma his own mother's transport and subsequent hospital stay had caused his sister-in-law. And now, Sylvia's entire life was in the hospital.

"Rocho is strong. I know I've been separated from her for too long, but she's been strong, both physically and mentally, by herself." Harry had to swallow so that he could continue. "She now has us. So, she'll fight extra hard."

"I know." Sylvia had to take several gulps of air before she was able to function. Finally, she stood on her own. "I must look a fright. I better clean up a little before seeing Rocho."

"She'll just be grateful you are here." Harry gently wiped the tears from Sylvia's cheeks. More and more, he was seeing exactly why his sister had fallen so fast and hard for the woman.

"Mr. Bishop?" Harry turned toward the entranceway where a small nurse was standing. The smile on the greying redhead was sweet and concerned.

"Besides, it's time to see Rocho now." Harry guided Sylvia toward the nurse who was waiting patiently. "I'm Harry Bishop. This is Renee's, aka Rocho's, fiancée."

The nurse nodded. "I'll let them know and make a note in her chart. If you'll follow me." The redhead turned without another word.

Harry maintained contact with Sylvia as they weaved their way through the maize that was a hospital. He only hoped that either was able to find their way out once it was time to leave.

Knowing Sylvia and the relationship she shared with his sister, they would have to kick her out before she left Rocho's side. And he couldn't blame her. Harry had felt the same. That was the birth of his daughter.

"I'll let them know at the nurse's station." The nurse once again had a beaming smile upon her face. "Visiting hours are another half an hour." Again, without waiting for a response, the nurse disappeared.

"Do you want to go in alone?" Harry wanted to see his sister more than anything, other than hold his wife and daughter. But he knew this was a moment for the couple to share.

"We can both go in. Forgive me if I do anything embarrassing." Sylvia squeezed Harry's hand. Up until that moment, she hadn't even been aware that he had held it the entire time they had been led to Rocho's room.

They continued to hold hands as they made their way into the observation room. Rocho had her eyes closed. The moment Sylvia sat next to her fiancée, azure eyes opened immediately.

While part of Sylvia wanted to ask what Rocho had been thinking, she already knew the answer. "How are you feeling?" Without thought, she brushed dark locks from her fiancée's forehead.

Rocho coughed several times before attempting to speak. "Been better." When Sylvia's hand came to rest on her cheek, Rocho leaned into the gentle touch. "How's the girl?"

"I haven't found out, yet." Sylvia glanced at Harry who nodded in understanding. "Perhaps your brother would be so kind as to find out for us?"

"I'll take my time. Maybe try and find some decent coffee for us." Harry patted his sister's knee before taking his leave of the two ladies.

Sylvia took a moment merely to stare into azure eyes. "You terrified me." She couldn't help it. The thought of losing Rocho remained fresh in her mind.

"I'm sorry." Rocho wanted to sit up and hold Sylvia in her arms. She remained too weak. Her body was itching like mad. What the Hades had been in the water and how would it affect her and the child?

"No need to apologize." Sylvia leaned down and brushed her lips against Rocho's. "You were being you. And I love you. But you better never do anything stupid like leaving me. Ever."

There was a comfortable silence between the two soulmates. It was broken by the slight wheezing from the mechanic. Sylvia was surprised her soulmate wasn't on oxygen.

It was about ten minutes later when Harry returned. "The little girl's name is still unknown. She's suffering pretty much the same thing that Rocho is. The only thing they do know is that the occupants of the car she was in didn't survive the crash."

"She's all alone." Rocho knew that sensation far too well. "Harry, I know you still have your practice back in Flint. And you were talking of moving back. But could you, well, see if the young girl has any family?"

A smile was instantly upon Sylvia's face. "You are in a hurry to get me knocked up." A serious expression hastily replaced the smile.

The Rocho's weary mind was slow in processing the fact Sylvia was teasing her. "I just want to make certain the girl is taken care of. And I don't want her winding up in foster care."

"I was teasing." Sylvia once again leaned in and kissed her fiancée gently on the lips. "I'm just as concerned about the young girl as you are. And if she is alone, I want to help. Now that the lawsuits are settled, we can start planning our future."

Rocho smiled sweetly as she reached up and traced Sylvia's cheeks. "You were crying." There was the evidence of puffiness. "I'm sorry. This will be the last time I say it. And I hope I'll think before just leaping in feet first."

Harry cleared his throat. He placed the coffee he'd smuggled in on the small table next to the hospital bed. "I think I'll start on discovering what I can about young Jane Doe. It's getting late. They might attempt to kick you out. If they do, call me." He hated coming in between the soulmates, but he had to give his sister a kiss on the forehead. "And if you need me for anything else, call me. Let me know if stubborn here has a relapse of any kind."

"Don't worry, you'll be the first to know, after me." Sylvia reluctantly rose. She hugged Harry. "I'm sorry about the text. I just…"

A raised hand hushed Sylvia's apology. "I understand. You got me to the hospital. And you let me know that my big sis is a hero. Though I doubt she'll ever allow herself to see it that way."

"Nope." Sylvia winked. "You be safe. And kiss your wife and child for us when you finally get home." Harry nodded before waving to his sister.

Sylvia remained standing with her back to Rocho for several moments. "I'm on emotional overload." Finally, she turned to face her soulmate.

Before either could say a word, a tall, blond male nurse knocked gently on the door. "I hate to bother you, but I have to check on the patient." He slowly made his way to Rocho. "My name is David. I'll be your nurse until morning."

Rocho allowed herself to be poked and prodded. She answered the questions about how the rash was causing major itching. Her lungs were still annoyed from the lack of oxygen and swallowing of polluted water.

"They'll probably want you back on oxygen." David typed away on the computer. "And they'll want a dermatologist to see you for a second opinion." He turned toward Rocho. "Sorry to speak to you with my back to you. That was rude. Now, is there anything I can get you?" He sniffed the air. "I see you found the good coffee. If you want a snack, let me know. And if you want a cot to sleep on, let me know."

The last statement was directed toward Sylvia. "I can sleep in the chair. Thank you. As for food, I'm good. Can you tell us how long you think Rocho will be in here?"

David could hear the love and concern in the young woman's voice. "If I had to guess, Miss Bishop will be sprung in the morning. At the latest, sometime after noon. Wish I could be here to assist you ladies more. If you'll excuse me, I have to report back to Doctor Richmond and check on my other patients."

Once again, Sylvia watched until they were alone. She turned toward Rocho. "Screw the chair." Rocho took the hint. The mechanic scooted over so that there was room for her soulmate to snuggle next to her. "While the coffee sounds divine, I just want to nap with you until we're interrupted."

"Sounds good to me." Rocho hoped she could fall asleep. She knew holding Sylvia would help her soulmate. She only hoped holding Sylvia would aid her in sleeping.

Chapter 26

Morning came too quickly for Sylvia. They were disturbed every so often throughout the night. Rocho had been placed on a low concentration of oxygen to help her breathe easier and she'd had the consultation which led to more and more tests.

"Good morning, Miss Bishop." The doctor was taller and thinner than Rocho. His hair was thinning and greying. "I don't know if you remember me. I'm Doctor Jacobs. We've received the tests back."

Sylvia was sitting on the edge of the bed holding Rocho's hand. While she was anxious to know her fiancée's results, she also wanted to know how the little girl was doing. "So, what's the diagnosis doc?"

"Miss Bishop was quite lucky her exposure wasn't longer." Dr. Jacobs made his way to the end of the bed. "With some medication I've prescribed and some topical, her rash should clear up within the next month. I'd suggest making a follow up appointment with your family doctor, but preferably with a dermatologist."

"So, I'm going to be all right?" Though she would need treatment for longer than either wanted to wait to be married, it was overall good news. "And I can be discharged soon."

"I'm not your attending physician, but I'll make certain to speed up the process." Dr. Jacobs was now standing beside Rocho, opposite side as Sylvia. "A little birdie informed me you've been concerned about the child you saved."

Rocho managed to nod. "I'm not supposed to tell you any of this, but with the tenaciousness of your brother, I'm certain it won't be long before you hear it for yourself. Her name is Cindy Burns. Sadly, her parents were killed instantly in the accident that threw her into the river. She's suffering similar ailments as you are. I don't know if they've found any family members."

"My brother will find out." Rocho was pleased Cindy had a similar diagnosis. Though she did realize that it could be more dangerous for a child to endure.

"Of that, I have no doubt." Dr. Jacobs smile was beaming. "I have a feeling a force runs strong in this family. You ladies, if you you'll excuse me, have a good rest of the day."

"Thanks, Doc." Sylvia was surprised when the doctor bowed at the door before exiting. "I'm hoping this means we can get out of here soon." She made certain she was looking into azure eyes. "I'm just wondering if I shouldn't take the motorcycle back and get the Trans Am. Or get one of the cars from the lot."

"Breathe." Rocho, who was gratefully in an upright position, kissed her fiancée. "If it's just me, I'll be fine on the back of the motorcycle. We can take the back roads home so the speed isn't too great."

After a moment to catch her breath, Rocho continued. "And unless Harry can pull out a miracle, we'll be the only ones heading home."

As if he knew they were speaking of him, Harry waltzed in. Not only did he have coffees, he had breakfast. "Ladies, Jessica and Renee send their best. And I have some news." He yawned as he handed over the smuggled in food and caffeine.

They each took a moment to sip on their coffee before Harry continued. "Cindy Burns is 3. She was born in Lansing, in this very hospital but lives in Portland. Using my best private investigators, we found out that she has a cousin that lives in California. He's twenty and being contacted now."

Both ladies stopped eating immediately. It was Sylvia who found her voice first. "So, that means she'll have someone who will take her."

"That depends." Harry pulled up one of the visitor seats. He stretched out, his feet resting on the hospital bed. "From what I understand, Cindy's cousin isn't in a financial position to take care of her. And sadly, her parents were just barely making ends meet."

"So, there is hope." Sylvia couldn't help herself. "But not to completely get our hopes up." With one hand, she sought out Rocho's hand. With her other, she grabbed her coffee. "I might need a few more of these before we are through."

"Exactly." Harry held up his cup of coffee. "To both." They chuckled at the thought. "Seriously. I'll keep someone on the situation. And I'll keep you apprised. Just like you keep me apprised of everything. We're still heading back to Flint. But only to pack our things and finish any cases remaining."

Family. Rocho would at least have her brother, his wife and her niece in town. Sylvia was her number one family member. Always. "I have to ask. How is Mom?"

The color drained from Harry's face. "I didn't want to tell you until you were sprung from here. At eight this morning, Mom passed away. Dad is taking her body back to Mississippi. Neither of us is invited to the funeral."

Rocho nodded. In a way, she was kicking herself. She would never have the closure she might have had from actually seeing her mother. From what Harry had informed her, in the end, their mother was capable of very little speech.

"I'm sorry." There was a part of Sylvia that was far from sorry. Yet, she would never wish the death of another person. No matter how much she loathed that person or how much ill-will they had spread.

As one, the pair shrugged. "She wasn't much of a mother." Harry finished his coffee. "I came to update you, see when you're going to be sprung and see if I could beg to drive your motorcycle home."

Rocho chuckled. "Thanks for the food, the update, still not certain and there's only two people who will drive the classic. Maybe two more, depending."

Azure and emerald locked. They really had to stop this. If Cindy had family, wasn't it in the young girl's best interest to be placed with them? Now young Renee was another reason.

"I don't think Jessica will ever be comfortable with that if you are hinting that one of them is my daughter." Harry shook his head as he rose. He stretched. He hadn't slept only an hour the night before. "I need to walk around. I was hoping to remain until the doc releases you. But lack of sleep means I should head home."

"We understand. Why don't you head out now?" Sylvia reluctantly rose from her perch beside Rocho. "I can call you when we are settled back at home. I plan on waiting on your sister, hand and foot, for the next few days. The others can run the dealership."

Before Harry could answer, yet another doctor entered the room. Unlike the others, he wasn't the politest. "Miss Bishop, I've looked at your tests. I've conferred with the others who've treated you. Besides making certain not to overdo it and take the medications for the rash, you are free to go."

"What about Cindy?" Rocho didn't want to leave not knowing who would be taking care of the child. There was always social services, but she hated that thought.

"Who?" The young doctor, was barely as old as Sylvia. He definitely was lacking a bedside manner.

"The child that my sister saved." Harry decided he needed to step in. He could feel the seething already simmering just below the surface of his sister-in-law.

"Oh, the orphan." The man wouldn't even look them in the eyes. "All I know is she's stable and ready to be released. After I'm done caring for them, it's not my issues. I'll have the nurse in here with your discharge instructions and papers."

And just like that, the doctor had left the room. "And I thought he was just grumpy because of lack of sleep. I see he was born with a stick up his ass."

"Sylvia!" Rocho was laughing as she chastised her soulmate. Laughing wasn't the smartest thing in the world as it turned to coughing.

"Sorry about that." Sylvia was instantly by Rocho's side. She aided Rocho into sitting up slightly further so that she could rub the strong back. "I'll have to try and remember not to make you laugh for a little while."

"Probably for the best." The trio glanced up as yet another figure entered. "Miss Bishop's lungs have to recover from the water intake, but also some of the pollutants in the river. Let's get this paperwork over with so you can get home and on with your life. And no skinny dipping in the river."

Sylvia nearly pissed her pants laughing. Rocho would never skinny dip. At least her mechanic would never in some place so public as The Grand River. Now if they had a pool that was fully enclosed…

Two hours later, Rocho was finally lying in bed. The only reason she was allowed to be out of bed was if nature should call. If she needed anything else, Sylvia was more than happy to retrieve it for her.

While Rocho remained exhausted, sleep just wouldn't claim her. It wasn't because of Sylvia's continued doctoring. It was because her mind could not forget the young girl who she had willingly held in her arms until they could both be saved.

The mechanic suddenly felt as if she was back in the river. Rocho was freezing. Her entire body was shaking. It felt as if the air conditioning was on full blast.

By the time Sylvia entered the bedroom, she could have sworn Rocho's skin was blue. "Oh my God!" Hastily, she placed the hot chocolate on the stand next to Rocho's side of the bed. "Rocho? Are you all right? Do I need to call for an ambulance?"

"J…J…Just need to g…g…get warm." Rocho held out her hand. Sylvia understood immediately what her soulmate was begging for.

Sylvia divested herself of her clothes. When she pulled back the comforter, she noticed Rocho was fully clothed. "If you were up for it, I'd say let me get you as naked as me."

Rocho laughed, but it caused her to cough. "I…I'll take you up on that. Soon." She aided Sylvia the best she could with the removal of her own clothing.

Soon, the soulmates were holding one another. Sylvia nearly gasped when her body had first come into contact with Rocho's. She hoped it was merely a mental reaction and not some kind of setback.

Sylvia shifted until she was spooning her soulmate from behind. Absently, she was rubbing Rocho's stomach. The body she was holding was shivering still.

"Tell me, Miss Bishop." Sylvia nuzzled Rocho's neck. "Is our life together always going to be this interesting? First, we meet and it's love at first sight. Then, we do this dance a little. Finally begin to admit our feelings. Then there's the sexual harassment lawsuit and my father being an asshole. Discover I have a long lost sister. Your mother shockingly returning to exonerate you. And then, you are this amazing hero."

Rocho had felt her body begin to respond. It wasn't merely a sexual response. Finally, her body temperature felt as if it was returning to normal.

"I guess there's only a few more things left for us to do." Rocho managed to turn so she was looking into emerald eyes. "We need to make this permanent. We need to have kids. And we need to continue to love and live our life so that our children can be proud of us."

"If you weren't rash covered…" Sylvia kissed her fiancée soundly. Rocho definitely understood exactly where this would lead to. "There's a part of me that wants to anyways."

The mechanic groaned. "I definitely understand." Rocho held Sylvia firmly against her body. "I don't know what I would have done if we hadn't met. I don't want to know. I can't wait until we can be married and settled down and…" It was the last thoughts for both as they drifted off to sleep.

Chapter 27

"Aunt Sylvia!" The woman in question turned at her name. The dark-haired girl who was nearly a mini version of her wife was running toward her. "Where's Cindy?"

Sylvia should have known. Since adopting Cindy over five years ago, the cousins were inseparable. "I think Cindy is in the garage with her mom."

"Thanks." And with that, Renee was off to seek her cousin and her Aunt Rocho. Sylvia shook her head as she placed the plates on the picnic table.

Five years since they had met. Five years since they had been put through the ringer. Five years since they had been married. And five years since they had adopted Cindy.

"Don't overdo." Sylvia turned at the sound of her sister's voice. Kaz had the hamburger patties on a platter. They would also grill chicken and hot dogs. "Don't want Rocho having a heart attack."

Sylvia chuckled, though she knew that her wife would overreact if she began lifting or carrying too much. "She's hovering enough. Don't need her hovering more."

Kaz placed the tray down and helped her sister into a sitting position. "She is quite the protective person. And you enjoy every second of it."

Cheeks reddened, ever so slightly, as Sylvia couldn't hide the truth. "I do enjoy being taken care of." At that moment, she felt the powerful kick. "And so does Rocho's son. My goodness."

"Can I?" Sylvia nodded at her sister's request. As Kaz felt the next kick. "Wow. He could be a field goal kicker. The Lions need one. Desperately."

"Don't they always?" Sylvia's heart was warm. After her mother had died, she had never had family. And she knew Rocho had not thought she had family at all.

A squealing sound came from the garage. Sylvia's gaze turned that way in time to witness Rocho carrying Cindy under one arm and Renee under the other. All three were covered head to toe with grease.

"There's my girls." Sylvia shook her head. This was her life. This was a typical Sunday afternoon. Harry was over by the grill preparing it for the meat. Jessica and Elizabeth were inside making the side dishes.

The only thing that would change was who would host the grill out. Elizabeth and Kaz had been together, officially, for three years now. Though they had dated for the entire time they'd known one another, they hadn't moved in with each other until three years ago making it official.

"Clean them up." Rocho nodded before disappearing into the house. Sylvia wondered if her mother was looking down from heaven or with them at that very moment and was proud of who she was and what she had done with her life.

The dealership was one of the most profitable dealerships around. But it wasn't the money bringing in that made her such a success. Sylvia had many scholarship programs in place, along with organizations that helped the LGBTQ community.

Yes, Sylvia decided, her mother would be extremely proud of her. As Rocho's arms slipped around her, she knew that this was the life she was always meant to have. She was grateful her wife had done the one thing she had begged of her. "Don't ever leave me."

Other works by Agnes H. Hagadus

Sam/Abby Series

ANOTHER TIME ANOTHER PLACE:

Join Sam & Abby as they fight exes, the mob and their families to find a happily ever after.

https://www.amazon.com/Another-Time-Place-soulmates-journey-ebook/dp/B01IYM663U/ref=sr_1_4?s=books&ie=UTF8&qid=1470103288&sr=1-4&keywords=agnes+hagadus

Cover by:

http://www.shiralynlee.com/

COMING HOME:

Sam & Abby have been separated against their wills. Yet their hearts call out to one another. Join them for their journey home.

http://www.amazon.com/Coming-Home-soulmates-Journey-Book-ebook/dp/B00RMB7ZHQ/ref=pd_sim_351_1?ie=UTF8&refRID=10D1XH39DBHQ3MCPZFEB

Cover by:

http://www.dreams2media.com/

SAFE HARBOR:

Sam & Abby have settled in Middletown. As always, trouble seems to find them. Join them as they fight mobsters, the past and family members.

http://www.amazon.com/Safe-Harbor-soulmates-abby-Book-

ebook/dp/B0161DW81S/ref=sr_1_2?ie=UTF8&qid=144400389
7&sr=8-2&keywords=agnes+hagadus

Cover by:

http://www.shiralynlee.com/

EUROPEAN VACATION: WALKER STYLE

Sam & Abby are finally enjoying their honeymoon. It takes them to Europe. The problem? New and old enemies make their vacation anything but.

https://www.amazon.com/European-Vacation-Walker-Style-soulmates-ebook/dp/B01N6V5AQ1/ref=sr_1_1?ie=UTF8&qid=148571569 5&sr=8-1&keywords=agnes+hagadus

Cover by:

http://www.shiralynlee.com/

SAM AND ABBY: THE FINAL ADVENTURE

Sam & Abby have had many adventures. This is the ultimate one. Will it finally lead to their happily ever after?

https://www.amazon.com/dp/B07W2VKJJV

Cover by:

http://www.shiralynlee.com/

Emily/Tabby

DISTANCE OF THE HEART:

Emily is called back to California as her parents face different health issues. She leaves behind her soulmate, Tabby and their son, at a time when they are struggling to reconnect. Will the physical distance be too much for these two intertwined hearts?

http://www.amazon.com/Distance-Heart-Emily-Tabby-soulmates-ebook/dp/B01EGO1ZXQ?ie=UTF8&keywords=agnes%20hagadus&qid=1462104135&ref_=sr_1_2&sr=8-2

Cover by:

http://www.shiralynlee.com/

Kathy/Candy

ONCE BURNED:

Kathy is a firefighter who couldn't save her younger brother from a fire. It has left her badly scared and nearly devoid of emotions. Candy owns a bookstore/café. She, in her mind, is the reason her mother died and hasn't truly allowed love back in her life. When Kathy rescues Candy from a fire, everything changes for them both. But are they too badly burned?

http://www.amazon.com/Once-Burned-Candy-Kathy-Soulmates-ebook/dp/B00ZGFMFGG/ref=asap_bc?ie=UTF8

Cover by:

http://www.shiralynlee.com/

TWICE BURNED:

It's four months after the events that transpired in Once Burned. Can Kathy and Candy overcome all of life's obstacles to remain together? Or have they once again been too badly burned.

http://www.amazon.com/Twice-Burned-Candy-Kathy-Soulmates-ebook/dp/B017Y7MUL8/ref=tmm_kin_swatch_0?_encoding=UTF8&qid=1447713766&sr=8-1

Cover by:

http://www.shiralynlee.com/

Jessie/Thelma

WHERE THERE'S SMOKE

Jessie is training to be a firefighter and loves the ladies. She doesn't care only about those two things. Thelma is older and been burned one too many times. She can't even be open to friendship. Sparks are immediate. But is there more than smoke between these two?

https://www.amazon.com/Where-Theres-soulmates-jessie-thelma-ebook/dp/B01KXWZ3LK/ref=sr_1_6?ie=UTF8&qid=1472307593&sr=8-6&keywords=agnes+hagadus#nav-subnav

Cover by:

http://www.shiralynlee.com/

KINDLING

Jessie and Thelma have opened a bed and breakfast. Their romance continues to kindle, but can they help others kindle new romances? Or even face what the world has to put them through?

https://www.amazon.com/Kindling-soulmates-jessie-thelma-Book-ebook/dp/B07CMDMGXX/ref=sr_1_3?ie=UTF8&qid=1525450775&sr=8-3&keywords=agnes+hagadus

Cover by:

http://www.shiralynlee.com/

TRANSITIONS

Vacation is over for Allison, Geraldine, Lucy and Dallas. It means back to life. Life means many things and many transitions.

For Allison it means where to work and live and whether to pursue a relationship with Geraldine. For Geraldine it means becoming true to herself and standing up to her hateful father. For Lucy, it means facing truths about her past she never knew. And for Dallas, it means possibly giving up her vocation to be with the woman she loves.

https://www.amazon.com/Transitions-agnes-hagadus-ebook/dp/B089KTD3YM/ref=tmm_kin_swatch_0?_encoding=UTF8&qid=1591192931&sr=8-3

Cover by:

http://www.shiralynlee.com/

Erica/Emerald

THE SPEAKEASY

Erica Chase has posed as her twin brother since she was ten. She took over her father's bar, The Speakeasy. She's done everything and anything to make it successful. The only thing is denying herself love. Emerald Knight has taken care of her sister since she was a youth, doing nearly whatever it takes. The singer uses her bosses to gain whatever she can. When the bar owner and singer meet, it's a battle of the wills.

http://www.amazon.com/gp/product/B01BI0SXQI?keywords=agnes%20hagadus&qid=1455457126&ref_=sr_1_5&s=books&sr=1-5

Cover by:

http://www.shiralynlee.com/

GEORGIA NIGHTS

Erica and Emerald have left Chicago after learning of property belonging to Erica's mother. As in Chicago, trouble seems to follow them everywhere and it's not the singer. Can they survive past and present enemies?

https://www.amazon.com/Georgia-Nights-soulmates-Erica-Emerald-ebook/dp/B0777PJF7S/ref=sr_1_2?ie=UTF8&qid=1511976932&sr=8-2&keywords=agnes+hagadus

Cover by:

http://www.shiralynlee.com/

Andrea/Alicia

LIES IN THE DARK:

Watch as Andrea and Alicia face all the things that go bump in the night. Who to trust, including a vampire who saved Andrea as child, is the biggest question.

http://www.amazon.com/Lies-Dark-Soulmates-Andrea-Alicia/dp/1511800585/ref=sr_1_3?ie=UTF8&qid=1432820302&sr=8-3&keywords=agnes+hagadus

Cover by:

http://www.dreams2media.com/

FRIEND OR FOE:

Andrea and Alicia have found one another and continue to fall in love. There are so many forces out there, who is a friend and who is a foe?

https://www.amazon.com/dp/1515392260

Cover by:

http://www.shiralynlee.com/

THE TERROR WITHIN:

Andrea and Alicia face the ultimate battle. It's not the ultimate evil, though it will torment them in every way it can. It's the terror that resides within each of us.

http://www.amazon.com/gp/product/1519622171?keywo
rds=agnes%20h%20hagadus&qid=1449535679&ref_=sr_1_9&s
r=8-9

Cover by:

http://www.shiralynlee.com/

STAND ALONES

4 POINT PLAY:

Jenks & Beth were born weeks apart and grew up
together. Watch as they take the journey from friendship to
marriage.

http://www.amazon.com/4-Point-Play-Agnes-Hagadus-
ebook/dp/B00NRSO4GI/ref=sr_1_1?ie=UTF8&qid=143282030
2&sr=8-1&keywords=agnes+hagadus

Cover by:

http://www.dreams2media.com/

DILAPIDATED SOUL

Michelle Franklin has a dark past. One that has eaten
away at her soul and closed herself off from truly loving. With
the help of the woman who loves her, she's about to face that
dark past. Will she survive? Or will it be too much to bear…

https://www.amazon.com/Dilapidated-Soul-Agnes-
Hagadus-
ebook/dp/B01I42DCA0/ref=sr_1_5?ie=UTF8&qid=1468627798
&sr=8-5&keywords=agnes+hagadus

Cover by:

http://www.shiralynlee.com/

BONDED SOULS

Elissa is a thousand old vampire who avoids mortals. One day she stumbles upon Cassandra, an eight-year-old mortal, at an orphanage. Something happens that causes the vampire to take the young girl with her. They discover they have a bond unlike they could ever have imagined

https://www.amazon.com/dp/B07Y2GXH35

Cover by:

http://www.shiralynlee.com/

MILE HIGH CLUB

Evie is a pilot who used to believe in commitment until she was cheated on. Now, she loves having a different woman in each hub. Andy's life has never been her own with her mother attempting to control her life, even who she dates. Both their lives change when the pilot and flight attendant work the same flight. But will it be forever?

https://www.amazon.com/Mile-High-Club-agnes-hagadus-ebook/dp/B08B9ZK8KC/ref=sr_1_3?crid=1IF19L8RO3SNF&dchild=1&keywords=agnes+hagadus&qid=1592488946&sprefix=agnes+h%2Caps%2C181&sr=8-3

Cover by:

http://www.shiralynlee.com/